Strung Out to Die

Doug Fletcher Mysteries
Book 15

Dean L. Hovey

Print ISBNs
Amazon Print 9780228631019
Ingram Spark 9780228631026
Barnes & Noble 9780228631033
BWL Print 9780228631040

Table of Contents

Chapter 1

As Grace Watanabe crested the hill approaching the Manzanar National Historic Site, she was surprised to see a Toyota Prius parked alongside the entrance road with the driver's door open. Drawing closer, she noticed that there seemed to be something entangled in the barbed wire fence behind the car.

Grace, who was not a morning person, was driving to Manzanar to open the site. Still half asleep and sipping iced coffee from her travel mug, she assumed an animal had run into the fence the previous evening, and that one of the rangers was checking it out. *Yes, there's a ranger there. Wait, why is he tangled in the fence?*

Pulling off the access road and parking near the Prius, Grace trotted to the scene, her mind unable to comprehend what she was seeing. At first, she thought someone had dressed a mannequin in a Park Service uniform and tangled it in the wire as a joke. Getting closer, she saw blood staining the ranger's shirt.

"Oh geez! It's Red Petersen!" Stopping a few feet behind the abandoned Prius, Grace dialed 911.

"Inyo County 911. How may I assist you?"

"There's a dead ranger at Manzanar."

"Where is Manzanar, and are you sure the person is dead?"

"Manzanar is a national historic site off the highway. It's where the Japanese Americans were relocated during World War II."

"Can you provide a nearby crossroads?"

Grace, who'd driven to her ranger job on the same route for 37 years, looked over her shoulder at a passing car on the highway. The shock of the discovery caused her mind to go blank. "There's no crossroads. The entrance is right on the highway. You can see the guard tower from miles away."

"Which highway?"

Becoming infuriated with herself and the dispatcher she replied, "There's a long name for the highway. The Grand something or other."

"Is there a road number?"

"Of course, there is. I'm standing here staring at a dead body and the highway number isn't coming to mind."

"Is the historic place on 'The Grand Army of the Republic Highway'? That's Highway 395."

"Yes," Grace sighed. "Can you send someone?"

"You said there's someone dead there? Are you sure the person is deceased?"

Cocking her head, Grace watched several flies buzz around the victim's neck. "I'm reasonably certain. I mean, there are already flies circling his body."

"Do you know the deceased person?"

"I'm pretty sure it's Erik "Red" Petersen. He's the only red-headed ranger here."

"I've dispatched a deputy. What's your name?"

"Grace. Grace Watanabe. I'm a ranger here."

"Ms. Watanabe, can you stay at that location until the deputy arrives?"

"Yeah. Sure. This is where I work. I'm technically on duty now."

Ending the 911 call, Grace punched in her superintendent's phone number. "What's up, Grace?"

"Red is dead. I found his body when I arrived at the visitor center this morning. The Inyo County dispatcher is sending a deputy."

"Red is dead? Was he in an accident on the highway or..."

"It appears his throat was cut. His Prius is parked outside of the entrance and his body is hanging from the barbed wire."

"What the hell?" Ed Richardson asked rhetorically. "Everyone liked Red."

While not looking directly at the body, Grace tried to keep the growing hysteria out of her voice. "Clearly, not everyone liked Red."

Chapter 2

Converting a back bedroom into a home office offered me privacy and fewer interruptions, allowing me to dig through piles of US Park Service cold cases. The downside was the lack of interruptions left me sitting in my chair for hours at a time without mental or physical breaks from the files. The silence, compared to the constant background noise and interruptions of working in my North Padre Island National Seashore office, seemed like a godsend. After a few weeks of working from home, I discovered that I missed walking to the break room for a cup of coffee where there was always a ranger to speak to. The topics of weather (hot and humid), and sports teams (I didn't care) seemed inane, but they offered me a chance to stretch and talk to someone besides my wife. They also brought me up to date on North Padre Island National Seashore gossip, as well as updates on new stores, restaurants on the island, and Texas politics.

I missed all that as I walked to my home kitchen and poured my third cup of coffee from a carafe that had been cooking down since I brewed it at 6:30 AM. A splash of creamer diluted the acidity and nearly covered the burnt flavor. I was pouring the dregs into the sink when the front door opened and Jill, my wife and investigative partner, walked in. Quickly assessing the coffee situation, she shook her head. "Let's buy a Keurig. Every cup is fresh."

"The old Mr. Coffee machine still works."

Jill stared at the tarry residue in the carafe. "I know it just kills you to throw away things that are still functioning but think of it as moving ahead in technology. We got rid of our Blackberries, and now we have Android cell phones with more functions."

"I never owned a Blackberry. I had a flip phone I used to make phone calls. I never needed all that other stuff."

"I'm continually amazed that an intelligent man can't throw away a coffee maker that came in a box with Joe DiMaggio's picture. When did he die?" Jill pulled out her phone and started pressing the buttons. "There. A second-generation Keurig will arrive tomorrow by 7:00 PM. It's coming with a K-cup sampler pack so you can decide which flavor of coffee you prefer."

Unhappy with the turn of events, or possibly about losing the argument, I rebelled. "I like coffee-flavored coffee. I don't need a sampler pack of foo-foo drinks."

Jill walked over and turned her phone so I could see her screen. "All the options are coffee flavored. There's Donut Shop blend,

Hawaiian blend, Blue Mountain blend, Nantucket blend, and more. I didn't buy you the assortment with hazelnut and cinnamon bun flavors."

My cell phone, still sitting on the desk in the other room, chirped. Dashing back to the office, I accepted the call and activated the speaker function before it rolled over to voicemail. "Fletcher."

"I've got an investigation you're not going to like," my boss said.

"Great, Jack. You seem to find a lot of those."

"I don't *find* them, Doug. They just show up."

"Do your other investigators get distasteful investigations, or do you save them all for us?"

"Most of our investigations are more straightforward. I need your detective expertise and Jill's diplomatic skills in places I wouldn't send my other investigators."

Curious about the conversation, Jill leaned against the office door. "So, you've got another ambiguous case with political implications you'd like us to take?"

Jack laughed. "Jill, you make it sound like you have a choice in your assignments."

Jill sat in the chair next to the speaker. "So, what's the case?"

"A ranger was found dead in Manzanar National Historic Site yesterday morning. One of the other rangers came in to open the visitor center and found Erik "Red"

Peterson, who'd been on duty the previous afternoon, dead. His throat had been cut and his body was draped over a barbed wire fence."

Frowning while deep in thought, Jill asked, "Is Manzanar the World War II Japanese relocation camp?"

"That's it. The location is just west of Death Valley National Park. It's in California, not far from the Nevada border."

"Was there something special going on with that ranger?" I asked. "A recent divorce or breakup? Financial problems? Gambling?"

"According to the superintendent, the victim was congenial and well liked."

"Is there something going on at the site?" Jill asked. "Are they having protesters or is anyone suing the Park Service?"

"Richardson says, there's always a low level of discontent among several groups. People show up on special occasions to hang prayer ribbons on the monument or a person might picket the gate. None of that has been going on recently."

"You mentioned a political aspect to it," I said.

"The Inyo County Sheriff's Department was called to the scene. They apparently have problems with shipments of Mexican drugs moving up the highway past the site. The sheriff is convinced that the ranger was either dealing drugs, or he was killed by someone when a drug deal fell apart."

"Is there any reason to believe the dead ranger *was* involved in the drug trade?" I asked.

"Not at all. By all accounts, Erik Petersen was a boy scout. He drank only to be sociable. He wasn't in a relationship with any of the female rangers, although some of them thought he was cute. The superintendent was with the county deputies when they searched Petersen's apartment, and they didn't find drugs or drug paraphernalia. It's highly unlikely he was into drugs."

"Maybe he stumbled into a drug deal," Jill suggested.

"That's an angle to consider," Jack replied.

"Why do you want us involved?" Jill asked.

"The superintendent told me the sheriff isn't even going to look at any of the protestors or other parties with potential issues. The sheriff told Richardson that if the Park Service wanted something else investigated, he'd have to find someone to do it."

"That doesn't sound political," I replied. "The sheriff is looking one way. We can look the other."

"The problem may come if you find a murderer who isn't part of a cartel. The sheriff might not be willing to accept that result. It would call his total focus on the drug aspect into question, which would make him look bad.”

Jill grinned at me and said, “A smartass former St. Paul detective told me to collect evidence, then let it lead me to the motive and murderer. By finding the solution first, cops tend to pick and choose evidence that fits their preconceived decision.”

“Does Jill always refer to you as a smartass?” Jack asked.

“She does, and I want to file a harassment complaint.”

“No problem,” Jack replied. “Fill it out on the Park Service Human Resources database. Make sure to cite specific incidents and the dates they occurred. The Park Service will have an inspector general or legal counsel contact you to discuss your complaint.” Jack paused. “Oh wait, that won’t work because Jill does all the computer paperwork. You probably don’t know how to pull up a form in the HR database.”

Snorting, Jill replied, “He’s a dinosaur, Jack.”

Ignoring Jill’s dig, I asked, “Which airport is closest to Manzanar?”

“You can take your pick. Las Vegas, Reno, and LA are all about two hundred miles away.”

“Great,” I replied. “Centrally located in the middle of nowhere.”

Jack laughed. “Fletcher, you were the person who told me he hated big cities.

There are no big cities near Manzanar. You'll love it."

"How soon do we need to be there?" Jill asked.

"The body was found yesterday. The superintendent called me this morning after talking with the sheriff. I think the sooner you get there, the sooner you can stop the sheriff from running too far down the wrong rabbit hole."

"We'll book flights and start packing," Jill replied as I ended the call. Looking at me, she asked, "What are you thinking?"

"I think this sounds suspiciously like the Hawaiian case where the ranger had decided what happened, sent in his report, and closed the case before looking at the evidence."

Jill patted my arm. "Don't worry, I won't make you go on a helicopter ride with a suicidal killer on this trip."

"That won't be a problem," I said as I walked to the bedroom and took out a pair of well-worn suitcases. "You will *never* get me on a helicopter again. NEVER."

"It wasn't so bad. Your eyebrows grew back after the fire." She looked at the small carryon I'd opened and gave me *the look*. "You need the big suitcase. Your uniform and bulletproof vest won't fit in a carryon."

"I hadn't planned on being shot, so I wasn't going to bring my vest."

Pulling the large suitcase out of the closet, she rolled it to me. "We didn't plan on being shot in Wyoming. Yet, there we were in the middle of a gunfight. Pack your vest."

Staring at the suitcase and contemplating the hassle of checking and collecting the bags at the airport, I paused. "The airlines lose checked bags."

"Fine. Wear your vest on the plane while we're flying."

The prospect of sitting in an airline seat wearing a bulletproof vest, along with the undue attention we'd attract, made my decision easy. I set the carryon aside and opened the larger suitcase.

I noticed Jill's smirk as I packed the vest as the bottom layer in the suitcase. "I really don't need to bring a uniform. We're investigators, we can dress casually. Tell me what you know about Manzanar."

"I heard it's located on the site of a Japanese American relocation and internment camp. People were uprooted from their homes, jobs, and businesses, then sent to Manzanar. It was one of the ten relocation centers built in the western US during WWII. That's about all I've heard."

"By today's standards the internment of a whole group of people seems incredible. There are rules and laws about unlawful arrest, seizure of assets, etc."

"Pearl Harbor had just been bombed by the Japanese Imperial Navy. There was a lot of distrust and fear of anything Japanese. Things were different."

"Yeah. As a kid I remember hearing stories about German immigrants who changed their names, so they sounded more American." Intrigued, I asked, "How do you know all this history of the internment camps?"

Jill smiled. "Maybe I stayed awake in my history class."

Chapter 3

After looking at a map of Manzanar and speaking with the government-approved travel agency, Jill booked flights into Las Vegas. I called our friend Matt Mattson, asking if he or his wife would water our plants and keep an eye on the house while we were gone.

"Of course, we'll water the plants and chase away the burglars," Matt replied. "When are you flying out?"

"Jill booked flights to Las Vegas for tomorrow morning."

"Hang on, Doug." I waited while Matt passed the information to his wife, Mandy. A moment later, Matt was back. "Mandy says supper will be served at 6:00. Bring your departure information because she's driving you to the airport. She added that there would not be any discussion about that arrangement. She *is* driving you to the airport. You won't take an Uber. Understood?"

"Yeah. Tell Mandy the message is understood. Can we bring something for supper?"

"No. Just pack your bags and get your butts over here at 6:00. Mandy is walking out of the door to buy groceries."

Jill walked into my office as I ended the call. "Are we going there for supper, or is Mandy preparing a traveling feast to be delivered here?"

"Did you listen in from the hallway?"

"No, I just know Mandy. She'll have to pick us up before 6:00 tomorrow morning to make our flight."

"And we both know her hair will be perfect, and her makeup will be done. I suspect she may have to stay up all night just to be prepared to deliver us to the airport."

Jill turned to leave and said, "I'm sure that's all part of her debutante training."

"She can't leave the house unless she looks like she's *put together*," I said to the empty doorway.

From down the hall, Jill responded, "You're catching on, dear."

* * *

The aroma of boiling shrimp preceded our arrival at the Mattsons' door. I handed over a growler of Lazy Beach beer when Matt met us at the door. "I have beer," he replied, looking at the brown half-gallon glass jug. "But this looks more interesting."

Jill pushed past us and was met with a hug in the kitchen. Looking over Jill's shoulder, Mandy smiled and said, "Y'all get your fannies in here. The shrimp are done, and the margaritas are poured."

Over dinner, we shared what we knew about the case. Jill provided the details on which plants needed watering, and Mandy chatted about her improving golf scores, which she attributed to a new putter.

Matt carried the growler of beer onto the patio while the ladies cleared the dishes. Closing the door, he refreshed our mugs of beer as I sat in a chair overlooking the lawn. "I spoke with Ed Richardson, the Manzanar Park Superintendent," Matt said as he settled into his chair. "He warned me that the Inyo County Sheriff will not be pleased that the Park Service is sending investigators. The sheriff views the case as his, and your assistance will not be appreciated."

"Yeah, I got a little of that from Jack when he called to tell us about the case. Jack said the reason he assigned the case to us was because of the political considerations. He thinks Jill can keep the sheriff at bay while I dig into the case."

Looking over his shoulder at the women through the patio doors, Matt said, "Jill is good, but Richardson made it sound like mere diplomacy will not overcome the sheriff's stand. You may want to return to Las Vegas and catch a couple of shows rather than sitting in your local motel room."

"The travel agency booked us into the Mount Whitney Motel. It sounds like the pool and cable television are their big attractions. If we're really blocked from the investigation, I think we'll call Jack and tell him we're changing our flights and returning to Texas. I'm too old, cynical, and grumpy to stay where I'm unwanted."

Matt's smile and stare were hilarious. "Gee, I wouldn't have used those adjectives to describe you. I must be too polite."

"But you're not arguing about my choice of words."

"Not at all. I'm just saying I'm too polite to describe you like that."

I lifted my beer mug and touched it to Matt's. "A toast to cynical park rangers everywhere."

After sipping his beer, Matt shook his head. "You know, park rangers don't get cynical like old cops. We just get tired of smiling and acting interested in the repetitive questions our visitors pose."

"Like telling people why they can't keep the silver coins they find on North Padre Island National Seashore beach?"

"That, and politely telling people that smoking marijuana is illegal in the park and asking visitors to pick up the debris from their picnic tables and campsites, and deposit it into the provided waste receptacles before they leave."

I leaned back in my chair as the patio door opened. Jill and Mandy joined us. Sensing that they'd interrupted a conversation that was inappropriate or about them, Mandy put on her best debutante smile and asked, "Which one of us were you talking about, dear?"

Matt shook his head. "We were talking about getting old and cynical. You two were not the topic of our discussion."

Mandy's smile went from forced to softer when she turned to Jill. "As much as my mother taught me to be polite, tolerant, and considerate, young people try my patience. The poor young thing who rang me up at the grocery store didn't know how to make change. She was counting out seven dimes and eight pennies to give me seventy-eight cents in change. I suggested three quarters and three pennies would be better, and she looked at me like I was speaking a foreign language. It made me wonder how she passed third-grade math."

Jill stared into her margarita glass. "Doug's cynicism runs deeper. Sadly, it's starting to rub off on me." Glancing my way, she added, "There are still nice, polite, and genuine people out there, but we usually deal with folks at the other end of the spectrum."

Mandy's forced smile returned, and she looked at me. "Can we move to a happier topic?" When none of us offered conversation, she said, "When we were teens, my best friend, Alli, took me to the swimming hole and suggested we go skinny dipping."

All three of us were stunned. Matt, who'd been married to Mandy for thirty years said,

"You never told me you'd been skinny dipping."

"I never said that *I* went skinny dipping. Alli drove me there, but there was no way I was going to strip down to *my altogether* in front of a dozen other people."

Cocking her head, Jill asked, "So, you just sat there and watched the others swim naked?"

"Well, I didn't stare at them. That wouldn't be ladylike." Mandy paused, then added, "But I did learn more about male anatomy than any textbook or girls' discussion ever taught me."

Intrigued, I asked, "Like what?"

Getting a sly smile, Mandy replied, "I'd never heard about cold water shrinkage. And the whole circumcision discussion had never come up before that."

Hiding my smile by taking a drink of beer, I said, "Those don't seem like topics that would come up among debutantes."

"I know!" Mandy replied. "It was eye opening. On many levels." She paused then looked at the three of us. "Now wasn't that a more pleasant discussion than talking about getting old and cynical?"

Checking her watch, Jill said, "As entertaining as this has been, we need to go home and get some sleep. I don't want to be tired and hungover on the plane ride."

Matt stood and gathered the empty margarita glasses. "And I thought you were going to suggest running into the surf buck naked."

Shivering as if she was chilled, Jill shook her head. "No thank you."

Following Matt into the kitchen, I asked, "How would an arrest for public nudity affect my Park Service pension?"

Jill responded, surprising me, "I caught a bunch of young rangers skinny dipping while I was the park superintendent at the Ozark National Scenic Riverway. I put the fear of God into them by telling them they'd been verbally reprimanded, and any additional events would result in written reprimands that would go in their permanent files."

Matt nodded. "I would act tough, but realistically, I wouldn't ruin someone's career over something that trivial."

Mandy hugged us on the front steps and admonished us not to injure ourselves on our walk home. While hugging me, she whispered, "Don't get caught skinny dipping on your trip."

Laughing, I replied, "Mandy, we'll be in the desert, next to Death Valley. I don't think there is enough water there for a skinny dip."

Chapter 4

I looked around as we waited for our connecting flight to board in Dallas. "There aren't any children here. I don't recall ever being on a flight without noisy kids."

"We're flying to Las Vegas, Doug. It's not a family travel destination."

"Why did you choose Las Vegas over Reno or Los Angeles?"

Jill picked up her bag as the desk announced our flight's pre-boarding. "The travel agency suggested it. Apparently, the flights are always full, so they're cheap. Since it was a toss-up in terms of driving distance, and there's far less traffic than driving out of LA. I agreed with her."

Approaching the gate as pre-boarding started, I adjusted my windbreaker, making my badge visible to the gate agent. She nodded and scanned the boarding pass I'd loaded on my phone. "Have a nice flight, Mr. Fletcher."

I entered the jetway and was halfway down before I realized Jill wasn't behind me. I stopped and waited. A few moments later she walked down, wearing a sheepish grin. "What was the delay?"

"The agent asked if we'd be disturbed if the flight crew conducted a cash raffle on the flight. I said, 'no problem.'"

"A raffle?"

"If you want to participate, you write your name or seat number on a one-dollar bill that is thrown into a basket. The flight attendants collect all the money, then draw a winner. The winner gets all the money in the basket."

"Why did the gate agent ask you about the dollar bill raffle?"

"I think the law about gambling on a plane flying over Texas, New Mexico, and Utah might be murky."

"I've never heard of anything like an in-flight raffle on a flight," I replied as we reached the plane doorway.

"The Las Vegas flights are different. I guess the flight crews have fun, although some of the passengers start their Vegas drinking binge enroute, and they sometimes get a little rowdy."

Seeing my badge, the flight attendant smiled and leaned close. "I'll move you up to first class if there are any open seats." Seeing Jill's badge, she added, "Cool! We never get female cops on our flights. Welcome aboard."

Taking our seats in the coach section, I looked around. "We'll never get upgraded on this flight. There are too many Vegas high rollers who are willing to pay for first-class tickets."

As predicted, we weren't upgraded. I chose not to throw a dollar into the drawing, but Jill pulled a bill out of my wallet and wrote her seat number on it. The winner was a young woman apparently part of a group flying to Las Vegas for a bachelorette party. Although that group bought a lot of drinks and got loud, they weren't obnoxious and the people around them seemed to enjoy their revelry.

"What happens at a bachelorette party?" I asked Jill.

"I've never been to a bachelorette party, so I couldn't tell you. What happens at stag parties?"

"I was dispatched to a few rowdy stag parties when I was a St. Paul cop. I can't believe women would do the things drunken young men..."

I got a look. "Really? You don't think a bunch of drunk young women would act differently from a group of drunk young men?"

I looked at the laughing, singing young women. "I withdraw that argument."

"I think there's a bell-shaped distribution of peoples' drunken stupidity. The extreme, like me, shrink into a corner and get very quiet or will leave. Then there's the other extreme, becoming totally uninhibited and anything goes."

"The people at that end of the bell-curve are the ones we see as cops. They behave normally when sober and have jobs. Get a few drinks in them, and they become sociopathic, willing to step beyond the bounds of what's morally or legally acceptable."

Leaning nearer to get heard over the increasingly rowdy people around the bridal party, Jill asked, "Do you think that's what happened to our dead ranger? Someone was angry with him when they were sober, but after a few drinks their displeasure turned into murderous hatred?"

"If the murderer was a sociopath, that could be the case. There are also psychopathic people who will act on their aggressions without needing alcohol to lower their boundaries. Most premeditated murders are committed by psychopaths. Second-degree murder, those committed as part of a fight or other crime, are most often committed by sociopaths."

"Like a guy who's mad at the world and picks up a bottle on his way home from work. He takes a few drinks, then takes out his frustrations on his wife or girlfriend."

"I saw a lot of that as a St. Paul cop. There really aren't that many truly psychopathic people out there. I think a lot of them get locked up."

"So, what would make someone so angry they would kill a park ranger?"

"That's why I asked Jack if the guy had an angry roommate or girlfriend. Most murders are committed by someone known to the victim."

"The sheriff seems to be focused on a drug angle."

"He may be spot on. If the ranger was using drugs, or dealing, he might've gotten crosswise with a dealer. Or, he may have been dealing himself and ran into someone who couldn't pay or wanted more than they could afford."

Leaning closer so I could hear her over the increasingly vocal bridal group, Jill said, "Okay, that's probably where the sheriff is looking. If we let him pursue that line of investigation, where will we look?"

"If it's not personal, the murder is probably related to someone who's unhappy with the park."

"Perhaps a family member of someone who was held there?"

I watched the bride, who was wearing a tiara, stand up and lead the plane in a Taylor Swift song while I thought about Jill's comments. "I think virtually all the people who were interned during the early 1940s are probably dead. If that was the motive, it could be the grandchild of an internee. But I don't see that kind of anger flowing down through three generations."

"Really?" Jill asked. "Think about Israel and the Palestinians. Their hatred goes back thousands of years."

'That's a festering sore. There are people picking at that scab and stirring up the hatred. I don't see that with the Japanese American internees."

"Okay. Let's talk about festering sores. Which tribe was ousted from this area and moved to a reservation?"

"I don't know. That'd be a great topic to research on your phone after we land."

"Jack mentioned protesters who showed up occasionally to picket and hang banners. We need to know what their issues are and who is leading the protests."

I closed my eyes and thought. "Most protesters aren't killers. There are protests going on all the time. Hell, there are professional protesters, like the ones we met in the Everglades. They move from protest to protest, just to be an irritant to 'the system.' Most of them are non-violent. I think they just like seeing their faces on the news."

The bride moved into the aisle and started dancing. A flight attendant moved quickly to keep the aisle clear. A second flight attendant made an announcement over the speaker that safety was their number one objective and the aisles needed to be kept clear. She suggested that anyone not going to the restroom stay in their seat with the seatbelt buckled loosely around them.

Jill looked at me. "We helped with the one drunk guy on a flight, but I haven't been trained to handle a riot."

Laughing, I replied, "A shot of pepper spray would probably quiet them down, but it would spread to everyone in the plane. They'd have to make an emergency landing."

We watched the bridal group, now having a subdued discussion with the lead flight attendant. "I think they're being advised to quiet down."

After a few minutes of silence, I said, "We need to know why there are protesters at Manzanar. There might be one kook in the group who took the issue too seriously and went off the deep end."

Jill wrinkled her nose. "Sometimes there's friction between the rangers. I've never seen it get too out of hand, but there have been some park romances that turned sour."

"Jack told me that everyone loved the victim."

"Do you think anyone would tell you they hated a murder victim?"

"It happens. Not often, but it happens."

"Yeah, about as often as the killer loses his wallet or cell phone at the murder scene."

"That happens too," I said, wiggling my eyebrows. "There is no intelligence test for being a murderer."

Chapter 5

Once out of the Las Vegas area, we discovered that most of the four-hour drive was through the desert. As we neared Manzanar, the eastern slope of the Sierra Nevada mountains provided a change of scenery. We passed through a few towns, but the region was surprisingly void of civilization.

After I'd commented on that, Jill replied, "It's high desert. There's no water." Using her phone, she'd done searches on Manzanar, protests, and history during our entire four-hour drive. "As a matter of fact, one of the 1990s protests in the Manzanar and Lone Pine area was over water rights that were sold so the water could be diverted to California cities and farms. There are people who want to reclaim those water rights so the area can be developed."

"How long ago did that transfer happen?"

"Some time in the mid-twentieth century."

"That water isn't coming back. I'm sure farmers somewhere else are growing crops with it, and golf courses are green. They'd have to turn off the spigot to those existing uses."

"That doesn't mean people won't protest over water rights again. There are people protesting about everything. A lot of the issues are moot or nonsense. That doesn't mean there aren't protesters willing to picket over any cause."

"Yeah, I remember women picketing on a street corner in Roseville. They wanted the city council to declare Roseville, Minnesota a nuclear-free zone."

"I didn't know there were nukes in the Minneapolis area."

'There aren't. And the nearest nuclear power plant is a hundred miles away. Just the same, there were nuclear protesters."

With a few keystrokes, Jill was at another site. "People are protesting the mining of uranium in that region. Apparently, there were test holes and mines all over the Southwest. The protesters want a moratorium on uranium mining and exploration."

"That seems like a more reasonable protest issue than water rights. I remember that coming up when we were in northern Arizona. As I recall, there were people getting sick and dying from radiation exposure due to the old mines," I replied.

"As my smartass husband recently said, protesters don't need to be reasonable or rational. If there's an issue, someone will have a burr under their saddle about it." Jill's phone chimed and she looked down. "The Manzanar turn is in one mile."

Moments later a watchtower came into view. As we approached, it became clear the old guard tower overlooked the Manzanar entrance. An unoccupied sheriff's department car was blocking the road next to a stone shack at the historic site entrance to turn away any visitors. I turned into the exit driveway and eased past the cop's car, noting the empty entrance guard shack. Another sheriff's department vehicle was parked outside the impressive visitor's center that resembled an airport hangar. Parked in front were another sheriff's car, two Park Service pickups, and an assortment of civilian vehicles.

Compared to the rest of the rustic, wooden buildings, the visitor center looked modern and out of place in the stark brown landscape.

"It looks like a cop party," I quipped as I parked in an open slot next to one of the pickups.

"I feel like I should've worn a coat," Jill said as we stepped out of our rental car. "I expect a frosty reception."

"Put on your vest," I said as I opened the trunk lid to access our suitcases.

"Why?"

"We need to look like real cops," I said as I removed my vest from my suitcase. "If the sheriff's department thinks we're government bureaucrats, they'll ignore us."

Jill smiled as she fastened the Velcro straps on her vest. "We *are* government bureaucrats, and I suspect they'll ignore us no matter what we're wearing."

"They don't need to know that."

Entering the building, we found a portion of the visitor center lobby had been converted into an incident room with historical displays arranged around the walls. Half a dozen people sat around the table alongside two whiteboards covered with pictures and handwritten notes. A tall, slender ranger stood when we walked in. The heads of the others turned, but they didn't leave their seats.

"I assume you are the Park Service investigators," the man said as he approached us.

Offering my hand, I replied, "I'm Doug Fletcher, and this is my partner, Jill."

"Ed Richardson, Park Superintendent," the man said. He gestured for us to follow him into a remote corner in front of a pictorial display of the camp taken in the 1940s. The others returned to their discussion at the table. Richardson made sure we were out of earshot, then turned his back to the table and whispered, "Thanks for coming. This is out of control. I need some open minds to sit in on this discussion."

Glancing past Richardson, Jill looked at the uniformed people sitting around the table. Two wore sheriff's department brown uniforms. The others wore Park Service green and tan. "How is this out of control?"

"The sheriff's department is convinced Red was involved in the narcotics trade. They're trying to find evidence to support that theory."

"I take it that you don't think that was the case."

"Red was as straight as an arrow. I mean, he didn't ever have more than one beer when we socialized, and there's never been a hint that he's been involved in any drugs. The sheriff's department dismantled his car and apartment searching for drugs." Richardson nodded toward a gangly male ranger. "When they didn't find any, they accused his roommate, Todd Overland, and the rest of us of cleaning them out so Red wouldn't be accused."

"Was there anything else sketchy going on in Erik's life?" I asked.

"Nothing sketchy comes to mind. He had dated a girl from Lone Pine, but they broke up a while ago. I don't think there's been anyone in his life since then."

"We've heard about camp protesters," Jill suggested.

Richardson rolled his eyes. "The park had an occasional picketer when the site first opened. Aside from a peaceful annual pilgrimage of internee families, there's been nothing recently."

"What were they protesting?"

Richarson shrugged. "It varies. Water rights. The establishment of the site itself. The treatment of the internees. The theft of sacred Native land." Richardson paused. "Most recently, someone heard we were going to sell the property to a developer and two people protested that."

"Sell a national historic site?" Jill asked.

Glancing at the people around the table, Richardson shook his head. "I know. It was crazy. I went out and talked to the two protesters myself. A college-age man and woman. I assured them that no Park Service site had ever been sold to a private party."

"Did they accept that?" Jill asked.

"They left within ten minutes of our discussion, and I haven't seen them again." Sighing, the superintendent nodded toward the table. "I should introduce you to the team."

The rangers stood as we approached the table; the deputies didn't. "Folks, these are the investigators from the National Park Service Investigative Services Branch, Jill and Doug Fletcher. This is Grace Watanabe, who discovered Red's body. Todd Overland was Red's roommate. Becky Stipe is our most senior ranger. Kevin Roberts and Tonya Marshal are seasonal rangers."

I shook hands, noting that both Grace and Becky appeared to be in their fifties and wore uniforms that showed a little wear. Grace, who had Asian features, was tiny and slim. Becky was more matronly. Both had hair streaked with gray. Todd was gaunt and appeared tired while Kevin and Tonya appeared to be fresh out of college and their uniforms looked new. Kevin had a two-day growth of dark beard, and Tonya's dark hair was braided in cornrows. None of them smiled, apparently grieving the death of their colleague.

The older of the two male deputies, whose brass nameplate showed his name was Jones, watched while we shook hands with the rangers, then said, "I'm sorry you've wasted your time. This case is cut and dried."

"Really?" I asked, taking the empty chair next to him. "That's fast work. Who was the murderer?"

"Some Mexican cartel flunkies. They're probably back in Tijuana drinking Corona and bragging to their buddies about killing a *gringo* cop."

"Are there a lot of cartel hits here?" I asked.

The younger deputy, whose name badge showed Kellen, replied, "The highway is an artery of drugs flowing from Mexico into California, Utah, and north. We had a body dumped along the highway a couple of years ago. It's been quiet since then. We expect more violence as the drug flow increases and fentanyl becomes a bigger portion of the mix."

I leaned back and looked at the murder scene pictures posted on the boards. "I was a St. Paul detective. I've seen a few cartel hits.

I've never seen them use anything but a pistol for a hit and the cartel killers are in too much of a hurry to get away to do anything but leave the body lying in a heap. Someone took time to arrange this murder scene."

Looking irritated, Deputy Jones glanced at the board. "Their violence is evolving. We think they were trying to leave a message with this killing."

"Like what?" I asked. "Did they cut out his tongue, like he was an informant? Did they stuff his mouth with money like he was skimming profits?"

Deputy Kellen glared at me. "This was a 'don't mess with us' message."

"Ah," I replied. "Erik did something that irritated the cartel, and they wanted people to know not to repeat it." I nodded, then leaned my arms on the table. "So, what were they warning people about? What had Erik done?"

"Cartels don't need a reason to warn anyone," the deputy said. "They just want people scared of them."

I nodded in agreement and said, "I've seen that. They like to come in and take out some tough guy in a rival gang as a statement. Was the victim tough, heavily armed, or even in a gang?" I looked at the pictures of the victim' body more closely and said, "I don't see any gang tattoos."

Sighing, the older deputy glared at me. "We're still investigating that angle."

Trying to de-escalate the rising tension, Jill leaned forward. "We're here to assist you with *your* investigation. What can we do to help move things ahead?"

The corner of the older deputy's mouth twitched, like he was tempted to smile. "Where are you staying?"

"The Mount Something Motel."

"Have you checked in yet?"

"No, we decided to stop here first."

Pushing himself back, Deputy Jones nodded. "I'll tell you what. Check in to your motel and leave your cell phone number with the superintendent. I'll give you a call if we come up with something for you to do."

Knowing we'd been dismissed, I stood. "What time are we meeting here tomorrow morning?"

Jones sighed and looked irritated. "I don't know that we'll be here in the morning. I'll have the superintendent call and let you know when we're getting together again."

Kellen leaned close to Tonya, used a stage whisper, and said, "I wouldn't hold my breath while awaiting that call."

Tonya rolled her eyes, then sighed in resignation.

Jill took out a business card and wrote her phone number on the back. Sliding it across the table to Deputy Jones, she said, "Here's my cell phone number."

Without looking down, Jones pushed Jill's card toward the superintendent. "Ed will call if there's anything for you to do."

The superintendent walked us to the door. Jill looked over her shoulder at the deputies who went back to interviewing the rangers. "I feel like a crumb that's been brushed off the table."

Richardson walked outside with us. After the door closed, he let out a breath. "Yeah, welcome to the realm of the irrelevant, unappreciated, and unwanted. Now you know how I've felt for two days. The only time I've been useful is when I accompanied them to Red's apartment." He paused, then looked at me. "What are you planning to do?"

"We'll be here at 8:00 tomorrow morning. If the deputies aren't around, I'd like to speak to all your rangers to hear what they know. If the county won't let us be part of their plans, we'll run a parallel investigation."

"Are you going to look into Red's drug connection, too?"

Shaking my head, I said, "If the deputies are already on that aspect, and it's as unlikely as you make it sound, we'll strategize and look at other possibilities."

Richardson grabbed my hand as if it was a lifeline. "I am so glad you're here. I'm sick of being pushed aside and ignored while they chase something that seems illogical. And you heard them say they think Red's killer is already in Mexico. They're not going to put any effort into identifying him."

"Did the state crime lab process the scene and recover evidence?" Jill asked.

"The county has their own forensics guy. He took a bunch of samples, but I don't know what he did with them."

"Do you have his card?" I asked.

Richardson snorted. "The deputies wouldn't let us anywhere near the forensics guy. They were 'preserving the crime scene.'"

In the rental car, Jill buckled her seatbelt and turned toward me. "They're trying to find evidence to support their preconceived theory."

Starting the car, I nodded. "And they're not finding any supporting evidence. They'll muddle along for a week or two, then file the case as unsolved with their notes indicating it was likely the result of drug gang violence."

"What are we going to do about that?" Jill asked as I drove out of the parking lot.

"First of all, you're going to find a map to our motel. Secondly, you're going to ask Yelp for the best nearby restaurant."

Pulling out her phone, Jill started a search. "And thirdly?"

"We'll eat supper, then go back to our motel where we'll find something interesting on the hotel's expansive cable network."

"I'm not eating any red meat tonight," Jill said as she waited for something to load on her phone.

"Fish or chicken only?"

"I'll eat anything that doesn't look like the bloody mess in the pictures they'd posted on the board."

"I forget that you haven't developed insensitivity to gruesome crime scenes."

"I haven't, and I don't want to." Seeing something on her phone, Jill said, "Here's our motel, the Mount Whitney Motel. It's in Lone Pine."

"That sounds like a mom-and-pop place. Isn't there a Holiday Inn or Best Western?"

Ignoring me, Jill slid her finger across the screen. "The Season's Restaurant has four and a half stars. It's within walking distance of our motel."

"Is that your walking distance, or mine?"

* * *

Both the motel and restaurant felt like they'd come from an earlier, simpler time. They were well-maintained and clean. The workers were young adults who greeted us with smiles. After accepting menus, I was surprised to see Jill smiling at me.

"What?"

"Finding places like this reminds me of why I hate big cities. People aren't rushing around here, acting like they're too important to deal with others, and stressed out beyond belief."

"You're saying this feels like home."

45

"Yeah," Jill replied as she picked up her menu. "It does."

While perusing the dinner options, I said, "I'm surprised you're not stressed out about the investigation."

"What's there to stress about? We're locked out by the sheriff's department. I know you're brainstorming because you think the sheriff is barking up the wrong tree. We'll meet with Ed Richardson tomorrow morning, then we'll start looking in a different direction."

"You're amazingly calm. Jack thinks that you're going to smooth things over with the sheriff and get us into the thick of it."

"I've accepted that there are things I can't change. I'm not going to stress out over a couple of deputies who've made up their minds. The only thing we can do is show them they're wrong."

Our waitress returned, holding her order pad open. "Did you two want something from the bar before you order?"

"I'll have a local tap beer," I replied.

"I'd like a red wine," Jill replied. "Which would you suggest?"

The waitress' grin told me that was an amusing question. "Well, we're on the back side of the Sierra Nevada mountains. The wineries on the other slope are world-renowned for their reds, especially zinfandels."

"That sounds good," Jill replied.

Continuing to hold her pen over the pad, the waitress asked, "Which one?"

"Pick something good that won't bust my per diem allowance."

"I think the Chatom Vineyards zin fits the bill." As she wrote, the waitress asked if we'd made our dinner choices.

Handing her my menu, I replied, "The French dip sandwich looks good."

"Fries, slaw, or a salad?"

Looking at Jill, I paused. "I'll have a salad with Italian dressing."

Jill smiled and handed her menu to the waitress. "I'll have the brook trout with a baked potato and salad. I'd like French and blue cheese dressings on the side." When the waitress left, Jill leaned close so the people at nearby tables couldn't hear her. "What's your gut telling you about the murder?"

"We need to find out who among the protestors has the most to win or lose."

"I'm sure that would be developers if they can get water rights. They stand to make millions."

I shook my head. "They're irrelevant. The Park Service isn't going to turn over a historic site. How big a deal are the water rights? I know water rights were behind the Sedona case."

"It's moot. According to the internet, water rights were sold decades ago. There are farms and cities relying on them. No one is going to cut them off. Not happening."

"What's left?" I asked.

"People whose grandparents were interned. I suppose they might want financial reparations for the harm done to their families."

"You can check, but I think reparations were paid to the families years ago."

Jill leaned back. "Then that's it. I don't think there's anyone else who stands to benefit."

"There must be Native tribes who were pushed off the land and put on reservations. Maybe some of the tribes are fighting for land lost in old treaties." I thought for a minute, then added, "or the people fighting against uranium mining."

"The park has nothing to do with uranium," Jill countered.

"The park is a lightning rod for protests against the government."

"The superintendent said there wasn't much recent protest activity."

I thought for a moment, then said, "That brings us back to the traditional big three murder motives: love, money, or drugs. The sheriff is chasing the drug motive. We need to know if the victim had a current girlfriend or if money was involved."

"Think more broadly. Maybe the victim had a boyfriend. Maybe there was a love triangle."

"Those are good questions for tomorrow." Our drinks arrived before we could continue brainstorming. I held up my beer. "I declare the office closed. No more investigative discussion."

* * *

Though not a gourmet delight, dinner was tasty and satisfying. As we drove to the motel, Jill said, "I'm a little worried about Mom. She's putting up a good front, but I don't think she feels well."

Not prepared for the change of topic, I composed my thoughts. "My mom and Chet see them every day. If there's something to worry about, one of them will call you."

Satisfied with that answer, Jill relaxed and looked out of her window as we drove through town. "I don't like this situation. The Park Service is being shut out, and I'm not sure there's anything we can do about it."

"There's plenty to be done, just not with the sheriff's department."

Jill turned toward me and replied, "It's unlike you to display optimism."

"I'm not being optimistic. I just know there are a lot of things the sheriff's department is overlooking. We'll dig around on the fringes of their drug investigation. Something may pop up."

Jill pointed a half block ahead of us. "Pull into that gas station."

"We could wait until tomorrow to fill up."

"No. Pull in here."

Unsure about Jill's sudden concern about our gas level, I turned into the gas station and parked next to a pump. Jill got out of the car and walked inside, leaving me with the impression she needed the restroom more than I needed gas. I topped off the gas tank and paid at the pump with a credit card. I was waiting for my receipt to print when Jill walked out carrying a shopping bag.

"What did you buy?" I asked as I buckled up and started the rental car.

"Something to snack on while we're watching television."

Glancing at her, I expressed surprise. "You never snack."

"I felt like having popcorn while watching a movie."

"Did you buy soda pop too?"

A grin crept onto her lips. "California gas stations sell wine and beer."

"So, we're going back to the motel where you're going to choose a pay-per-view romantic comedy. Then, we'll eat popcorn and drink wine?"

"I bought you a six-pack of beer."

"That's very considerate, considering I don't care for wine." I paused, then asked, "Why were you suddenly overtaken with the urge for munchies and a movie?"

"They'll take my mind off the investigation." I waited for more. Eventually, Jill added, "I might feel romantic after a cute movie and a couple glasses of wine."

"You're going to ply me with alcohol, then have your way with me?" I asked.

"That usually works."

Laughing, I turned into the motel parking lot. Jill handed me the bags while she unlocked the room. Inside, she used the television remote to review the movie options while I carried in our suitcases.

"My only request is that you don't choose a movie involving a disguised prince who falls in love with the librarian. I think we've seen that one about five times."

"Fine. No Hallmark movies. How about Sandra Bullock and Ryan Reynolds?" Jill studied the movie information. "Betty White is in this one."

I opened the wine's screw cap and poured some into a plastic glass. Handing it to Jill, I opened the giant bag of popcorn and then opened a beer before joining her on the bed. We watched the opening scene, and I commented, "Well, Sandra Bullock isn't Miss Congeniality in this movie."

"She's kind of bitchy. I bet she softens as the movie progresses."

We'd finished half the popcorn and a beverage refill for each of us before the movie ended. Jill snuggled into my shoulder for the last half hour. As the credits rolled, she said, "I'm getting my hair done tomorrow after we meet with the superintendent and his rangers."

"Why?"

Turning off the television, then nestling against me, she said, "Hair salons are a hub of information. When I have my hair done in Port Aransas, I learn more about what's going on than when I watch the news or read a newspaper."

I rolled onto my side, so our noses were nearly touching and slid my hand under her shirt. "That's inspired. You're turning into a creative investigator."

After one kiss, Jill pushed herself away. "Hold that thought."

"Where are you going?" I asked as she stood.

"I'm going to slip into something...flannel. I know you find that irresistible."

"Does it reach to your ankles?" I asked as the bathroom door closed.

"Of course, it does."

Chapter 6

There were eight vehicles in the Manzanar parking lot when we arrived at 8:oo the following morning. Inside, we found the visitor center rearranged as if the sheriff's department had never been there. Ed Richardson broke away from a discussion with a group of rangers when we walked in.

"The deputies are gone?" Jill asked as he greeted us.

"They're off doing their investigation. They 'no longer require our input,' so they took their toys and left." Nodding toward the gathered rangers, he said, "Let me introduce my staff."

A male and female ranger ended their conversation as we approached. The middle-aged woman stood and put out her hand. "We met yesterday. I'm Grace Watanabe."

The young, male ranger reached past Grace to shake my hand. "Everyone calls me Casey."

"Casey was off yesterday," the superintendent explained.

"I'm Doug and this is my partner, Jill."

Jill was intrigued by the way Casey had introduced himself. "Everyone calls you Casey. I take it that's not your *given* name."

Grace jumped in before Casey replied. With her eyes sparkling, she said, "His name is Krispin Charles O'Brien the fourth."

The look Grace got told me Casey wasn't happy about her sharing that information. "Only my parents call me Krispin. It's an old family name. I prefer to be called by my initials, K.C."

"We get that," Jill replied. "Only Doug's mother calls him Douglas. And only when he's in trouble."

The other rangers gathered around as we introduced ourselves. "I'm Becky, we met yesterday."

Next was Todd Overland, who was Erik's roommate. Behind him was Tonya, whose personality seemed larger than life. The last ranger to introduce himself was Seth Cline. After Tonya, anyone would've seemed like an introvert, but Seth seemed especially reserved, saying nothing except, "I'm seasonal, like Tonya."

Following the introduction, Richardson said, "I'm sorry about yesterday. The sheriff's department is calling the shots and we're out of the information loop."

Jill looked at Grace. "You discovered Erik's body, right?"

Grace turned solemn and nodded. "It was the worst day of my life."

"Did you notice anything about the crime scene that provided a clue as to what happened or who might have attacked him?" I asked.

Shaking her head, Grace replied, "There was nothing there. I mean, Red was just hanging on the wire."

Jill touched Grace's arm. "Put Red's image out of your mind for a moment and close your eyes. What else did you see and hear around the immediate area?"

Closing her eyes, Grace paused. "Flies. There were dozens of flies buzzing around him." Grace's eyes blinked open. "There aren't many flies here. That's weird."

"There are flies everywhere," Jill said, reassuringly. "That's good. The presence of flies means he'd been dead for a few hours. What else?"

"His Prius was there, with the driver's door open. Other than Red's car and body, nothing else seemed memorable."

"Were there tire tracks?" I asked.

"There were tracks from Red's car." Grace paused again. "There was another set of tracks, like someone had driven off the road when they passed by."

"Did you notice anything about them?" Jill asked. "Were they close together, like they'd been made by an ATV, or maybe dual tires like on a truck?"

Grace closed her eyes, trying to envision details. "I don't recall much. I think the tire tracks were more like a car had driven off the road. They weren't knobby and were wider than an ATV, but not like a big truck. I suppose they might've been made by a pickup or car."

"That's good," Jill said, encouraging Grace. "What else did you see? Were there footprints?"

"I didn't notice. I kind of stared into the distance when I called 911. I didn't want to look at Red's body."

"Was he wearing his uniform?"

"Yeah. There was blood all over his tan uniform shirt, running down onto his..." Grace choked up and stopped.

"Onto his uniform pants," Jill suggested.

Grace nodded. "I've never seen so much blood."

"Was it dried blood, or fresh?" Jill asked.

"It wasn't fresh. I mean, it was dark-colored, like it had once been redder, but had turned kind of thick and burgundy-colored as it soaked in and dried."

"What did you smell?" I asked.

"Smell?"

"Smell is a strong sense. It sometimes gives clues our eyes miss."

Grace drew a breath. "I didn't smell anything unusual. It always smells dusty here. You know, because it's a desert."

"You didn't sense a metallic smell, like the blood?"

"Yeah, a little."

"Did you notice the lingering smell of aftershave, perfume, sweat, or anything else unusual?"

Grace drew a breath, then frowned. "There was a faint smoky odor. Like a wood stove, campfire, or something."

"That's good," Jill said, encouraging Grace to continue.

I gestured for Ed Richardson to join me as I walked to a corner away from the others. "Grace smelled wood smoke. Is there a neighbor who heats with wood?"

"There aren't any nearby residences. I've never smelled wood smoke here."

"What would Grace have smelled burning?"

"We're in the desert, so there aren't any forest or grass fires here. I don't know what she might've smelled."

"Did the sheriff's deputies recover any tire track impressions or footprints?"

"Who knows? They kept us in the visitor center while their forensics people processed the scene. I have no idea what they might've found."

Accepting that Ed had no knowledge of the investigation, I nodded toward Jill and the other rangers. "Casey wasn't there that morning?"

"He was scheduled for later in the morning, in case we had a noon and early afternoon rush of visitors."

"And the others weren't here either?"

Richardson shook his head. "I spread their shifts out during the week, so we have at least two people here at all times. I schedule more staff and volunteers on the weekends, when we get the most visitors."

"But Erik was alone when he closed the park?"

Richardson paused. "Seth closed the entrance at five o'clock, checked to make sure all the visitors were gone, then he went home. Red locked up the visitor center and probably left a few minutes later."

I saw Jill talking with Seth as the other staff members stood around them. Most were engaged and interested in the discussion. Casey frequently checked his phone, like he was bored or expected a text from someone. "Casey seems like a square peg in a round hole."

"He's offered up a couple of reasons for being here, the most likely having to do with crashing his father's Maserati. I think he was banished from the house. I overheard him tell Grace his father wanted him to learn the value of hard work and money."

"Do you have many volunteers who work here?"

"We have two volunteers who come in on the weekends to help with souvenir sales. They weren't scheduled to be here the day of Red's death."

"Was Erik's body visible to someone driving by on the highway?"

Richardson looked toward the entrance door. "I suppose it might've been. I mean, anyone driving by might've seen Red's Prius parked by the fence if they looked that way. They might not have seen the car in the dark. In the morning, they might not have realized that the body hanging on the fence was anything but trash."

"What do you mean?"

"It's the desert. Stuff blows around and gets caught in the barbed wire. If they'd seen it, I suppose someone might've thought a tarp had blown in and was tangled in the wire."

We rejoined Jill and the rangers, who were now chatting about the site and visitors. Jill turned to me and shook her head slightly, indicating that Grace and Seth hadn't provided any additional details.

"Has there ever been another death at this site?" I asked.

All the rangers looked at Grace, who'd obviously been employed at the site longer than anyone else. Her brow furrowed as she thought. "The last person who died here was probably a detainee during the war."

"Did many detainees died here?" Jill asked.

Grace, who the others deferred to as the historical expert, exhaled and focused on a window that overlooked the memorial. "About one hundred and fifty people died in the camp. Many were elderly and a few were stillborn children. Most were cremated.

Their remains were removed to other cemeteries when their families were released from the camp in 1945. There were nine graves left after the camp closed. Two were elderly men who had no family here. One was an unnamed stillborn baby whose body was never claimed."

"But no deaths since the camp closed?" I asked.

The rangers all shook their heads but looked toward Grace to answer. "No," she replied.

"Are there ever demonstrations by the surviving families?" I asked.

"They weren't uncommon through the '50s and '60s. As the survivors died, the protests became less prevalent. Ronald Reagan signed the Civil Liberties Act of 1988, which gave the detainees, and their families, a formal apology and paid them reparations. The protests ended after that." Grace continued, "A few families make a pilgrimage here each spring, but it's not a protest as much as it is a memorial ceremony."

Casey added, "We tell visitors the protests ended until 9/11. That brought a groundswell of survivors' families stepping forward to make sure Arab Americans didn't suffer the same fate as the Japanese Americans did after Pearl Harbor. There were a few picketers in the weeks after 9/11. When it became clear that the government wasn't going to undertake another unconstitutional roundup of innocent civilians, the protests died."

Tonya said, "Like Grace said, there's an annual pilgrimage here by survivors' families. They're always quiet and very respectful."

"So, you don't think Erik's attack would be retaliation from a survivor's family?" I summarized."

Grace shook her head. "None of the survivors' protests were ever violent. They wanted to vent their grievances, but they never harmed anyone."

Tonya smiled. "The Japanese American community is very polite and respectful. If there was a violent protest, it would be from some other, less civilized group."

Her comment intrigued Jill. "Give me an example of a less civilized group."

"A lot of the environmental protesters are more radical. The animal rights protesters release animals from research facilities and burn down labs."

"But they're not an issue here," I said.

Richardson shook his head. "I think Tonya is just pointing out the more radical and militant protest groups. Neither animal rights nor environmental groups have targeted National Parks. They have much more attractive targets than Manzanar."

"We heard about local water rights protests," Jill suggested.

Richardson wrinkled his nose. "We're not a target for them. Yes, the government allowed the water rights to be diverted elsewhere. The US Park Service wasn't part of that."

"So, who might be unhappy about the Park Service's Manzanar site?" I asked.

The door opened behind us, and Kevin Roberts walked in. Seeing us already in conversation, he grimaced. "Sorry. Um. My battery was dead. I had to get it jumped."

Richardson nodded his understanding. "You met Doug and Jill yesterday."

"Yeah," the latecomer said as he shook our hands.

"I just asked who besides the families of the internees would be unhappy with this site. We discussed people who might be generally unhappy with the government."

Kevin nodded his understanding but didn't add anything.

The rangers and superintendent looked among themselves, waiting for someone else to speak. Casey said, "I think that's the problem. We can't think of anyone who has a grudge against the Park Service. Everyone seems to think we provide a useful service by educating people about what can happen when the government does something terribly wrong."

"That leaves us searching for someone with a motive to target Erik," I replied.

Richardson shook his head. "We've asked ourselves a hundred times who would want to hurt Red. The answer is always, 'no one.'"

"That leaves us with some random killer who happened upon Erik and took out his personal frustration," I said. "The murder scene seems staged. Is there something symbolic about the way Erik was found?"

Shuddering, Grace replied, "His arms were spread out like Christ's crucifixion. But he didn't die from that; someone cut his throat."

I looked at Jill. "We should talk to the medical examiner. I'm sure he recovered some evidence from the victim's body."

After it was clear no one had anything more to offer, the superintendent walked us to our rental car. "I'm sorry we couldn't provide you with more information. There just isn't any rational reason for Erik's death."

I stopped next to the car. "I think you summarized the situation very well. There is no rational reason, so there must be an irrational reason that set off the killer."

"Like what?" Richardson asked.

"Maybe the killer had an abusive, red-haired father; Erik somehow triggered him to react while he was having a psychopathic episode."

"That happens?" Richarson asked.

"Sadly, it happens way too often," I replied. "Our prisons are full of irrational murderers."

"How do you catch someone like that?"

"Everyone at a crime scene takes evidence with them and leaves traces of themselves behind."

"The sheriff's department took all the evidence."

"I'll talk to the medical examiner. Maybe he's outside their sphere of influence. He might have something the deputies are choosing to exclude from consideration."

"I don't know anything about a medical examiner. The deputies were talking about the county coroner."

"That makes sense," I replied. "Rural areas often have a coroner who refers difficult cases to a pathologist or medical examiner. Where is the Inyo County Coroner's office?"

"I assume the coroner's main office is in Bishop, near the courthouse. I think there's an office in Lone Pine, too." Richardson put out his hand. "I'm so glad you two are here. For the first time, I feel like we have an advocate in this investigation."

Shaking Richardson's hand, Jill added, "We'll look places the sheriff's department doesn't know to look."

His interest piqued, Richardson asked, "Where?"

"I'm going to the hub of all gossip and information."

"Where are you going?" Richardson asked.

"To the hairdresser," Jill replied. "Stylists are usually tight-lipped. But everything that happens in any town is discussed at the salon.”

Richardson snorted. “I’d never have thought of that.”

I nodded. “Jill and I are usually overlooked by local law enforcement. It’s easier for us to apply our unique life experiences to gain useful information from alternative sources.”

* * *

Jill buckled her seatbelt as I started the rental car. “Seth was very quiet.”

“Do you mean quiet, as in hiding something? Or, quiet as an introvert?”

“Introverted. Most rangers are talkative and outgoing. I liked to hire theater majors as tour guides. They know how to project their voices and add charisma to their banter. Seth looked like he wanted to melt into the background.”

“Interesting,” I replied as I backed out of the parking spot. “Kevin didn’t have much to say, either.”

“I think he was embarrassed about being late.”

“He just stood there.”

“Not everyone is an extrovert, Doug.”

I chuckled.

“What?” Jill asked.

“I was just thinking about your Uncle Chet. He has something to say even when he has nothing to say." I paused, then asked, "How is Bill, the new horse?"

"It took a while for the other horses to accept him."

"Ah, the new kid on the ranch got the cold shoulder."

"Introduction to a new herd takes time, Doug. He'll eventually find his place in the pecking order."

"We should probably send your dad a check for hay. Before we left, he was grumbling about the cost of having another horse on the ranch."

"Dad likes to grumble. I've learned to ignore him. Besides, Chet had a truckload of hay delivered and I paid the farrier and vet bills. It's not costing Dad anything except that there's a horse in a stall he used for storage. Bill is in the pasture most of the time anyway."

"Someone has to clean the stall."

"It gets Dad out of Mom's way, and she doesn't have to listen to his grumbling. We're providing two services by having another horse there."

I looked at Jill skeptically. "You really believe that don't you?"

Jill shrugged. After a moment she asked, "Did you notice the bumper stickers on Kevin's pickup?"

It took me a second to shift mental gears from discussing Jill's ranch back to the Manzanar case. "Not really."

"Most rangers have 'Save the Whales' and 'Hug a Tree' bumper stickers. Kevin's were about the Second Amendment and guns."

Trying to be clever, I said, "Kevin's providing diversity."

Jill looked at me skeptically. "Sure. That's one way to look at it."

"Call the coroner's office to set up a meeting."

After a brief conversation, Jill nodded. "We'll see you this afternoon." After ending the call, she turned toward me. "The coroner agreed to meet us at the funeral home in Lone Pine at 3:00."

"At the funeral home?" I asked.

"He's the local mortician."

Chapter 7

A brief call got Jill an immediate appointment for a haircut and blow dry. "Come along and read the magazines in the waiting area while they're doing my hair," she said.

"I'm really not into *Cosmopolitan, The Ladies Home Journal,* or *Parenting Today.*"

"You're not there to read. Pretend to read and listen to the conversations."

"I'll read the email on my phone," I replied.

"Whatever. Just keep your eyes and ears open. If nothing else, you'll get a view inside the female psyche by listening to the conversations between clients and the hairdressers."

"I'm not sure that's a place I want to see," I replied.

"It might help you understand your mother."

"Like I said, I'm not sure I want to acquire that knowledge."

Jill reached over and ran her fingers over the nape of my neck. "You're a little shaggy. Maybe they could trim your hair, too."

"I think it'd cost triple my average barbershop haircut to get trimmed in a salon."

"Don't think of it as a haircut. You're paying an informant."

I sighed but didn't argue.

"Did you notice Casey's haircut?" Jill asked.

"Not really. Why?"

"He was shaggy, in an expensive, rich kid way."

"I thought shaggy was bad. You just said I was shaggy, so I should get trimmed."

"Casey's hair was carefully shaggy. It costs a lot of money to look stylishly unkempt."

"Huh. Are you saying I'm stylish?"

Snorting, Jill replied, "No, you just look shaggy."

Chuckling, I nodded. "I heard Dolly Parton on a talk show. She said it cost a lot of money to look trashy."

"Hmm. Trashy isn't the adjective I'd use to describe her. She's an incredible talent and a businesswoman. She's probably done more for American literacy than anyone since Andrew Carnegie."

"What? Explain that comment."

"Andrew Carnegie built libraries in thousands of small towns across their entire country. Because of him, people had access to reading material. Dolly's charity gives away children's books. Because of her, thousands of underprivileged children are being read to."

"Huh, I didn't know that. There are some really fine people in this world. Too bad we end up dealing with the ones on the other end of the spectrum."

"Fletcher, you really know how to kill a moment, don't you?" Jill pointed to a row of buildings ahead of us. "There's the salon."

* * *

Walking down the sidewalk, I asked, "Aside from the expensive shaggy haircut, what are your thoughts about Casey?"

"I haven't really formed any thoughts about Casey. Do you find him suspicious?"

"The superintendent told me Casey was here because he'd crashed daddy's expensive car and has been banished to help him understand the value of a dollar."

"That sounds plausible. I don't see anything there that would make him a murder suspect."

"The problem with narcissists who don't appreciate the value of things is that they sometimes devalue people, too."

"Do you think Casey killed Erik just because he didn't value him? That seems pretty far out."

"Who was the last person to see Erik alive?"

The twinkle in Jill's eye told me I'd asked the wrong question. "I suppose the killer was the last person to see him alive."

"Who closed up the park and supposedly left Erik alone when he should've stayed around for coverage?"

"I think they said Seth, the seasonal ranger, was the other person on that night."

"Not Casey?"

"No, I'm sure Seth was on that last night."

Following Jill into the salon I felt uneasy, mostly because I didn't know salon etiquette. We were greeted by an attractive young woman with henna red hair. Catching me staring, she smiled, "This color might go well with your skin tone. No, wait, you're blushing. Red really won't work for you."

Lacking a witty response, I replied, "Probably not."

Continuing to revel in my discomfort she looked at the computer and said, "Unless your name is Jules or Stacy, I'm guessing you don't have an appointment."

"I was hoping someone could squeeze me in for a trim. If not, I'll just read this." I picked up the magazine at my fingertips.

"Hmm, I wouldn't have pegged you as a *Marie Claire* kind of guy."

Glancing at a cover I focused on the first topic. "I really want to know how miracle beauty tips could change my life."

Reaching her limit of the inane conversation, Jill interrupted. "If there's no time for a trim, maybe you could get him in for a pedicure."

The girl's eyes lit up as she smiled at me. "What color toenails would you prefer?"

Having never considered a pedicure, the color of my nails had never crossed my mind. "Natural?"

"That's so dull." She glanced at my badge and gun. "I suppose you'd endure endless teasing in the cop gym if you showed up with lilac toenails."

"Can someone fit in a trim?" I asked.

Glancing at the computer the girl replied, "If you don't need a wash and blowout, Angelica can trim your hair while her client's frosted tips rest." She turned to Jill. "Ramon will be with you momentarily."

With the receptionist gone, I leaned close to Jill. "I sincerely hope this is worth the humiliation."

Jill's smile was disarming. "For me, it already is."

A woman with one side of her head shaved and the other side with long black hair stepped up to the counter. "Since you're the only man in the place, I assume you're Doug, my next client."

"That's me."

Nodding toward an empty chair at the end of a long row, she said, "How heavy of a trim do you want?"

I approached the chair while trying to ignore the shaven part of her head. "Clean up the edges and make it less shaggy."

My stylist draped a maroon sheet over my lap and shoulders. "My name is Angelica. What variety of cop are you?"

"I'm a Park Service investigator."

While surveying my head, Angelica considered what she was about to do. "What is there to investigate in parks? I mean, are we talking about people digging up plants or stealing petrified wood?"

Angelica combed and snipped my hair, "Crimes like that are usually handled by the law enforcement rangers. We often handle assaults, murders, and missing people."

The snipping stopped. "Murders? In parks?"

"It happens," I replied. "Right now, we're helping the sheriff's department investigate the death of a ranger at Manzanar."

Resuming her clipping, Angelica said, "I heard about that. The local cops think it was drug related."

"That's one theory. We're looking at all aspects of the ranger's life and other things happening at Manzanar."

"Nothing happens at Manzanar. I mean, I was there as a school kid, but it's not like going to Death Valley or Yosemite. There are just dusty buildings and a monument there."

"What murder motives would you consider in this case?" I asked.

"Isn't it always drugs? I mean, we're close to Mexico, so the cops are always stopping cars and searching them for drugs."

"Don't you think there might be something else?" I asked. "I heard there've been protesters at Manzanar."

Angelica switched from scissors to an electric trimmer to even my sideburns and trim my neck. "There really haven't been that many protests. It's not like anything there is current. It all happened like a hundred years ago. Like, who cares?"

"Someone cares," I replied. "Maybe one of the families of an interned person was taking revenge."

Turning off the trimmer, Angelica brushed the hair from my neck, then shook off the sheet. "Do you want to know what I think?"

I stood and took out my wallet. "I'd love to hear a different theory."

Angelica took the twenty-dollar bill I handed her, then looked like she expected more. I dug out another twenty, thinking this was the most expensive haircut I'd ever had. "I think one of the county deputies did it."

Stunned, because no one had ever suggested foul play in the sheriff's department, I frowned. "Why would a deputy kill a ranger?"

"Some of those guys are on real ego trips. I mean, they get off on pulling people over, then tearing their cars apart looking for drugs. I think one of the deputies got torqued because the ranger told him to buzz off."

"Have other people been killed by the sheriff's deputies?"

"People disappear. The cops blame it on the drug cartels. I think it's the cops who are killing them. They never find the bodies because they don't look very hard."

"The ranger's body wasn't hidden."

"Listen, Doug. I've got to get back to my frost customer. If you're really curious about the stuff the deputies are pulling, talk to Harv at the chopper shop. He knows all their secrets."

I returned to the lobby and opened a *Ladies Home Journal* and scanned articles on home decoration that were more palatable than beauty tips for marital bliss. Voices came from all corners of the shop, making it hard to focus on a particular discussion. The person nearest to me was discussing her daughter-in-law's miscarriage. While tragic and sad, it got me no closer to a murder motive.

I picked Jill's voice out of the chatter and listened to her discussion and Ramon's replies. He seemed to know no more than Angelica did, although he seemed less forthcoming with opinions, making me suspicious. Having the only male voice, I was able to pick out his comments from the chatter.

Jill listed some of the possible motives or groups who might have a motive. Ramon discounted each of them, especially the drug motive. He paused after one of Jill's comments, while studying her hair. "Ms. Jill, a nutcase killed that guy."

Jill smiled. "All murderers are nutcases, Ramon."

"This one is even more of a nutcase than the people who kill their spouses and girlfriends. This killer had something special against that ranger."

"What makes you say that?"

Lifting Jill's chin, Ramon studied her damp hair. "That ranger had red hair, right?"

"That's no secret, and probably not a murder motive."

Satisfied with the cut, Ramon picked up a hair dryer. Before turning it on he said, "What if that is exactly why he was murdered? What if someone hated that ranger because of his red hair."

"Who hates redheads?" Jill asked.

Ramon paused with the hairdryer, ready to start Jill's blow out. "I come from Mexico where there are legends about red-haired people. Some are revered while others hate redheads, almost as if they're demons." Starting the dryer ended the conversation. Jill tried to get Ramon to say more after he finished, but he was done.

After peeling off several twenty-dollar bills, Jill thanked Ramon, who smiled. "It's the red hair," he said in parting.

"Who kills redheads?" I asked as we walked away from the salon.

"Ramon said some ethnic groups consider redheads to be demons."

"I'm not sure I buy into that."

Jill stopped by the car fender. "Is it any more far-fetched than any of the other theories we're considering?"

"My hairdresser thinks a deputy killed Erik."

"Ramon said Angelica has a thing against cops. They're socially profiling and keep pulling her over for all kinds of minor violations. She's likely to throw out the theory that a cop was the killer."

After getting into the car, I suggested that Jill look up redhead demons on her phone.

A few keystrokes later, Jill leaned back. "We have to narrow the search. I've got tens of thousands of hits. Everything from a book named *The Red Headed Demon* to posters of red-haired demons, to websites claiming that all female redheads are demons."

"Focus on the US Southwest and Mexico."

"I'm down to several thousand hits, but the pool is still too large."

"Try demons in Southwestern lore."

Paging through the hits, Jill signed. "Most of these just talk about the myths of hot-tempered redheads. Like this one, 'Redheads...Angels or Demons.' Here's another, 'Are redheads descendants of cats?'"

"Some people have too much time on their hands," I replied. "Who has time to make up all that stuff and post it?"

Entering a new search, Jill leaned back. "This one is great. According to the Old and

New Testaments, all redheads are reprobates, beginning with Satan and all his demons."

I snorted. "We should be looking for a holy roller who thought he'd killed off Satan."

"Do you have any better theories?"

"What tribe was displaced from this area?"

After a few keystrokes, Jill replied, "It appears there were several tribes, or Native communities who occupied this area. The Paiute-Shoshone were displaced in 1863. Currently, there is a 'Bishop Community', and they are composed of federally recognized Mono and Timbisha tribes residing in the Owens Valley Indo County."

"Try searching each of those with redhead myths."

Jill looked at me. "How far do we want to chase this wild hare?"

"Do you have something better to do?" I asked.

"I'm getting mostly the same hits. Wait, here's something new. Nephilim was a red-haired giant." Jill paused as she read. "This would be perfect. The Nephelium were a tribe of red-haired giants descended from angels, adept at combat."

"Are they Paiute?" I asked.

"No, they're Biblical." Jill entered something into her phone, then held it to her ear. "How's my godson?"

I glanced at Jill, wondering why she'd chosen this moment to call our friends Jamie and Liz Ballard in Flagstaff.

"Is Jamie around?" she asked, inquiring about my former investigative partner, Jamie Ballard. We'd used Jamie, who was a Navajo Nation police officer, as a resource on a couple of investigations. I assumed she was going to ask him about Native American myths involving redheads.

Jill put the phone on speaker and held it out between us as I drove into a strip mall and parked. "What's up, Jill?" Jamie asked.

"We're investigating a death at Manzanar National Historic Site. The victim was a red-haired ranger, and it was suggested that we look into Mexican and Southwestern mythology for a red-headed demon."

"Doug put you up to this, didn't he?"

I leaned close. "Jill has the phone on speaker and I'm sitting next to her. She decided to call you all on her own."

"I've never met a red-haired Navajo. As far as I know, there aren't any red-haired Navajo demons."

"The Manzanar site is in Owens Valley, California. Jill searched and found that this area was inhabited by the Paiute and Shoshone tribes until they were driven out and put on a reservation in 1863."

"And you think some crazy Shoshone killed a redheaded ranger because of something that happened 150 years ago?"

"My hair stylist suggested we look at Southwestern and Mexican mythology to find a red-haired demon."

Liz had been listening in and asked, "You're getting investigative tips from barbers and hairdressers?"

"Come on Liz," Jill kidded. "Who hears more gossip and inside information than a stylist?"

"It sounds like you're grasping at straws," Liz replied.

I leaned close to the phone. "The local sheriff's department is blaming drug runners for the crime and aren't looking beyond them. We're locked out of their investigation, so we're trying to find some other motive for the ranger's murder."

Jamie replied, "So, you immediately thought it was an Indian who killed the guy."

Knowing I was being baited, I replied, "We looked at all of the people who have picketed the camp or who have some other grudge against the park service. We discounted the families of the Japanese Americans interned there because the crime of their relocation has been admitted and the families financially compensated. There's also the issue of water rights. We know that many tribes are asking the courts to reopen discussions about treaty rights and then this suggestion of Native demons popped up."

We heard Jamie and Liz speaking in the background while we waited. Jamie came back a moment later. "Can I call you back in a couple of minutes?"

"Sure," I replied.

Ending the call, Jill cocked her head. "Do you think he's going to do some research for us?"

"Who knows? Jamie says so little it's hard to know what's on his mind."

Pocketing her phone, Jill looked at me as I turned onto the street. "What now?"

"Let's think about the other protesters. The water rights issue seems settled."

"Water rights are a big issue. But I think you're right, I don't see that as an issue someone would kill a ranger over."

"And the Park Service isn't going to shut down Manzanar and sell it to a developer."

"A couple of parks have been decommissioned, but Manzanar is one of the few sites commemorating the Japanese American relocation and internment. I can't see that as an issue. It's not like the Manzanar site has any great development value."

I tried to think of any other reason someone would target a Park Service site. "Is there any mining or oil drilling activity in the area?"

"There aren't any oil derricks or mines nearby. I suppose Manzanar might be sitting on top of a lithium deposit, or some rare mineral only found in Africa or the Far East, but someone would've drilled test holes around the area to determine if there were valuable minerals underneath the park."

"That leaves us trying to find a motive in Erik Petersen's personal life."

Jill grinned at me. "It's time for you to recite the common murder motives."

"Love. Money. Drugs."

"The sheriff's department is all over the drug angle. That leaves us with money and love to investigate."

"Erik was living in Lone Pine because there isn't any on-site housing, right?"

"I've got Erik's address in my notes. I think the sheriff's office said he was renting a house with another ranger." Paging through her notebook Jill stopped. "His roommate is Todd Overland." She read me their address and punched it into her mapping feature. Within a minute, her phone prompted me to take a left turn.

Erik and Todd's rental was a modest house on a street lined with other small houses, a few with children's toys in the yard. Most appeared to be typical of the places where working folks live. I could smell microwave popcorn before I rang the doorbell. Out of uniform, the gangly young man who answered the door looked like he might've just graduated from high school.

"Hi, Todd, do you have a few minutes to answer some more questions about Erik?"

Todd looked over his shoulder as if he expected someone to be standing there. "Actually, now isn't the best time."

"Who is it?" A woman's voice called from somewhere inside the house.

"More cops asking about Erik."

A shorter, chunky young woman with dark hair appeared in a door down the hallway. She looked a few years older than Todd. "Invite them in. Don't make them stand outside like they're Jehovah's Witnesses."

Todd stepped aside and pulled the door open. "Come in."

After introductions were made to Lexi Cruz, we were invited into their living room where a movie had been paused. A big bowl of popcorn sat on the coffee table with two cans of beer alongside the bowl. Jill and I sat in chairs facing the couch where Lexi and Todd had been seated while watching television.

"Tell us about Erik," Jill said after removing her notebook from a shirt pocket.

Todd leaned back and blinked. "I told the county cops everything."

Lexi elbowed him and gestured with her head toward Jill. "Quit being a jackass and answer Jill's question."

"Erik was a nice guy. He paid his half of the rent and utilities, and he cooked a lot of our meals."

"He sounds like an ideal roommate," I said.

Lexi's glance at Todd made me think everything wasn't perfect. "Is there something you wanted to say?"

"Erik was always around. I mean, like, always. He was nice and everything, but it was like he didn't have a life except for work."

"No privacy?" Jill asked.

Todd looked at Lexi, then shrugged. "It's sometimes nice to watch a movie with just the two of us and no audience."

"I thought Erik had a girlfriend," I said.

Lexi wrinkled her nose. "They broke up ages ago."

"Can you quantify ages ago? Weeks? Months? Years?" Jill asked.

Lexi and Todd looked at each other. "Three weeks?" she replied.

Todd stared at her. "It was right after they went to Death Valley to help clean up the flood mess."

"His girlfriend was a ranger?" I asked.

Shaking her head, Lexi replied, "She volunteered to help."

"Did he break it off, or did she?" Jill asked.

Lexi rolled her eyes. "It was definitely Hailey who ended it. Red told us she wasn't into camping *at all*. I mean, the whole zero-carbon-footprint-tent-camping-experience was the end of it for her."

"So, no hard feelings on her part?" I asked.

Lexi looked at Todd before answering. "Erik was gutted. I haven't seen her since the break-up." Pausing, Lexi stared at Jill.

"You're looking for a motive. There's no way Hailey killed Erik. She left him."

"What is Hailey's last name?" Jill asked.

"Qualls. Hailey Qualls."

"He wasn't stalking her or doing anything to make her crazy?" I asked.

"She ghosted him," Lexi replied. "No answers to texts, phone calls, or emails. He got the message and just moped around with us."

"That must've been tough on you," Jill said.

Todd grimaced. "We had, like, no privacy. He was always here."

Lexi discerned the meaning behind Jill's question and shook her head. "*We* had nothing to do with Erik's murder. I mean he was clingy, but he was starting to catch on that we needed some time away from him."

"What was Erik into?" I asked.

"He was heavily into some character playing games," Todd replied. "He played a scheduled online game every Saturday with some of his high school friends. Aside from that, he didn't do a lot of socializing. I mean, he'd have a beer with people, but he wasn't ever into the bar scene."

"And sometimes we could hear him playing Minecraft or some violent zombie killing game in his room. I think he was embarrassed about that."

"Do you think any of the gaming people ever got angry with him?" Jill asked.

"Those games aren't terribly competitive," Lexi replied. "I mean, you get killed by the zombies once in a while, but it's not like you'd actually kill another person over those stupid geeky games."

"So, you two can't think of anything in his social life that would have been a threat?"

Lexi and Todd shook their heads.

"Did he have any family problems?" I asked.

"He didn't have a lot to do with his family. I mean, he saw them a couple of times a year, but there really wasn't any friction."

"Where do his parents live?" Jill asked.

Todd thought for a moment. "I think they are in some Minneapolis suburb. The county cops asked us that. I think they contacted his mom and dad."

"Did Erik have money problems?" I asked. "Gambling issues?"

The response to each question was a headshake. "Like I said, he paid half of all the bills every month. Erik was a responsible geeky guy. I can't think of anyone less abrasive than him," Todd replied.

Nodding, Lexi agreed.

Todd added, "Erik was an okay guy. Needy, but helpful and nice. The other rangers loved him. He'd cover shifts for people who had conflicts, and he'd socialize if there was a celebration. He's the kind of guy you'd like for a brother."

Jill folded the notebook and put it into her pocket. "The kind of guy you'd like for a brother, but not as a boyfriend."

Lexi shuddered. "He was way too dorky for me. I'm sure there's someone out there who would appreciate a guy like Erik, but not anyone I know."

"Was there something in particular about him that put you off?" I asked.

Lexi looked at Todd. "I don't know how to explain it. I mean, he was nice, but he never got happy or sad. He just had this even, boring life."

"It's like he didn't have any adrenaline," Todd added.

"Was he religious?" Jill asked.

"He never went to church," Lexi answered, "but I had a sense that he had been religious. Maybe his parents dragged him to church and burned him out. I don't know."

"It's not like he was an atheist who argued about God and the meaning of life," Todd said. "He just wasn't a religious kind of guy."

Jill and I thanked Todd and Lexi, then we walked to our rental car. Jill looked bewildered. "It's hard to imagine someone being angry enough at Erik to kill him."

I started the car and pulled away from the rental house. "Yeah, boring isn't a common murder motive."

Jill looked at me. "Not common but not unheard of?"

"It's more of a suicide thing than a murder motive."

"I'm hearing an 'although.'"

"We got called to an assault where the wife was beating on her husband. She'd made plans to have dinner with friends. The husband told her to go ahead, he was planning to watch television."

"I assume alcohol or drugs were involved?"

"I think it was an issue of her not taking medication rather than using illegal drugs."

"Hearing those stories makes me happy that you're past that period of your life. I don't think I'd have handled you sharing those stories with me on a regular basis."

"I share those stories with you now."

"True, but they're historical, not current."

I turned into the motel parking lot. "Dealing with a ranger who's been murdered and hung on a barbed wire fence is better?"

"That's semi-historical. I didn't actually see the body. I can deal with this." Jill looked around. "Why are we back at the motel?"

"I thought we'd order pizza while we watched television."

"Didn't you just tell me about the woman who was beating on her husband because he wanted to stay home and watch television rather than going out with her?"

I backed out of the parking spot and stopped at the street. "I'm fine with going out. It's a little early to eat, and thought we'd exhausted the restaurant options."

"We've only been to one restaurant."

I gestured with my fingers like I was entering information into a phone. "Great. See what other gourmet restaurants there are in town."

With her phone halfway out of her back pocket, Jill paused. "Actually, I did that search last night. There's a mom-and-pop place down the street from where we ate."

"Do they serve wine and beer?"

Sighing, Jill flicked her fingers, indicating I should start driving. "Let's drive around town to get a better feel for Lone Pine. I'm sure we'll find somewhere to eat."

Jill's phone buzzed and she retrieved it from her pocket. "Hi, Jamie."

Switching it to speaker mode, I heard Jamie say, "I'm on the road. I should be there sometime mid-morning."

"You're driving to Manzanar?" I asked.

There was a long pause, then Jamie said, "It's complicated."

"Explain that," I said.

In his usual abrupt manner, Jamie replied, "Tomorrow."

I sighed and looked at Jill who asked, "Is Liz with you?"

"No."

"You could've brought your family along and I could see my godson."

"Not this time."

"Did Liz have to work?" Jill asked.

"Probably."

As exasperating as Jamie's abrupt answers were, I asked, "Can you answer a question with more than one word?"

There was a pause, then Jamie replied, "If I'd needed more than one word, I would've used it. I'll see you tomorrow."

The dial tone sounded before we could ask for more details.

Jill looked at her phone and her eyes went wide. "We're supposed to be at the coroner's office!"

Chapter 8

Jill looked up the Inyo County Coroner's Office and found the address in Lone Pine. The directions guided us to a funeral home a block off the main street. The parking lot was empty except for a Toyota Landcruiser parked near the main entrance. I looked at Jill. "You're sure this is the coroner's office address?"

Double checking her phone, she nodded. "This is it."

We parked next to the Toyota and walked into the lobby of the funeral home a few minutes after 3:00. I could hear a Billy Joel song coming from an open door down the hallway. I startled the office's occupant when I knocked on his doorframe.

Glancing at his watch, the man quickly stood and composed himself. Smiling, he said, "You must be Jill Fletcher and her partner."

"I'm Doug, the partner," I said as I walked into the office and offered my hand.

"I'm Aaron Hawes, the Inyo County Coroner." Smiling and shaking our hands, he gestured toward chairs at a small table. "How can I help you?"

I noticed the coroner's casual dress and demeanor. Most funeral directors wore dress slacks and button-down shirts. Wearing a knit golf shirt and khaki pants, Aaron Hawes looked like he'd just walked off a golf course.

"We'd like to talk to you about Erik Petersen's death."

"What would you like to know?"

"Did you remove the body from the murder scene?"

"Yeah. When the California Bureau of Investigation techs finished gathering evidence, they helped me recover the body. I brought it back here. Doctor Jonas came over later that afternoon and did an autopsy."

"He did the autopsy here?" Jill asked.

"The hospital doesn't have a morgue, so he used my prep room." Aaron reached over to his desk and picked up a stapled sheaf of paper. "Here's his report."

I looked at the standard autopsy coversheet which included a body outline marked with the knife wound to the neck. The cause of death was listed as exsanguination due to a knife wound.

Aaron spoke to Jill as I scanned the report. "It was pretty straightforward. The victim died from the neck wound."

"Did the doctor speculate on how the victim had been subdued prior to being slashed?" I asked.

"He said the lack of defensive wounds indicated the victim had probably been drugged before the attack. He took blood and tissue samples. I don't think he's received the results of the testing."

"Were you able to recover any evidence from the body or the victim's clothing?"

Hawes shook his head. "The CBI techs went over the body with tweezers and plucked every stray hair, fiber, or fragment they found. There was nothing left to recover when I got to the scene."

I went back over the report as Jill asked, "I assume you're the funeral director?"

Aaron smiled and nodded. "My brother and I own the mortuary. My main role as coroner is to recover deceased bodies. Most of the time, the cause of death isn't in question. When there is a question, if the family wants an autopsy, or when there's a suspicious death, I call Doc Jonas and ask him to perform an autopsy."

"You and your brother own the funeral home?"

"We bought out the previous owner when he retired."

"Isn't it stressful operating a business with your sibling?"

Aaron smiled. "We have our moments. For the most part, we split the work and the duties. I handle the coroner job, so that gets me out from under Jon's feet."

Flipping back to the front sheet of the report, I offered it to Jill, who shook her head. "Was there anything unexpected in the murder?"

Aaron stared at me for a moment. "You mean aside from a kid having his throat slashed and being strung up on the barbed wire?"

"Sorry. Of course, a murder is unexpected. I mean, did you discover anything that might reveal who murdered Erik, or anything that might point to a motive?"

"Such as?"

"Was his mouth stuffed with money? That's a cartel thing done when they want to send a message about someone siphoning money out of the drug sales."

"The only strange thing was that there were no signs of a struggle. It's as if the victim stood there and let his killer tie him to the barbed wire fence. That's what made Doc Jonas take the blood samples. He thought it looked like someone had drugged the victim before hoisting him onto the wire."

"That would mean there was more than one person involved in the murder," I surmised.

The coroner rubbed his chin. "It's really strange. There were no signs of a struggle, I mean, aside from the slashed throat. And there weren't a lot of footprints, so there couldn't have been a bunch of people subduing him. For that matter, the contusions on his wrists were limited to the restraining wires. There wasn't any bruising to indicate he'd been roughly held in place while the wire restraints were put into place."

"What do you think happened?"

Aaron glanced at his office window while composing his thoughts. "Do you think he knew his attacker and let himself be tied to the fence?"

Jill grimaced. "Don't you think it's more likely that someone held a gun on him and forced him to stand still while he was tied up?"

Aaron's head shook and he drew a breath. "I don't know that I'd stand still while someone tied me to a barbed wire fence, even if they were holding a gun on me. I'd fight or run."

"Unless Erik was a pacifist," I suggested.

"Or he thought being tied to the fence was going to be the endpoint," Aaron said. "His killer might've convinced him not to resist."

"Do you have his clothing?" I asked.

"The sheriff's office took his clothes. I think they sent them to the CBI."

"Is there anything we can learn from viewing his body?" I asked.

"I've already cleaned and embalmed his body for the return to Minnesota. I didn't think anyone other than his family would be interested in seeing his remains." Aaron paused, waiting for me to say we were through. "It's not like you can't see him if you want to. His parents are coming for a viewing and will be bringing the clothes they want him to wear for the funeral."

I looked back at the autopsy report. "Tell me about the cut to his neck."

"It was a single slashing cut with a very sharp blade. It cut through the jugular and carotid."

"His attacker would've been sprayed with blood," I suggested.

The coroner thought for a second before responding. "I don't think the average person is prepared for the volume and trajectory of blood that comes from a cut artery. My guess is that the attacker was probably doused with blood spurting from the carotid." Seeing the pain on Jill's face, he added, "The victim bled out very quickly and probably felt little pain."

"I'd expect a cut like that to hurt like hell," Jill suggested.

"Have you ever cut yourself with a razor blade?" the coroner asked. "The cut from a sharp blade doesn't hurt for a few moments. I'll tell his parents that Erik was dead before his body experienced any pain."

"Will this be a closed casket funeral?" Jill asked.

A smile flickered on the coroner's face. "Funeral directors have tricks to hide almost any injury. My brother patched up a woman who'd been hit by a train so her sister could view her body. It wasn't quick or easy but, in the end, the victim's sister was at ease seeing the victim in her casket."

"May we see Erik's body?"

"Certainly," the coroner replied. He led us down the hallway to a locked steel door. The room we entered was as neat and clean as any hospital morgue. A stainless-steel table was the centerpiece of the room, standing on a white tile floor. Hawes opened a refrigerator door and wheeled out a cart with a blue sheet covering what was obviously a body. With gentle care, he folded back the sheet, exposing Erik Petersen's pale face and shoulders.

Jill bent over to examine Erik's head and neck. "It appears Erik had a natural crease in his neck."

"The magic of Superglue and cosmetics."

Standing, Jill took in the entirety of the scene. "If I didn't know better, I'd say he was asleep."

"That's the look we strive for," Hawes replied. He lifted the sheet covering Erik's left wrist exposing torn skin where he'd been bound. "I didn't spend any time on his wrists; they won't be visible under the lower casket lid."

Jill nodded. "Thank you. I'm sure his parents will be comforted by your great work."

Recovering the body, Hawes nodded. "Thanks. People don't realize how much work goes into the process."

Jill looked at me and sighed as Hawes returned the body to the cooler. "This stop hasn't provided many leads."

"We know the killer was sprayed with blood. If we can find his clothing, we can tie him to the murder."

"Don't you think he disposed of his clothes immediately?"

"For some reason, people are willing to throw away their shirt and pants, but they think they can clean up their belt and shoes," I replied.

Aaron Hawes rejoined us near the table. "Is that all you need?"

"I think so," I replied. "Unless you can identify the killer for us."

Hawes shook his head. "I'm sorry, but there wasn't anything with the body that identified the attacker."

"Attackers rarely leave their wallets at the scene," I said as Hawes escorted us into the hallway and locked the door behind us.

"If there's anything else I can do for you, don't hesitate to call."

* * *

As I drove away from the funeral home, Jill commented, "Seeing Erik's body like that was so...sterile. It's a huge step away from the grisly pictures posted on the board the day we arrived."

"That's the funeral director's job. He erases all evidence of the cruel attack and makes the body appear at rest."

Jill considered that for a few moments before commenting, "I wish he could do that to my memory. All the grisly bloody scenes are chemically etched in my brain."

"That's why soldiers suffer from PTSD. They see and do things a civilian never experiences—terrible things that haunt their dreams. EMTs, firemen, and cops have the same problem. An average citizen is unprepared to deal with violent trauma."

Jill's phone buzzed and she struggled to remove it from her pocket before the call rolled over. "Jill Fletcher," she said without looking at the caller ID.

I recognized Jack Pardee's voice and watched Jill's head nod as he spoke.

"I'm pleased that Ed Richardson reached out to you. I wish I had anything to add to what you already know. We just left the coroner, who had nothing new to add other than to point out that the killer was likely sprayed with the victim's blood during the assault."

Jill listened for a few more moments, then ended the call.

"The boss is checking up on us?" I asked as Jill pocketed her phone.

"Jack had a call from Ed Richardson. He wanted to let us know how much Ed appreciated our involvement."

"Our involvement won't mean shit if Erik's killer isn't identified."

"Richardson felt left outside of the information loop. With us involved, he feels like he's got a horse in the race."

I chuckled. "Too bad his horse started the race a day after the gate was opened."

"Maybe his horse is the only one running in the right direction."

"How would you feel about a burger and fries for supper?"

"I can feel my arteries hardening."

"You ate beef when you were growing up."

"At forty, I discovered that I don't get enough exercise to burn off a daily burger and fries. I've also discovered that my GI tract likes more fiber than I get from fast food."

"You haven't commented on my risk of getting scurvy lately."

"Somehow, you manage to eat enough vegetables and fruit to ward off scurvy and rickets. Let's try one of the mom-and-pop places near downtown. I'm sure we'll each find something we like."

I passed a café with a sign advertising home cooking and parked down the street. There weren't a lot of diners inside, but it wasn't dead, either. The aroma of fried chicken filled the air. The waitress nodded toward a booth as she scurried by with a tray of food. She walked to our table as we sat, then handed us menus. "Tonight's special is broasted chicken with mashed potatoes and your choice of soup or salad. What can I get you to drink?"

Jill glanced at the menu, then replied, "I'll have a Diet Coke and the special with a salad."

I waited while our server jotted Jill's order in her pad. "I'll have a California burger with fries and a side salad."

"We've got house-made Italian dressing, blue cheese, or French."

After noting our salad dressing choices, the server walked away. Jill looked around and said, "This feels like the small-town cafés in South Dakota."

A man looked over from a nearby table, then excused himself to the woman he was with. Uninvited, he pulled a chair up to the end of our booth. "We don't see a lot of unfamiliar cops in town. I'm Ed Goshen, the Lone Pine mayor."

Jill and I introduced ourselves. "We're here investigating the Manzanar ranger's murder."

"Sad thing. The county sheriff seems to think it's somehow drug related."

Not wanting to get into politics, I nodded. "It might be."

"Where are you two stationed?"

"We operate out of Texas."

"Dallas?"

"North Padre Island National Seashore," Jill replied.

"You're not average Park Service rangers."

"We're investigators with the National Park Service Investigative Services Branch.

We investigate crimes in national parks around the US."

Goshen nodded as our server approached with a tray of food. "Feel free to call if there's anything I can do for you while you're here. I think you'll find my office is more hospitable than the sheriff's department."

"That was kind of him," Jill said as she spread a napkin on her lap.

"He's a politician. They have to shake hands. It's their nature."

Chapter 9

I awoke to the sound of the shower. The alarm clock showed 5:12, which caused me to groan and roll over. After a few minutes, I gave up on sleep and turned on the early network news. The shower sounds stopped as I flipped through the networks. I'd settled on ABC, only because it was the first station not showing a commercial, and then my phone rang.

"Yeah," I said, assuming it was either my mother or my in-laws calling from South Dakota.

"I'm sitting in the Totem Café."

"Jamie?"

"Drag your butt out of bed and get moving."

"Where is the Totem Café?"

Jamie let out a breath. "On Main Street, in downtown Lone Pine."

Jill emerged from the bathroom drying her hair. "Who's calling at this ungodly hour?"

"Jamie."

Jill took the phone from my hand. "Hi, Jamie. Where are you?"

I couldn't hear his short response. Jill replied, "Yes, I'll have him dressed and sitting next to you in fifteen minutes. It's the least we can do after you drove all night to get here." She ended the call and handed the phone back to me. "You heard him. Put clothes on. We're going to meet Jamie for breakfast."

I got up from the bed and took underwear from the suitcase. "I'll shave and shower."

It took twenty minutes for my quick shave, shower, and the drive to the café. As expected, Jamie was sitting at a table near the back of the café watching the door. Three mugs and a thermal carafe of coffee were already on the table.

Jamie smiled and stood, hugging Jill as we approached. "How is my child's godmother?"

"I'm good, Jamie. You look amazingly refreshed for a man who drove all night."

Ignoring Jill's implied question, Jamie turned to me and put his hands on my shoulders. "My captain sends his regards to *Ivanbito*."

"Have you decided to call me a buffalo, too?" I asked, smiling.

Jamie sat as Jill poured coffee. "It seems to fit. A big animal who charges ahead regardless of the obstacles before him."

"It appears that married life has softened you. I think you've gained a few pounds."

Jamie, still slender, had added a bit more bulk to his frame. "Regular meals do that."

Glancing at my waist, he said, "It appears your stomach is pressing against the top of your belt buckle, too."

Trying to change the topic, Jill asked, "Why did you drive all night? There's nothing pressing about our investigation."

The waitress delivered a fresh carafe of coffee. "Would either of you like cream or sugar?" she asked, handing us menus.

"Thanks, no," Jill replied.

"Do you have a breakfast special?" I asked.

"If you're in a hurry, we always have a toasted English muffin egg sandwich. Otherwise, it's just the usual fare on the menu."

"Give us a minute," Jill suggested.

As the waitress departed, Jill leaned close to Jamie so the diners at nearby tables wouldn't hear her. "Why did you rush here?"

"You requested information and I have it."

"You could've told us over the phone."

Shaking his head, Jamie removed a notebook page from the pocket of his plaid shirt. He unfolded and flattened the small sheet of paper. It read *Si-Te-Cah and Lovelock Cave.*

I looked at Jamie, expecting him to explain what I'd read. "What is the significance of that?"

Our waitress arrived and Jamie refolded the note and put it into his pocket. "Have you decided?"

Jamie nodded. "The trucker's special with firm eggs and crispy hashbrowns."

I glanced at the menu and read the trucker's special, which included one of almost every breakfast item. I noticed Jamie's smile, which might've been a challenge. "I'll have two eggs, over easy, with whole wheat toast."

Jill ordered oatmeal with all the fixings.

As our waitress walked away, Jill asked, "What's the significance of your notes?"

"Legend says the Paiutes defeated a group of red-haired giant demons, the *Si-Te-Cah*, at the battle of Lovelock Cave."

"You could've told us that over the phone," Jill said, sipping her coffee.

Jamie stared at his coffee mug while composing his response. "I talked to my captain about it, and we agreed that two white cops asking about the *Si-Te-Cah* might not get a straight answer from Native people and might stir up a pot of trouble. A Navajo Nation Police Officer might get a very different response."

"You said the demons were defeated in this cave battle," I replied.

Jamie looked me in the eye, "Many Native cultures believe that demons can't be killed. They are often shapeshifters who change into a different form, then come back again later."

"You think a Paiute saw our red-haired ranger and thought he was a *Si-Te-Cah*?"

"What I think is irrelevant," Jamie replied. "You may be looking for someone who saw your victim as a demon and struck him down."

Our breakfast arrived, ending our discussion. The waitress refilled our coffee mugs, asked if there was anything else we needed, and then left with the emptied thermal coffee carafe.

Jamie took a bottle of hot sauce from the rack of condiments, salt, pepper, and napkins, then shook a liberal dose of it onto his eggs and hashbrowns. Jill stirred brown sugar and raisins into her oatmeal and asked, "Do you think there are people who still believe in demons?"

"I *know* there are people who believe in demons. I also know there are psychopathic people who are capable of murder because of their beliefs."

I took a bite of toast and thought. "I'm having a hard time with this."

Jamie ate a huge forkful of pancakes. "Do you have any better leads?"

"We've only scratched the surface," I replied.

Jamie nodded. "So, you haven't got anything better."

"The local sheriff's department is convinced the murder is drug related," Jill replied.

"There are lots of drugs everywhere," Jamie conceded. "Was your victim shot and left in the desert?"

"His throat was cut after he was strung up on a barbed wire fence," I whispered.

"That doesn't sound like either a drug deal gone bad or a gang enforcement killing."

I shook my head while swallowing a bite of food. "That's why we're looking at different things."

"Someone mentioned Indian lore about red-haired people to you, right?"

"Actually, he said Mexican and Southwest mythology," Jill replied.

"Where did that lead you?"

"To pages and pages of stories about redheads being crazy and volatile."

Jamie nodded, knowingly. "And to me."

"We reached out to you because we thought you might have better historical resources than the internet provided," I said."

"Where was the body found?" Jamie asked.

"At Manzanar National Historic Site."

"Which tribe was displaced from that area?"

Jill dug out her notebook and read, "Shoshone, Paiute, Mono, and Timbisha."

"The Bishop Paiutes were formerly known as the Paiute-Shoshone tribe. The Mono and Timbisha are Bishop Paiute clans," Jamie clarified. "There's also a Paiute-Shoshone reservation here, in Lone Pine."

"All of them consider the *Si-Te-Cah* demons?"

Jamie nodded. "Probably like Judeo-Christians see Satan as a demon."

"Where is the Bishop Paiute reservation?" I asked.

Giving a smug grin Jamie replied, "In Bishop."

"Fine," I said. "Where is Bishop?"

"It's about fifty miles north of here on Highway 395." Jamie paused, and then continued, "Keep in mind that not all Paiutes live on a reservation."

"However," Jill interjected, "a visit to the tribal leaders might be a good starting point."

"Pretty much," Jamie said.

"I don't suppose you've already contacted them?" I asked.

"I have to leave something for you two to do."

Jill set down her spoon and picked up her cell phone, walking outside. A minute later, she returned and said, "I have the name of the Lone Pine tribal president and her phone number."

Jamie looked troubled. "What's the problem?" I asked.

"The president deals with the management of the reservation resources. We need to speak with elders."

"I don't know the difference," I admitted.

"If you wanted local history, would you approach the mayor, or would you go to the librarian?"

"Ah."

Jill punched a number into her phone and stood. "I'll get a suggestion from the president."

Glancing at Jill as she walked away, Jamie leaned close. "You make a good couple. She has the brains."

Knowing I was being set up for a punchline, I went along anyway. "What do I bring to the relationship?"

Jamie smiled, "Ah, you don't know either?"

"Smartass," I said as the waitress delivered our bill. Jamie made no move to accept the bill, so I handed the waitress a charge card.

"I figure the Park Service can afford to buy my meals if the Navajo Nation Police cover my car, gas, and motel."

"We'll figure something out," I replied.

Smirking, Jamie replied, "You always do."

Jill returned a few minutes later. "Halona Mid-Thunder is the president of the Lone Pine Paiute-Shoshone Reservation. She was gracious, and after I explained our interest in tribal lore and demons, she gave me John Standing Bear's name and phone number. He's documenting the Paiute oral history. She said he'd be a good resource for us."

Jamie filled our coffee cups and said, "I assume you've spoken with the dead guy's co-workers. What did you find out?"

"There are two senior rangers who've worked at the camp a long time. One of them discovered the body. She's pretty messed up."

Jill nodded. "Grace is a mess. Most of the rangers seemed to like the victim, Erik. We went to the victim's apartment and met his roommate, Todd, and the roomie's girlfriend. They seemed like normal young people."

"No unpaid rent or hostility over housekeeping or food?" Jamie asked.

I thought for a second. "It was almost like the victim was too nice."

"Do you think they're hiding something? Sometimes the killers portray their victims as best friends while in truth they're hiding a deep hatred."

"We didn't talk to them for a long time, but I wasn't getting the sense that their answers were anything but truthful."

Jill shook her head. "There's something weird about Lexi. She's like ten years older than Todd."

Jamie raised his eyebrows. "Maybe he's into cougars?"

Rolling her eyes, Jill said, "I don't think Lexi is cougar material. I got the impression she's made herself available and he's not unhappy with that. It seemed like she might've been happy that Todd's roommate was out of the picture."

"Like, now she can walk around the apartment in her underwear?" Jamie asked.

"More like, 'now I can move in and give up my apartment,'" I replied.

"That's a pretty thin murder motive."

"People have killed for less."

Jamie nodded. "Billy the Kid shot a guy for snoring."

I glanced at Jill, who was suddenly grinning. "What? Spit it out."

"There have been nights when snoring would've put me close to being a murderer."

"Too much information," Jamie said as he stood and stretched. "Why don't you two call the historian? In the meanwhile, take me to your motel and I'll nap."

Walking to our vehicles I kidded Jamie. "I thought you could track around the clock for three days and nights."

"That was before I was married and had a child."

"Marriage changed your ability to track?" Jill asked.

"I can no longer crawl into bed and sleep for twenty hours when I feel like it."

Chuckling, I replied, "Wives and children need to be fed and entertained."

Nodding her agreement, Jill said, "Life is simpler when you're single." Realizing how that sounded, she reached out and took my hand. "But the tradeoffs are worth it."

Rolling his eyes, Jamie unlocked his car using the remote. "Is our motel far away?"

"*Our* motel?"

"I assumed we'd stay in the same place."

"They may not have a vacancy."

With his eyes smiling, Jamie replied, "I'm sure there's space on the floor in your room for a sleeping bag."

"That's not happening," Jill said as she opened her car door. "Stereo snoring *would be* a murder motive."

* * *

The motel had a room for Jamie. I was prepared to help him carry his bags, but he pulled a single backpack from the trunk of his car. "You're traveling light," I observed.

"A toothbrush, a pair of underwear, and a spare uniform shirt are about all I require." I started to follow, but he stopped me. "Find something to do for a while, then call me after I've slept a couple of hours."

Jill was leaning against the fender, punching information into her phone. "We need to interview Erik's ex-girlfriend to see if her version of their breakup is the same as we heard from Todd and his girlfriend."

"Have you located her?"

"Hailey Qualls has a Facebook page, a Twitter account, a TikTok page, and..."

"I get it. She lives her life online. Where can we find her?"

"She appears to work at Pine's End Realty. At least, their logo shows up in lots of her posts. Their office is only a block from here."

Jill put her phone away. "Come on. The walk will do you good."

I pointed to the car. "There's something you need to learn. It's easier to chase someone when you're in a car than when you're on foot."

Jill walked back to the car. "Why would Hailey run?"

"We never know how someone is going to react when a cop shows up. Some people have a reason to run, like an outstanding warrant. I swear that others have guilty consciences and sprint any time they see a badge."

There were very few cars parked on the street, so we parked nearly in front of the realty office. A young woman looked up from the reception desk when we walked in. "May I help you?"

I glanced at the four office doors lining the area's back wall. Two were closed, one was open with no lights on, and the fourth was lit with a woman apparently speaking on the phone. There were nameplates next to the doors. Realizing none of them said *Hailey*, I turned to the blonde receptionist who wore too much makeup and looked anorexic. "Do you have a moment to talk to us, Hailey?"

The young woman frowned. "Do I know you?"

"I'm Doug Fletcher, a National Park Service investigator. This is my partner, Jill."

"Park Service?"

"We're investigating Erik Petersen's death," Jill explained.

Hailey's smile melted. "OMG! That was so terrible."

"Could we borrow an office to speak privately with you for a few moments?" Jill asked.

Nodding to a table across the room past the last office, Hailey said, "There are confidential files and stuff in the offices. Can we talk over there, at the meeting table?"

"Sure," Jill replied.

As we moved across the room, Hailey said, "Wow, I'm slipping. Would you guys like a bottle of water or a cup of coffee or tea? We keep some for our clients."

Jill shook her head, but I accepted a cup of black coffee. Jill and I walked to a table in a secluded corner while Hailey popped a K-cup into the coffee maker. I studied the walls which were plastered with printouts of current real estate listings and recent sales. Delivering a steaming cup of coffee and motioning for us to sit, Hailey said, "The realtors meet clients here, rather than in their offices." We sat in swivel chairs at a table capable of seating six.

"When did you last speak with Erik?" Jill asked as we sat.

Hailey's look went from perky to sad. "It was like three weeks ago. I told him I had to move on with my life."

"Was there a fight or argument that precipitated the breakup?"

"Erik didn't fight. That was part of the problem. He didn't have any..."

"Any what?" I asked.

"Sparkle. Yeah, Erik lacked sparkle. He was just monotone gray. He thought doing dull stuff was fun. I tried to get him to go to bars and movies. He thought zero carbon footprint camping in Death Valley was a big adventure."

"We heard you didn't enjoy the Death Valley trip," I said.

Hailey paused, then nodded. "Oh, you've already talked to Todd and Lexi."

Not answering her question, Jill said, "Tell us about Death Valley."

"It was a nightmare. I mean, sleeping in a tent? Really? With families in tents and campers a few feet away. You could hear every kid whining and people arguing."

"Is that why you broke up?" Jill asked.

Hailey shrugged. "That was the end. Erik was nice and polite, but he didn't know how to have fun. There's more to life than eating popcorn in front of a television and sitting around a campfire so you smell like smoked sausage."

"Your breakup was amicable?"

"Not really. I mean, I wasn't trying to break up. I just wanted him to do something adventurous. But he couldn't react. He just sat there and listened to me looking like a sad puppy. I walked out and ghosted him when he tried to contact me."

"Ghosted him?" I asked.

"I stopped replying to his emails and texts. I thought he'd get the message."

"Did that work?" I asked.

Hailey looked away from me and stared out of the window. "Not really. Erik showed up at my apartment and wanted to talk. I told him there was no point and asked him to leave."

"And that was the end of it?" Jill asked.

Hailey looked at Jill, then shook her head. "Erik showed up here at the office with flowers. I asked him to leave. That same night he showed up at my apartment. I told him to leave, but he wanted to reason through whatever he'd done wrong. My brother was visiting and when Tanner overheard us, he got into Erik's face, and they walked to Erik's car together. I didn't hear from Erik after that."

"Did the confrontation between Erik and your brother get physical?" I asked.

Hailey looked at her hands. "I don't think so. Tanner can be a little gruff, but I don't think he would do anything more than take Erik's arm and lead him away."

"Do you have a new boyfriend?" Jill asked.

"I've met a couple guys, but there's nothing serious."

"No one who would be jealous of Erik?" I asked.

"I don't talk about my exes. Besides, who would be jealous of Erik? He wouldn't have evoked jealousy even if there was a new guy in my life."

"How long were you and Erik dating?" Jill asked.

"We were together for a couple of months. Erik may have thought we were serious, but there wasn't ever any chemistry between us. How can there be chemistry when one of the people doesn't react?"

"You agreed to go camping with him," Jill said. "That sounds like there must've been some chemistry."

Hailey looked annoyed. "Hooking up with someone is one thing. Emotional attachment is something else."

"Is that how Erik felt?" I asked.

A middle-aged woman's head poked out of an office, then looked at us. "Excuse me, did you have an appointment?"

Hailey panicked, "Eloise, um, no. They're here to talk to me."

Jill smiled and twisted in her chair, exposing her badge. "Hailey is helping us with an investigation. We're sorry for intruding in your workspace."

The woman sighed and nodded. "Hailey, I need the signed Romanski purchase agreement and mortgage pre-approval letter when you're through."

"Are we through?" Hailey asked.

"Was Erik in love with you?" I asked.

"Probably. I don't know. He thought a hook-up was love. I didn't."

"Did Erik have problems with anyone?"

"Problems?" Hailey asked. "Like someone who was mad enough to kill him?"

I nodded. "Or someone he rubbed the wrong way at the park?"

"He loved Manzanar and telling visitors about the history. I mean, that's the only time he ever sparkled."

"How about his co-workers?" Jill asked.

"His boss is nothing. I mean, he lets the rangers get away with too much. He doesn't yell at people who show up late or even when they miss their shifts. Erik used to get irritated with him. Ed isn't a killer."

"How about the other rangers? Did Erik get along with them?"

"Most of them were kind of in the background. You know, non-entities. They're there, but they're not a team."

"Erik must've commented on that," I said.

"Yeah, he really wanted to be part of a team. Erik and Todd got along well enough to share the apartment, but they weren't BFFs."

"How about the others?" Jill asked. "Was there friction among the other rangers?"

"Erik said the two old women treated him like a son. I think the Japanese American woman taught him a lot about the camp. Grace?"

"So, Grace and Becky mothered him. How about the others?"

"The rest were okay. I mean, the Nazi and the narcissist were annoying, but I think they irritated everyone."

"The Nazi and the narcissist? Which ones were they?"

Hailey paused while trying to remember names. "The rich kid, who went by his initials. He was into himself and trying to impress everyone."

"Erik didn't get along with Casey?" Jill asked.

"Casey was above it all. I mean, he'd sometimes show up at a bar, but only to make sure we knew about his money, perfect outfit, and how much smarter he was than everyone else."

"Did Casey and Erik hate each other?"

Hailey shook her head. "Hate is too strong a word. I think Erik viewed Casey as an irrelevant irritation."

"And the Nazi?" Jill asked.

"He's a right-wing gun nut." Hailey lifted her head when she remembered the name. "Kevin. I think all the rangers disliked Kevin's politics. He called them tree-hugging communists."

"It sounds like Kevin and Erik had problems," I said, hoping to dig deeper.

"Erik said he just walked away from Kevin's ideological rants. Neither of them was going to change the other." When we didn't speak, Hailey looked at each of us, then added, "Whoa, it's not like they'd kill each other over their stupid political views or Kevin's immigrant prejudice."

"Racial prejudice?"

Hailey smiled. "Kevin thought any *foreigner* should go back to wherever they'd come from. Grace told Kevin that her family had been in the US longer than his ancestors. He told her to move back to Japan. He was always bitching about the *wet backs* coming across the southern border. He was very disappointed that the Mexican border wall wasn't finished."

Eloise stepped into the open area, looking stern. "Hailey, I need those files now." She turned and stalked off.

Jill stood and thanked Hailey.

"Do you know anyone who disliked Erik enough to kill him?" I asked as I stood.

"Who dislikes a puppy?" Hailey asked. "Erik was just a lost puppy who wanted to follow me around."

After we exited the building, Jill walked close alongside me. "I think Hailey kicked the loyal puppy who was following her around."

"It sounds like her brother did the kicking. If Hailey's telling us the truth, she tried to let him down easy, and Erik wasn't receiving the message."

"Some guys are a little thicker-headed than others."

"I don't get this whole hook-up-not-being-love thing," I replied.

Jill pulled my arm around her. "You're just an old-fashioned romantic."

"Me? You're the one who wasn't into one-night stands."

"Okay, so we're both old-fashioned," Jill replied as a couple rushed past us and entered the realty office.

"I think we can discount Hailey as the killer. She's just a wisp of a girl. There's no way she slashed Erik's throat and strung him up on the fence. Besides, that story was so pathetic, I can't believe she made it up." I thought about what Hailey had told us. "The Nazi thing is disturbing. If Erik had been Hispanic, I'd be very suspicious of Kevin."

"I don't like narcissists. Hailey made Casey sound like a sociopath. As you've pointed out, a sociopath will sometimes overreact to situations."

"What's Casey's motive? Erik was too frumpy?"

After a moment of thought, Jill said, "Maybe Erik wasn't deferential enough. He wouldn't bow down and kiss Casey's ring."

"I think that's a stretch."

Jill leaned on the car as I unlocked it. "The person whose story isn't pathetic is Lexi. She struck me as manipulative. I think she wanted to have Todd alone. She didn't want his clingy roommate around. Maybe she needed a place to live, and Erik's bedroom vacancy was planned, not accidental."

"She's years older than Todd. That makes me suspicious of her motives."

"I'm older than you are. Should people be suspicious of my motives?"

I raised my eyebrows, trying to be suggestive. "Definitely."

"Please don't do that eyebrow thing. It makes you look like Groucho Marx."

"Where does Lexi work?" I asked.

"I don't think she told us," Jill said as she got into the car.

Chapter 10

We sat in the idling rental car while Jill searched the internet for Lexi Cruz, residing in Lone Pine. It only took a couple of minutes for Jill to hit pay dirt. "I can't believe how much information these young people put on the internet."

"Her employer, for instance?" I asked, hoping to drill down to Lexi's pertinent job information without getting a monologue about what her last meals had been.

"She's the assistant manager at a sporting goods store," Jill replied as she studied Lexi's online presence. "She lists herself in a relationship with Todd Overland. She'll be thirty on her next birthday. She likes Terry Pratchett and Neil Gaiman books, and her favorite movie is *Eating Cake in Bars*."

"Where's the sporting goods store?"

After a few keystrokes, Jill replied, "About two blocks down, on the opposite side of the street."

The store wasn't large but was jammed with every variety of hiking, camping, and fishing gear imaginable. A retiree was ringing up a young family's purchases, which were mostly Mount Whitney t-shirts and sunscreen. In the back, we found Lexi restocking fishing gear. Although she was kneeling and focused on the shelf, she sensed our presence and looked up. "The park cops are all over," she sighed. "Are you buying or harassing?"

"Have you got a second?" Jill asked.

After looking around to make sure no customers required her assistance, she nodded toward the counter in front of the hunting rifles. When we were well away from any customers she asked, "What's up?"

"We spoke with Hailey. Your account of the breakup with Erik matches hers."

"Like I told you, Hailey dumped Erik, and he was devastated."

"That leaves us without a motive or killer," I said.

"I thought the sheriff's department was calling Erik's murder drug related?"

I paused for a moment to see if she'd add anything more. When she didn't, I looked at the selection of pistols locked inside the glass-topped counter. "I'm not buying that theory. The cartels and drug dealers use guns." Looking farther down the counter, I nodded toward a selection of hunting knives. "I think the killer knew Erik personally and used a knife like one of these."

Glancing down at the hunting knives through the glass counter, Lexi frowned. "I can't imagine killing someone with a knife. I mean, that's cold."

"Stabbings are usually personal. The killer is in a rage and is exacting revenge or sating his or her anger."

"Maybe it was a road rage thing?" Lexi suggested.

"Erik was killed just outside of the Manzanar gate. It's not like he cut someone off in traffic." I paused again, but Lexi had nothing to add. "Are you certain there wasn't someone angry with Erik? Did he get into a fight with someone in a bar or make a pass at someone's girlfriend?"

"Erik? Are you kidding? He went out of his way *not* to irritate people. He never made a pass at a girl. He didn't know what a pick-up line was."

"Who benefits from his death?" Jill asked.

"Benefits?"

"Who profits from him dying? Did someone owe him money? Did he flash around a wad of cash?"

"Erik? You've got to be kidding. He was frugal and he mostly used a debit card when we went anywhere to eat or drink. Did Erik's killer steal his debit card?"

"We'll check on that," I replied. "Who else benefits?"

"Not Todd. He's the loser because Erik was paying half their rental expenses."

"Where do you live?" I asked.

Lexi froze. "Wait a second. I didn't kill him so I could move in with Todd."

"Are you living alone?"

"Yes, in a dumpy house that's full of mice and infested with bugs."

"But you *are* planning to move into Erik's bedroom, aren't you?"

Lexi's eyes narrowed. "I have a lease for another three and a half months. If I'd wanted to get rid of Erik, I would've asked him to find another place to live when my lease ran out. I wouldn't kill him." Lexi looked past me, then said, "Excuse me. I have customers."

"What do you think?" Jill asked as we walked away from the store.

"I think she's planning to move in with Todd. We should find out if the statement about her lease is true."

Punching information into her phone as we walked, Jill found Lexi's address. "She only lives a couple of blocks from here. We can walk past her rental."

While none of the houses in Lone Pine were palatial, Lexi lived in an older part of town where the houses were small, and many were run down. We stopped in front of a blue house in need of paint. "This is it?"

"According to my phone, this is where Lexi Cruz resides."

"I can see how it might be mouse infested."

A woman stepped out of the house next door. Glaring at us, she exhaled a cloud of cigarette smoke, then coughed. "Help you?"

"Is this where Lexi Cruz lives?"

"Who's asking?"

I unclipped the badge from my belt and held it up. "I'm a cop."

After another coughing fit, the woman flicked her cigarette butt into the yard. "Yeah. That punk kid lives there."

"Do you know who her landlord is?"

The woman's laugh was as raspy as her voice. "If you're planning to arrest the girl, you'll have better luck finding her at the gun store."

"What makes you think we're here to arrest her?" I asked.

"No particular reason," the woman replied. "It's just that renters in this part of town aren't the cream of the crop, if you know what I mean. Lexi is better than most because she's got a real job."

"Does she have a lease?" Jill asked.

The woman's laugh turned into a coughing fit. "Oh, hell no. She rents by the month. If she misses a month, the locks will be changed, and her stuff will be sitting on the curb the next day."

"Thanks," I said, stepping away from the house.

"Hey, what kind of cops are you? I recognize most of the local deputies. Hell, they've been here often enough over the years."

"We're federal investigators," I replied.

"What's she done? Is she growing marijuana up in the hills?"

"We don't know that she's done anything wrong," I replied. "We're just following up on leads."

"Hang on." The woman leaned heavily on the railing as she slowly climbed down the steps. Approaching us, she lowered her voice. "Lexi is okay, but her taste in men sucks. Her new boyfriend seems nice enough, but the two before him were shits. They'd come in at all hours of the night with their noisy pickups and leave booze and beer bottles in the yard. I don't know what she saw in them because she's okay for the most part."

"For the most part?" Jill asked.

"You're cops and you don't know that she's got a record?"

"A record for what?"

"I suspect it was marijuana and drugs," the woman replied. "I've seen cops take her out of here in handcuffs at least twice."

"What's your name?" I asked.

"Ione Cartwright. And before you ask, no, I wasn't part of the *Bonanza* television show."

"Thank you, Mrs. Cartwright."

"Give me a heads up if you're planning to arrest her. I'll need to get the place fumigated before I rent it out again. Lexi says the mice are bad."

"You could fumigate it now," Jill suggested.

Ione laughed. "Why? She's not moving out, and fumigation costs money."

As we walked to our car Jill waited until we were out of earshot and then asked, "Why would Lexi lie to us about her lease?"

"The lease would've taken away her motive," I replied as I unlocked the car.

"Do you think she'd be willing to kill Erik just so she could move in with Todd?"

I mulled the question as the car idled. "She'd have to be a psychopath to kill someone over a bedroom."

"She seems normal enough," Jill replied.

"That's the thing about psychopaths; they can act like normal people until something triggers them."

"I thought psychopaths were creepy and suspicious, like Ed Gein, the killer in Wisconsin."

I drove away from the rental house as I answered, "For every outwardly creepy psychopath, there are a bunch of clean-cut friendly psychopaths who charm their victims. My experience says there's ten of the charming ones to one of the creepy killers."

Sighing, Jill looked out of the window at Lone Pine. "I don't like to think about things like that. I prefer to think of psychopaths as creepy and rare." After a moment, Jill turned to me. "If Lexi is a psychopath, she has access to hundreds of guns, knives, and crossbows, all of them lethal."

"And Erik would've been at ease with her."

Jill shook her head. "I can't buy Lexi as the killer. How would she have lifted Erik's body up to hang him onto the barbed wire fence? He must've outweighed her by forty pounds."

"Maybe Erik let Lexi tie him up before she killed him."

Grimacing, Jill asked, "Why would someone let that happen?"

"I've learned to never underestimate the creativity of a criminal." I turned into the motel lot and parked alongside Jamie's car.

* * *

Answering my knock on his motel room door, Jamie appeared to be surprisingly wide awake. He stretched and invited me in. The bed was unmade, reassuring me that Jamie had gotten at least an hour or two of sleep while we'd been following up on Lexi.

"Give me a second to shower," he said, taking underwear and a uniform shirt from his backpack. "Did you discover anything about the roommate's girlfriend?"

"She works in a sporting goods store filled with weapons, and she lied to us about having three months left on her lease."

I waited while Jamie showered, reflecting on Lexi's lie about her lease.

Jamie emerged from the bathroom with wet hair he'd combed with his fingers. "Did you solve the murder while I was in the shower?" he asked, as he pinned a badge on his shirt and clipped his holster to his belt.

"No revelations came to me."

131

Jamie opened the door for me. "Take me to a tobacco shop."

"When did you start smoking?" I asked.

"Have I taught you nothing?"

With Jill now sitting in the driver's seat, I got in the back seat and asked, "What lesson did I miss?"

"I always bring a gift of tobacco when I meet a tribal elder. It's a sign of respect and demonstrates my understanding of Native customs." As an afterthought, he said, "Good morning again, Jill."

"Jamie wants to buy tobacco. Have you seen a smoke shop in town?"

Backing out of the parking spot, Jill replied, "I saw a small grocery store and a gas station. I'd guess either of them might have tobacco."

Jamie buckled his seatbelt and replied, "The gas station will have tobacco and hot coffee."

I leaned forward to talk with Jill while Jamie went into the station. "What response did you get from John Standing Bear when you called about a visit?"

After a short pause, Jill replied, "John Standing Bear is about as talkative as Jamie. He said we could visit him, although he didn't seem excited or pleased."

"Did he give you an address or just vague directions with landmarks like we got when visiting people on the Navajo reservation?"

"His address is on Zucco Road. I have no idea if he lives in a residential or rural area."

"What does your mapping app show you?"

Jill looked at me in the rear-view mirror. "The mapping apps aren't particularly useful in rural areas."

Jamie emerged from the gas station carrying a cardboard tray and a bag. Inside the car, he handed each of us a paper cup with a lid. "Black coffee for you two. Coffee and a doughnut for me."

"Thanks," I said, accepting the cup handed to me. "Aren't you afraid of being stereotyped as a cop by buying a doughnut?"

"I really don't care," he replied.

Jill activated the turn-by-turn mapping feature on her phone, which told her to turn south on Main Street.

"What do you know about this reservation?" I asked Jamie.

"It's one of several Paiute-Shoshone reservations. It's only 235 acres and Highway 395 runs through it. There are over a thousand registered tribal members, although only a quarter of them live on the reservation."

Following the directions, Jill made several turns leading us to Zucca Road where a sign displayed the tribal logo, a circle with an eagle flying over mountains. Jamie looked at the buildings as Jill drove slowly toward the address. "Prosperous reservation," he commented. "Nice houses, built too close to each other."

When Jill's phone told us we'd arrived at our destination, she turned into a driveway leading to a double-wide trailer set on a concrete block foundation. A pickup was parked in front of the garage and a rocky trail served as the sidewalk from the driveway to the front door.

Jill reached for her door handle, but Jamie put his hand on her arm. "Wait."

Confused, she asked, "What's going on?"

"The owner will come to the door when he's ready to receive us."

Jill looked at me in the rear-view mirror. I nodded, "It's a nice cultural custom. Jamie introduced me to it on the Navajo reservation."

A moment later the front door opened and a middle-aged man in jeans and a t-shirt waved us in. Holding the door open, not speaking or smiling, he let us pass into the small entryway. Jamie entered last and nodded to the man before presenting him a package of tobacco with both hands as if making an offering. "Thank you for meeting with us, cousin."

The man looked closely at Jamie's badge. A hint of a smile formed on his lips, and he accepted the gift. "Please take a seat in the living room."

The room was bright, decorated with native carvings, rugs, and paintings. Jill and I sat together on a loveseat while Jamie stood. "I'm Jamie Ballard, from the Navajo Nation. These are my friends, Doug and Jill

Fletcher, who work for the Park Service." Jamie paused, staring at me. "I consider them my brother and sister. They are the godparents of my son."

Apparently impressed by Jamie, Standing Bear introduced himself as the informal tribal historian and gestured for Jamie to sit in a chair next to him. "I was surprised by the call from Halona Mid-Thunder, asking me to speak with Park Service people. You're here for a history lesson?"

Nodding toward me, Jamie waited for my explanation. "We're investigating the death of the ranger whose body was found at Manzanar. There are many unanswered questions and many things to investigate. We hope you can help us understand the legend of *Si-Te-Cah*."

"I've recorded hundreds of conversations about a thousand demons and spirits. Why are you interested in *Si-Te-Cah*?"

"The ranger who was killed had red hair," I replied.

"Ah, and you think a Paiute killed him?"

"At this point, I have no idea who killed the ranger. All we're doing is trying to understand anything that might be construed as a motive. A wise man told us to investigate Mexican, Native, and Southwestern lore for red-haired demons."

Standing Bear looked at Jamie. "And you bring these people to my doorstep to accuse one of my brothers?"

"I bring them to you for understanding, cousin. Nothing more."

Standing Bear leaned back and studied me, then Jill. He drew a breath, then nodded. "The *Si-Te-Cah* or *Saiduka* were a legendary race of red-haired giants who lived in southern Nevada. Depending on the source, they were either demons or giant warriors. Legend has it that the Paiutes drove them into a cave. After shooting arrows into the cave and taunting the giants to come out and fight, the Paiutes built a fire at the cave's mouth. Some of the giants came out into a hail of arrows. The rest were asphyxiated inside."

"And this legend continues to be passed down?" I asked.

"Like I said, it is one of many pieces of oral history. The *Si-Te-Cah* legend was documented in the 1930s and is retold, as are many of the other great victories."

"Are there people who believe the story is real?" Jill asked.

Standing Bear smiled. "Is the story of the Battle of Jericho real? What's real is people's faith in oral histories. As you can imagine, I have spoken to dozens of elders and the details of the stories are rarely the same. Your Bible has the advantage of being written, which froze the narrative at some earlier time. Our oral histories continue to evolve, hence my interest in recording them."

"Is there more to the battle at the cave than just the legend of the red-haired giants?" Jill asked.

"Lovelock Cave was excavated for the accumulated bat guano in the early 1900s. The miners discovered artifacts that they threw aside until a California professor became interested in the 1930s. He did a proper archaeological excavation and recovered an extraordinary number of artifacts from the site, many dating to 1400 BC."

"Did he find the skeletons of red-haired giants?" Jill asked.

"He found the skeleton of a woman who was over six-feet tall, and a man who was nearly eight feet tall. Both had red hair."

"Wow," I said. "Are the skeletons in a museum?"

Chuckling, Standing Bear shook his head. "Sadly, the skeletons were misplaced. That said, they did save a fifteen-inch sandal. I believe that is in the Smithsonian Museum along with baskets, bones, and other artifacts."

"It seems odd that there would be a tribe of red-haired people here, in the Southwest."

"One theory says the hair of the cave victims was stained by the red iron oxide leaching from the rocks over thousands of years."

"Is there another theory?" I asked.

"The Vikings claim to have landed in the New World thousands of years before

Columbus came to rape, loot, spread syphilis, and kill the Native people. Some people think that the Vikings were taller than the Native tribes and might've had red hair. I know there was a red-haired mummy discovered in Oregon."

"How do the people of your tribe feel about the Manzanar Historic Site?" I asked.

"From what perspective?"

"Are they angry that the Park Service is there and operating it?"

Standing Bear cocked his head. "Manzanar is generally felt to be a memorial to the American subjugation of another minority. I personally feel that it's important to remind the whites of their illegal and immoral treatment of all minorities."

Jamie interrupted. "Are there any young people who are particularly unhappy with the treatment of the Paiutes by the government?"

"You're asking if anyone would kill a ranger because Manzanar is symbolic of the government occupation of what had been Paiute territory?" Standing Bear paused. "I think we've become pragmatists who rely on the courts rather than symbolic attacks on Park Service rangers."

"Do you think any of your tribal members might mistake a red-haired ranger for a *Si-Te-Cah*?"

Standing Bear cocked his head. "Where are you from, Doug Fletcher? Your accent sounds Midwestern."

"I'm from Minnesota."

Standing Bear nodded. "I thought I caught a bit of *Fargo* in your accent. The elongated vowels give you away." He paused. "Would someone attack a man wearing a plaid shirt and carrying an ax because they thought he was Paul Bunyan?"

Jill chuckled. "No, but an eco-terrorist might attack him to save a tree."

"Where is home for you, Jill Fletcher?"

"South Dakota."

Again, Standing Bear nodded. "Would any of the Lakota people attack a ranger at Mount Rushmore because the government stole that land after giving it to the tribe in a treaty?"

I interrupted Jill's response. "There are psychopaths everywhere, and among every race. All it takes is one person with impaired judgment to carry a grudge too far."

"Well put, Doug Fletcher. You're looking for a psychopath but haven't identified what triggered that person."

"Is there someone in your community who might overreact to a red-haired ranger? Someone whose judgment is clouded by hate? Someone who might be triggered by seeing a tall, red-haired ranger?" Jamie asked.

"I don't know of anyone here who thinks the *Si-Te-Cah* are anything but an ancient legend. Our children are more concerned about global warming and modern issues." Standing, our host signaled the end of our conversation. "I hope I've given you clarity on your question."

Jamie's face showed deep thought. "How many Paiute-Shoshone communities exist?"

Standing Bear put his hand on Jamie's shoulder. "Unlike our Navajo cousins, the Paiutes and Shoshones have been dispersed into many tiny reservations and communities spread across California, Nevada, and Utah. Some of our reservations have as few as thirty surviving residents. Others have as many as two thousand. I suppose you could say there are thirty recognized tribes."

"Would you expect any of them to hate the *Si-Te-Cah* more than any other?"

"Perhaps the Paiutes closer to Lovelock Cave might be more attuned to the *Si-Te-Cah* legend." Leading us out of the living room, the historian added, "You should talk to someone on the Bishop Paiute-Shoshone Reservation. Call Mary Peacham, the president. The elders I've spoken to on that reservation seem more interested in retelling the stories of great tribal victories. Keep in mind that the *Si-Te-Cah* are no more than an oral legend."

"Except for the missing eight-foot skeleton," Jill said as she stepped to the door.

Standing Bear smiled. "It's convenient for legendary skeletons to be missing, isn't it?"

"There is the fifteen-inch sandal," I said, offering my hand.

Shaking my hand, Standing Bear nodded. "I'm sure it's displayed alongside the cast taken of the Bigfoot print."

"What do you think, Jamie?" I asked as we got into the car.

"There aren't many Paiutes, and the odds of one being a psychopathic killer are small."

"Do the Paiutes use peyote as a part of their religion?" Jill asked.

"I don't think peyote turns people into killers," Jamie replied.

"But it might impair a person's judgment."

Jamie's response was a shrug.

Chapter 11

In the car, Jill asked, "What now?"

"I think the Bishop Paiute-Shoshone reservation is nearby," Jamie suggested.

I sighed. "The red-haired warrior/demon thing seems far-fetched to me. I'm more intrigued by Todd's lying girlfriend. I think she is more motivated to take over Erik's room than she's saying."

Jill looked at me in the rear-view mirror as she started the car. "There's an area near the Manzanar memorial where people on their pilgrimage have tied ribbons and strips of cloth to the fence. It might be interesting to look at them to see if anyone left hateful messages."

"They're prayer ribbons," Jamie said.

I replied, "I imagine they're asking for blessings to the loved ones who died there during their internment."

Jill drove away from the curb and turned toward the highway. "Since we're at a dead end, let's look at the prayer ribbons."

Jamie, who was usually quiet, stared out of the windshield. Jill noticed his unusual silence and asked, "Are you uncomfortable doing this?"

"The spirits are active there. It's not a comfortable place."

"It's a place where people go for closure," I said.

"No," Jamie replied. "It's a place where people go to weep for the dead, lost dreams, and bigotry. The spirits linger there because they're unable to move on. They're trapped by the remote, unfamiliar, and unhappy situation."

"I read that most of the people who died at Manzanar were eventually relocated to family cemetery plots. Wouldn't that free their spirits?" I asked.

"If you spill blood on the floor, you can wipe it up, but you can't remove the stain. So, it is with Manzanar."

"I think that's the point of making Manzanar a US National Historic Site," I replied. "We want to be reminded of what occurred there, so it never happens again."

"You have wiped up the blood, but the stain remains," Jamie reiterated.

Wanting to move the conversation on, Jill said, "Tell me more about prayer ribbons."

"They must be somewhat universal," I replied. "They were tied to bushes and trees around Devils Tower."

"That's right," Jill replied. "There were more than ribbons there. I think a lot of people were inspired to leave a message on anything a person could write on. We saw handkerchiefs, strips of cloth, and even an athletic sock with a message written on it.”

“Those were different from the ribbons left at Manzanar,” Jamie said. “I expect the Manzanar ribbons were left as memorials. The ribbons and strips of cloth at Devils Tower were probably prayerful requests for a blessing or healing.”

“All are left in sadness,” Jill summarized. “We need to look at them to see if someone left a ribbon in anger.”

“Huh,” Jamie said. “Prayers for revenge, not for healing?”

“Maybe prayers for things to be set right,” Jill opined, “or to be returned to an earlier time.”

“It’s hard for someone my age to imagine the Navajo living anywhere but where they are today.”

“Perhaps John Standing Bear’s work may be stirring up some ancient sentiments,” I said. “He’s recording the elders’ retelling of ancient battles and days of glory.”

Turning onto the highway, Jill said, “It’s like my high school American history class. History is marked by wars, not so much the periods of peace.”

“Historically, young Native men gained recognition by killing their tribal enemies,” Jamie explained. “In some tribes, a young man earned a feather for each enemy he vanquished. In some tribes, that meant touching your enemy, as in fencing. In others, it meant the taking of the enemy’s life. The chiefs with the elaborate headdresses decorated with hundreds of eagle feathers were revered by their people."

"That brings up an interesting question; how do today's young men pass into manhood? There aren't any battles for them to earn feathers."

"Times have changed," Jamie said, smiling. "Now, it's a matter of who has the cutest girlfriend and the fastest car."

"Somehow, that's not the same as earning battle feathers," Jill said as we approached the Manzanar entrance.

"You show off your conquests in culturally acceptable ways."

I stared at the barbed wire fence as Tonya waved us past the stone guard shack. "Until you hear the stories of the bad old days when young men earned their feathers with blood."

Kevin Roberts, the young ranger manning the counter in the visitor center, was surprised to see Jamie's uniform. It took him a second before he noticed Jill and me. "Ah, you're the investigators."

I introduced Kevin to Jamie. "We brought our associate from the Navajo Nation Police, Jamie Ballard."

Shaking Jamie's hand, the ranger said, "I'm Kevin Roberts. I met the Fletchers when they were here earlier." Looking past Jamie, Kevin said, "The superintendent isn't around. Is there something I can do for you?"

"We're going to walk around the camp and thought we'd check in, so you weren't surprised to see unpaid visitors wandering around."

"No problem. Thanks for checking in."

Jill asked, "How well did you know Erik?"

"I suppose I knew him as well as any of the other rangers did. We worked together, but that was it."

"Did you ever notice anyone expressing anger at the victim?"

"Red was laid back. He didn't make waves."

"Did you get your battery replaced?" I asked.

Kevin froze. "My battery?"

"You said you were late because you had to get your vehicle jump-started."

"Oh, that. I had a loose battery terminal connection. It's good now."

Suspecting Kevin had lied about his tardy arrival, then forgotten his lie, I said, "That's the price of having an older vehicle."

Kevin tried to move on from being caught in a lie. "Bankers don't like to make car loans to seasonal rangers. I'm stuck with my beat-up pickup for the time being."

Walking out of the visitor center, Jamie asked, "I wonder what else Kevin has been lying about?"

"He's not a practiced liar," I replied. "He forgot his lie as soon as the conversation moved on."

"How long does it take for a person to go from seasonal to full-time ranger?"

Jill thought for a moment. "It depends on a number of factors. If he's willing to relocate, he might be able to find a permanent job at another park in a year or two. If he wants to stay here, he might have to wait until one of the permanent rangers moves to a different park."

"That's a lot of uncertainty," Jamie said as we walked across the parking lot.

"There are a lot of people who want to be rangers and not a lot of openings for permanent rangers. I've seen dozens of people take seasonal jobs for a few years, then they move on with their lives. Others have part-time jobs to fill in during the off-season at the parks."

In the cemetery, we stopped near a section of barbed wire fence where dozens of colored ribbons and strips of cloth twisted in the wind. Together, we walked to the fence, reading the prayer ribbon messages as we walked along the edge of the cemetery, on the outer edge of the park.

"A lot of these are *kanji* and *kana* characters," I said. "I assume they were left by the families of the survivors."

"I see a couple of ribbons with no markings at all," Jill observed. "The people who tied them to the wire must've said a prayer and assumed that God heard them."

Looking through the fence, Jamie pointed toward the cemetery's white obelisk monument where several park visitors were gathered. "There are a bunch of colored streamers on the fence around the memorial monument. Let's look at them."

We walked together to the white stone obelisk. Passing an elderly Asian couple, Jill knelt and touched a small bit of fabric that was strung on twine hung between the fence posts. "These look like little children."

"Without an explanation, we'll never know what the artist was trying to say," I suggested.

Jamie stood with his hands jammed in his jean's pockets. "They're meant to commemorate the children."

I looked for a plaque explaining that viewpoint but saw none. "How do you know that?"

"Can't you feel it? I can almost hear their voices. Children who never knew anything but life inside this wire perimeter."

A family with three children joined us at the monument. The woman, who'd been watching silently, spoke, "The tiny rags represent the children. Many were born here and knew nothing other than life in the camp for their first four years of life. A few died here, a few stillborn and two or three from diseases."

Jamie paused and nodded toward the tiny tufts of fabric. "These aren't threatening, they're sad. The answers we seek aren't here."

With Jill examining each piece of fabric, Jamie took a cloth from his pocket and unwrapped a small string-wrapped bundle of grass the size of a cigar. The gathering group watched as he struck a match and lit the end of the bundle. Satisfied that it was smoking, he looked at the sky, then situated himself so he was facing north.

We watched as he dropped to his knees and bowed his head. Speaking softly, he repeated the ritual, facing west, south, then east. When he was done, he stood and waved the bundle, so the smoke dispersed, the scent of sweetgrass and sage carried on the mild breeze. He dropped the bundle and stepped on it to snuff out the burning embers.

"Honoring the spirits of those who suffered here."

"Are there many?" I asked, as Jill joined us.

Jamie stared at me for a moment, then said, "Their voices are deafening, can't you hear them?"

The Asian couple, with tears in their eyes, stepped forward. The man put his hand on Jamie's shoulder. "Thank you. You have honored the spirits of the people who lived and died here."

Feeling somewhat ashamed for being so focused on the investigation that I'd forgotten the significance of the monument and the site, I closed my eyes and listened. I envisioned children playing, mothers hanging laundry to dry, men working to build and repair the buildings. All seeming normal, except for the fact that all this was happening to American citizens encircled by barbed wire and supervised by soldiers in guard towers.

When I opened my eyes, Jamie was still staring at me. "I hear them."

Jamie nodded. "Go back another hundred years. Those relocation camps were called Indian reservations."

Jill listened to the discussion without interrupting. Sensing we were done, she said, "Humans have never been kind to each other. Those in power take advantage of the less fortunate. Add paranoia and stereotyping, and you have this. Or a reservation. Or a holocaust."

Staring at the monument, Jamie said, "We should learn from our mistakes."

I stepped towards Jamie. "We improve what we can control. As cops, we see the shittiest parts of society, and our job is to protect the meek and innocent from the cruel and evil. We do that one person at a time. Sometimes we're successful. Other times, we're not. But we keep trying."

Jill slipped her arm around Jamie's waist and took a step toward the parking lot. "This place is draining my energy. Let's get out of here. We skipped lunch. Let's have an early supper."

As Jill drove out of the parking lot, Jamie twisted to speak to me over the seat. "This place is filled with evil and sorrow. There's no way to separate what happened to that ranger from all the sadness and suffering of the past."

"There's a way," I replied. "We just need to find it."

Turning toward Lone Pine, Jill asked, "Does anyone have a supper suggestion?"

Jamie shook his head, then stiffened abruptly. "No sushi. I don't eat raw fish."

"We haven't seen a sushi place in town."

"Good. Don't search." Jamie paused, then said, "A pizza would taste good, although I'll eat most anything...that's thoroughly cooked."

"Is pizza okay with you, Doug?" Jill asked, looking into the rear-view mirror.

"That sounds good. I've had enough comfort food. Pizza would be a nice change."

* * *

Jill found a pizza place a few blocks from our motel. The early crowd consisted of a few people drinking at the bar. The bartender waved at us when we hesitated by the door. "Sit anywhere," he said.

A moment later, a middle-aged woman with unnaturally black hair rushed out of the kitchen. She filled three water glasses, put menus under her arm, and walked to our table. "I'm Miranda. Would you like something from the bar while you study the menu?"

I ordered a beer, Jamie chose Coke, and Jill asked for the house red wine. Perusing the menu, Jamie stopped with his finger on an item halfway down the page. "The meat-lover's special sounds interesting."

Jill closed her menu and smiled. "You two can split that and eat whatever you want from my veggie pizza."

When our drinks arrived, we ordered two pizzas and side salads. After Miranda left with our orders, I looked at Jamie, then Jill. "What are we missing?"

"Besides a motive and the killer's name?" Jamie asked.

"If we knew the motive, we'd be a lot closer to identifying the killer."

"Is there something so obvious we're overlooking it?" Jill asked.

"Give me an example," I said.

"Maybe Erik was up for a promotion to a different park. Maybe someone thought they'd be in line for that transfer if Erik was dead."

"No one mentioned that. I'd think Todd or Lexi would've said something if they knew Erik was relocating."

Finished with that discussion, Jamie looked toward the barflies when they broke out laughing. "I could live here. It's a little remote, but it's cozy."

Jill wrinkled her nose. "Having grown up in a rural area, I prefer the anonymity of bigger cities."

I looked at her with disbelief. "You hate New York and Washington, DC."

"Slightly bigger," Jill clarified. "Something with 30,000-50,000 people is perfect. Smaller towns don't attract big chain stores, so they retain a lot of their mom-and-pop stores and restaurants. I like towns big enough to not overwhelm you with snoopy people trying to know your every move."

Jamie grimaced. "I prefer a little isolation. A place away from town where you don't need to buy window shades would be perfect."

Jill leaned close. "Trust me, Jamie. There is *nowhere* remote enough that I wouldn't want window coverings of some kind."

"That's a woman thing," he replied.

Jill smiled and said, "The last time I checked, you were married to a woman."

Jamie grinned at Jill without replying.

Replying for him, I said, "I think Jamie is still working his way around those marital landmines, like the need for window blinds."

* * *

After eating more than half of the meat-lovers pizza, Jamie wiped his face and fingers on several paper napkins and leaned back. "It's early, but I'd like to go back to the motel."

"I suppose twelve hours of sleep might recharge your batteries," I replied.

Jill signaled the waitress and asked for our bill and a box for the remaining two-thirds of her pizza. Jamie watched as Jill slid her pizza into the box. "That will make a nice midnight snack if I wake up hungry."

Sliding the box to him, she said, "I'm surprised you're willing to eat veggie pizza. I thought you were a meat-lovers pizza guy."

Accepting the box, Jamie replied, "I'm a *good tasting food* kind of guy. Lacking something I prefer, I'm happy to eat something farther down the list."

Jill said, "That's right, you thought the freeze-dried food on our Wupatki hike was tasty when the rest of us were choking down a few bites."

"Sometimes it's more important to consume calories than it is to criticize the recipe."

We rode silently back to the motel, each of us with our own thoughts about the investigation and the murderer's apparent lack of motive. Jill parked in front of our first-floor room, situated next to Jamie's room. Taking the pizza box, Jamie wished us goodnight and disappeared into his room.

After setting our holsters on the nightstands, Jill sprawled on the bed. "It's too early to fall asleep. A Hallmark movie would be relaxing," she replied as I found the channel selections.

"That would be one end of the acceptable movie spectrum. Could we compromise on something nearer the middle?"

"As long as there's no violence, you can choose whatever you like. I don't need Bruce Willis blowing up stuff or a psychological thriller that will get my heart pounding."

"I think that leaves us with the Disney channel or Nickelodeon," I replied.

"Either of those would be okay."

I turned away from the television and stared at her. "I was being sarcastic."

Smiling, she replied, "That kind of blew up in your face, didn't it?" Standing, she pulled a flannel nightgown from her suitcase. "Find something romantic and we can snuggle until I fall asleep."

After watching her disappear into the bathroom to change, I continued paging through the television directory until I found a Jennifer Aniston movie that looked slightly romantic and not too violent. Jill emerged from the bathroom in her flannel pajamas and slid under the covers. "What did you find?"

Showing her the on-screen synopsis, I asked, "Does this meet your criteria?"

"It looks okay," She replied. "I don't suppose you have a bottle of wine in your suitcase."

Pulling a pair of boxer shorts and a fresh t-shirt from the suitcase, I pretended to search for wine. "Darn, I forgot the wine," I said before going into the bathroom to change.

I heard Jill chuckling as I returned from the bathroom. "It's good?"

"It's cute," she replied as she pulled the covers back on my side of the bed.

Getting under the covers I slid my arm under her pillow and turned so I could watch the television. Jennifer Aniston and her friends arrived on a secluded island and the boat pulled away from the wharf as they rolled their luggage toward a waiting limo. "I bet the geeky-looking guy is a serial killer."

"The geeky guy?"

"Didn't you catch the look he gave the boat's captain as he stepped onto the wharf? He's definitely going to kill everyone except Jennifer Aniston."

Jill turned toward me, frowning. "You could've kept that to yourself and let me be surprised."

"I might be wrong."

Five minutes later, they discovered the body of a Hollywood starlet floating in the resort's pool. Jill sighed. "At least the people are being killed off-screen, so we don't see the violence."

"I think the movie producer will be poisoned next."

Squinting at me, Jill asked, "Have you seen this movie before?"

"Nah. I just know the formula."

"They don't make movies with a formula."

"You're kidding," I replied. "Think about the Hallmark movies. They hand a screenwriter an outline involving an incognito prince and a poor working girl whose family owns a failing Christmas tree farm and tell him to fill in the dialogue."

"There is *not* a prince in every Hallmark movie."

"You're right. Sometimes it's an incognito princess and a farmer."

"Shh. They're talking about the drowned woman's body."

"Her necklace is missing," I replied.

A few seconds later, Jennifer Aniston points out that the dead woman's necklace is missing and declares that is the motive for her murder. Jill sighed, "Can you just quietly watch this and not give away the plot?"

"Probably," I said, turning onto my side with my nose close to Jill's ear. "You might have to distract me."

We'd stopped watching the movie and moved on to creating our own romantic scene when we heard the sound of breaking glass outside of our room. Wrapping my arm around Jill, I pulled her along as I rolled off the bed, placing us behind the mattress and away from the window. Tearing myself free from the bedding, I pulled my pistol from the holster, and peeked over the edge of the bed as I aimed at the door.

"What in hell was that?" Jill asked as tires squealed in the parking lot.

"Call 911 on the motel phone," I said as I pulled on a pair of pants and slipped on shoes. Stepping out of the door with my gun at my side, I surveyed the empty sidewalk and parking lot. Broken glass sparkled in front of Jamie's room. I edged toward his room to check on him as lights came on in other rooms.

The night manager raced out of the office and saw me. He immediately focused on my pistol and spun around, returning to the protection of the office.

"Jamie!" I called out when I got to the broken window.

"Yeah."

"Are you okay?"

"Do you mean other than having a broken window and a rock laying on the floor?"

"Physically, are you okay?"

I heard crunching glass inside his room, followed by the sound of the chain being released and the door being unlocked. Jamie stepped out of the room, wearing only jeans and tennis shoes, with a pistol in his hand. "Did you see the car?" he asked.

"I only heard breaking glass, then squealing tires. Were you cut by the glass?"

"Nah, the curtains stopped it. And the rock fell just inside the window."

A siren howled in the distance as I followed Jamie into the room. There was glass on the floor and a white rock lay halfway between the window and bed. Seeing black marks on the rock, I nudged it with the toe of my shoe. When it rolled, I could see writing, apparently made by a Sharpie marker. *NAVAJO GO HOME.*

Jamie read the message at the same time I did. "Like throwing a rock through my window is going to make me go away," he said.

"Someone thought it would."

Blue and red lights flashed against the drapes as the siren stopped. "Is your badge handy?" I asked. "The cops might get uneasy if they see the two of us carrying pistols."

Jamie set his pistol on the dresser and put on a uniform shirt that had been hung over a chair with his Navajo Nation Police badge pinned on the chest. "Let's talk to the local cops."

Tucking my gun into the back of my waistband, I followed him out of the door, careful to make sure the arriving cops saw my hands were empty. Jill, dressed in jeans and a sweatshirt, was already talking to a female Inyo County deputy who was standing next to her open car door. Another siren whined in the distance.

Looking at Jamie, the deputy asked, "Vandals?"

"There's a rock in my room that reads, 'Navajo go home.' It was targeted vandalism."

Looking at Jamie's badge, the cop frowned. "What's a Navajo Nation officer doing here in Lone Pine? You're a long way from your jurisdiction."

"I'm assisting the Park Service with a murder investigation."

The deputy frowned. "What murder investigation?"

"The ranger whose body was found at Manzanar," I replied.

"That's a drug smuggling thing. What's there to investigate?"

"Well," I said, "it appears that someone doesn't want a Navajo cop poking around the investigation. We were at Manzanar this afternoon, then ate supper at a pizza place. My Navajo police friend hasn't been anywhere else."

"We visited the Paiute-Shoshone reservation," Jamie added.

"Did you see the vandals or their vehicle," the deputy asked.

"We were in bed," Jill replied.

The deputy looked at her watch, then smirked. "At eight thirty? You must've come here from an eastern time zone."

Before we could answer, the motel's night manager jogged over from the office. "Hey, Gretchen. You got here quickly."

The deputy smiled at the manager. "I was in town getting coffee. Did you see any of this from the office?"

"I was watching TV. I wasn't paying attention until I heard breaking glass. I saw a blue pickup drive away."

"Did you get the license number?" the deputy asked as she made notes.

"Nah. It was gone before I thought to look at the license plate."

"Did you see the occupants?"

"Two guys wearing hoodies."

"Guys? That's the best you can do for a description?"

"I assumed they were guys. I didn't see their faces."

Gretchen relayed the description of the pickup and occupants to the dispatcher on her shoulder mounted radio mic. Turning to the manager she said, "I assume you haven't repaired your surveillance equipment since the last incident."

"Nope. The owners think having cameras is enough of a deterrent without repairing them, so we have actual video."

Gretchen looked at Jill. "And you were in the room next door?"

Jill dug her Park Service ID from her pocket and handed it to the deputy. Nodding toward me she said, "My partner and I are US Park Service investigators."

After making a note of Jill's name, the deputy looked at me. "You're a Park Service investigator, too?"

"Yes. I have a pistol in my waistband, behind my back."

"What room are you in?"

"My wife and I are in the room next door." Getting a frown from the deputy, I explained, "My wife and I are investigative partners. We're sharing a room."

"And you're investigating the murder at Manzanar, too?"

"That's why we're here."

A second Inyo Sheriff's Department cruiser raced into the parking lot with its lights flashing. More people started peeking out of their rooms to view the commotion. A male sergeant stepped from the second car and joined us. Jill held up her badge and credentials. "Jill Fletcher, US Park Service Investigative Services Branch."

"The park cops are still here?"

Gretchen pointed to Jamie's car with the Navajo Nation Police logo on the side, "And they've got a Navajo Nation cop with them."

Turning to me, the sergeant asked, "This is a vandalism call. How does that involve you guys?"

"Someone wants me to go home. They threw a rock through my window."

The sergeant frowned. "What makes you think you were specifically targeted?"

"The note on the rock says, 'Navajo go home.' That seems pretty specific."

"Huh. Who knows you're here?"

"John Standing Bear, the rangers at Manzanar, a gas station clerk, a waitress at the pizza place, and a bunch of people hanging out in the pizza restaurant bar."

"Would you have run across anyone running or selling drugs?" the sergeant asked.

Jamie glanced at me, frustrated by the sergeant and deputy's focus on the drug angle. "Not unless they were filling up at the gas station."

"The vandals were driving a pickup," I said, addressing the sergeant. "That doesn't sound like the usual type of vehicle used by drug smugglers."

"We see a little bit of every type of vehicle driving drugs north." The sergeant studied my face. "You've been around long enough to know that if it weren't for drugs, most cops everywhere would be bored and getting fat eating doughnuts."

"Why would people in the drug trade be unhappy about the arrival of a Navajo officer?"

The sergeant drew a deep breath. "Who knows what those druggies are unhappy about. Maybe your friend looked at one of them wrong while he was eating his pizza."

Chapter 12

By the time the sheriff's deputies left and Jamie was moved to a different room, all three of us were too wound up to sleep. "Let's eat supper," Jamie suggested.

"Really?" I asked, still feeling full. "Pizza wasn't enough?"

"That was hours ago," Jamie replied. "I could use something to tide me over until breakfast."

I looked at Jill for support, but she already had her car keys out. "A man's gotta eat."

The Totem Pole was empty except for a young couple when we arrived at 9:30. The waitress stopped refilling sugar containers and approached us. "We close in half an hour."

"Is the grill still open?" Jamie asked.

"Probably," she replied.

"I'd like a cheeseburger and fries with a Coke," he replied. "Which table would you like us to sit at?"

Sighing, the waitress pointed to a booth near the kitchen. "Anything for you two?" she asked Jill and me.

"Coffee, black," I replied.

Hesitating, Jill asked, "Do you have any herbal tea?"

"Sure," the waitress replied as she trudged toward the kitchen.

"I think we just made her long shift a little longer," Jill said.

Jamie dug a wad of money out of his pocket and set $20 on the table as the waitress returned with our beverages. He slid the money to her as she set his Coke in front of him. "I apologize for arriving so late. Here is your tip."

The woman accepted the money and then studied the three of us. "Cops don't usually tip very well."

Chuckling, I replied, "We're trying to change that stereotype."

Leaning close, the waitress smiled and said, "The boss says coffee is free for the local cops. You guys look local tonight."

Jill shook her head emphatically. "We're paying customers. None of this is free."

"Your order will be out as soon as the fries are done. By the way, you guys get the whole fryer basket since you're the last customers of the night."

Nodding toward the young couple finishing up their burger baskets, Jill said, "Ask them if they'd like more fries. They're our treat."

The young couple looked surprised when the waitress gestured toward us and explained our offer. The girl, who appeared to be a late teen, smiled and mouthed, "Thanks!"

Jamie looked less pleased. "I could have eaten a whole bucket of fries."

"You don't need them," I replied. "I don't want Liz to accuse us of fattening you up while helping us."

Jamie wasn't amused. "I burn it all off. I've got a high metabolism."

The waitress arrived with Jamie's order. After setting it in front of him, she asked if we wanted refills, which we accepted. The cook delivered a mountain of fries to the young couple, who looked excited, while a bit overwhelmed.

While topping off my coffee, the waitress glanced at my badge. "You're Park Service cops?"

"Yes," I replied. "Our hungry friend is with the Navajo Nation Police."

"Are you here because of that ranger who was killed by the drug smugglers?"

"Who told you he'd been killed by drug smugglers?" I asked.

"That's all the county cops talked about for a couple of days. It kind of became common knowledge."

"Do you get a lot of drug crimes here?" Jill asked as she stole one of Jamie's fries.

"There's not much crime in Lone Pine. The county cops stay on top of it really well. I think the drugs just move through here on their way north."

"Did you know Erik, the ranger who was killed?" I asked.

"He'd been in a few times. I mostly recognized him because he's the only person I've ever met with copper-colored hair."

"Did he ever strike up a conversation with you?"

The waitress, who appeared to be close to forty, shook her head. "He was quiet. I only saw him when he came in with a group of others. He seemed to always be on the fringes of the conversation. You know how introverts sometimes like to enjoy being with the group, but not really joining in the discussion."

"Did he seem to get along with everyone?" Jill asked.

"I suppose so. I mean, introverts don't tend to irritate people. It's the loud drunks who pick fights and irritate others." After checking her watch, the waitress returned to filling sugar, salt, and pepper containers.

"Everyone we have spoken with seems to have the same impression of Erik. He was quiet, and just along with the group."

Jamie ate hungrily as we talked, occasionally stopping to squirt more ketchup on his fries or to nod his head. After wiping his mouth, he leaned back and took a deep breath. "That should carry me through until breakfast."

I nearly choked on my coffee. "You just ate as many calories as most people consume in a day, and you *think it might* last until breakfast."

"I told you; I have a fast metabolism. I'll burn all these calories in my sleep."

Jill was focused on her cup of tea, apparently ignoring us. "Are you reading your tea leaves?" I asked.

"What was written on the rock?" she asked Jamie.

"Navajo go home."

Jill frowned. "Not 'Indian go home?' It specifically said, 'Navajo?'"

"Yeah. What difference does it make? The message is the same."

I got Jill's point. "There aren't any Navajo people here."

"It's not a big mystery," Jamie replied. "I'm driving a car with the Navajo National Police logo on the doors."

"Why single you out?" I asked. "The three of us have been doing the investigation together. Why hurl a rock at your room?"

"That's no mystery to someone with brown skin," Jamie replied. "We're singled out all the time. And because I'm a half-breed, I'm singled out by the full-blooded Navajo as well."

Jill shook her head and leaned close to Jamie. "Why would someone in Lone Pine throw a rock through your window with the message, 'Navajo go home?'"

"What's your theory?" Jamie asked.

Seeing Jill's point, I said, "We're in a town with a large Paiute Shoshone population. You look a lot like the local Native Paiute people. If some white person was going to harass you, they might not even realize that you're Navajo."

Rolling his eyes, Jamie replied, "Aside from my uniform, badge, and the Navajo cop car."

"Wouldn't it be more likely for a Paiute to call you out as a Navajo?"

Jamie stared at me while he thought. "Interesting."

Our discussion was interrupted when the waitress delivered our bill and cleared our plates. "I hope everything was good."

Jamie pulled out his wad of cash and handed her an additional $40. "It was great. Thanks."

I interrupted her dish-clearing effort and asked, "Do you get a lot of Paiute and Shoshone people here?"

The waitress smiled at Jamie. "Sure. Your money is the same as anyone else's."

"Our partner is Navajo," Jill said. "Does that surprise you?"

The waitress shrugged. "It doesn't bother me one way or the other. He's polite and tipped me nicely. I like customers like him."

"Did you recognize him as Navajo and not Paiute or Shoshone?"

"Not really."

"All Indians look alike," I said.

"Not at all," she replied, defensively. "Your friend has features like many of our local Native Americans. They're all unique.

Not all are handsome and not all are nice or mean. They're as diverse as my white customers."

"Thank you," I said, allowing her to finish clearing the table.

Standing, Jamie asked, "What was that about?"

"I think a Paiute threw the rock through your window."

"Why would...?"

I nodded toward the door. Outside the restaurant, I huddled with Jamie and Jill. "I think someone from the Paiute tribe doesn't want you poking around in this investigation."

"Why would they single me out?" Jamie asked.

"Because you might understand something that a white cop would miss."

"Like *Si-Te-Cah*," Jamie said.

"That, or some other aspect of the case that's uniquely related to the Paiute or Shoshone tribes."

"We've only spoken with the tribal president and historian," Jill said.

Jamie looked up and down the empty street, then nodded toward our rental car, "Let's go. I'm feeling suddenly vulnerable standing here."

Inside the car, Jill said, "I can't believe either the president or the historian would have thrown a rock through your window."

"I agree," Jamie replied. "But they told two people, who told two other people, and so on. I bet there are several hundred people on the nearby reservations who know there's a Navajo tribal cop poking around in the investigation of a dead ranger. It makes someone very nervous."

* * *

Back in our motel room, Jill set her pistol on the nightstand, retrieved a nightgown from the suitcase, and walked into the bathroom. I turned on the television and pulled up the channel listing. With Jill humming something, I chose a rerun of *the Tonight Show* with Dom DeLuise as the guest. I must've been laughing, because Jill poked her head out of the door. "You rarely laugh out loud," she said, holding the door open just wide enough for her head.

"These old comedians crack me up. They don't swear or make fun of anyone. They just talk about life." Jill backed away from the door and was ready to close it when I stopped her. "Hang on a second."

Ever modest, she edged over so her body was out of my line of sight. "What?"

I looked past her at the bathroom mirror, which gave me a view of her bare slender backside. I stared at the mirror for a second, then focused on her face. "You're lovely."

She frowned. "What are you up to?" When I refocused on the mirror, she realized the view I had, and she quickly closed the bathroom door.

171

"It's okay," I said to the door. "I'm your husband." I shifted on the bed and the television switched to QVC where a man and woman were extolling the value in a gemstone bracelet. "I'd buy that for you."

Sliding under the covers, Jill replied, "Turn off the TV, dear. I'm not much of a jewelry person." After setting the remote on the nightstand, I slipped off my shirt and pants.

Chapter 13

The next morning Jamie knocked on our door while Jill was dressing in the bathroom. "I saw a breakfast place in town," he said as he entered our room.

"Your life revolves around food," I replied as he sat in our only chair.

"If you'd spent your entire childhood either hungry or overstuffed, you'd understand that. Eat when you can."

"It sounds like the army: Eat when you can, sleep when you can, hurry up and wait."

"That sounds like my kind of life."

"It's not all bad. No decisions. It's not all bad except for the possibility of getting shot."

"How's that different from being a cop?" Jamie asked, examining the remaining portion of a granola bar Jill had left on the table.

Joining us dressed in jeans and a plaid shirt, Jill fluffed her damp hair. "How's what being different from being a cop?"

"Doug says the Army was like being a cop."

"Really? I didn't know you had to solve crimes in the Army."

"It's the boredom that's most similar," I replied. "Jamie's ready to eat breakfast."

Attaching her badge and holster to her belt, Jill replied, "Let's go."

* * *

The restaurant Jamie chose felt like a thousand other small-town cafés I'd eaten in. It featured a row of stools along a counter, a row of tables down the center, and a row of booths along the windows opposite the counter. A waitress zipped past and told us to sit anywhere.

"Coffee," Jamie said as the waitress passed. An Inyo County deputy looked up from his breakfast sandwich as we walked down the aisle. I recognized him as Deputy Kellen from our meeting at Manzanar. Kellen nodded but gave no indication we were welcome to join him. Jamie walked past him, choosing the most remote booth, and then sat on the bench facing the door.

I glanced at the lone middle-aged waitress whose straight black hair was salted with strands of gray. "I think our waitress is Paiute."

"Maybe," Jamie replied. "I read that more than half of the local tribal people live off the reservation."

"The south half of the Lone Pine is the Paiute-Shoshone Reservation. If not for the sign, I wouldn't have known we'd crossed into the reservation yesterday."

"What's our plan for today?" Jill asked as she surveyed the array of people seated at the counter and tables.

"I think we need to visit the Bishop Paiute-Shoshone tribal headquarters," Jamie replied.

"Do you think they'll know more than the local people here?" I asked.

"As outsiders, they might be more forthcoming about things happening in Lone Pine than the locals are."

Our waitress arrived with three coffee mugs in one hand, a steaming coffee carafe in the other, and menus tucked under her arm. "The special is an English muffin sandwich with egg, bacon, and cheese."

Jamie set the menu aside without looking at it. "I'll have a breakfast steak, two eggs, hash browns, and toast."

The waitress nodded as she wrote in her order pad. "A rancher's special," she said before turning to Jill.

"Oatmeal with raisins and brown sugar."

"I'll have combo number two with the eggs over easy and whole wheat toast," I said, handing the waitress my menu.

After collecting our menus, the waitress paused. "Are you the cops staying at the motel?"

Unsure of where the question was leading, I replied. "We are."

Nodding, the waitress said, "Motel guests get a ten percent discount."

As she walked away, Jill commented, "Another small town where everyone knows everything. She knows we're the cops staying at the motel."

"I wonder if she knows who killed the ranger?" Jamie asked as he picked up his mug and sipped the hot coffee.

"If nothing else, I bet she's heard two or three rumors about what happened," Jill replied.

When the waitress refilled our coffee, I asked, "What have you heard about the ranger who was killed at Manzanar?"

She nodded toward the deputy, now finishing his coffee. "The county cops said it was a drug deal gone bad."

Holding out her cup for a refill, Jill asked, "Does anyone else have a different opinion?"

The waitress, whose nametag indicated her name was Holly, shrugged. "I only know about the drug thing because I overheard someone asking a deputy. None of the locals seem very interested."

"Have you heard about any protests at Manzanar?" Jamie asked.

"What is there to protest? It's a National Park in the desert. No one cares except the Japanese families who come back to see where grandma and grandpa spent the war."

"Do the visiting families seem angry?" Jill asked.

After checking to see if any other customers needed her, Holly replied, "They seem more curious than angry, not that they'd vent to me."

"We heard something about water rights protests."

Holly frowned. "What water rights? I mean, the town could use more water if the city wanted to build out farther, but who are they going to complain to?" Seeing a customer ready to pay their bill, Holly rushed away.

"That was useless," Jamie said.

"I suppose we've just taken the temperature of the town's reaction to Manzanar," I replied. "It appears the locals think of Manzanar as an irrelevant place out in the desert. That's good information."

"It doesn't get us any closer to a killer," Jill said.

"Not true," I replied. "Her comments eliminate the mainstream locals as angry suspects."

Jamie smirked as he sipped coffee. "But leaves any kook, on or off the reservation, who might be irrational or psychotic."

A bell dinged in the kitchen, and Holly disappeared through the swinging doors. She returned carrying a tray with our order as I replied to Jamie, "There are crazy folks everywhere, and individuals are harder to identify than a group with a grudge."

Setting out our orders, Holly smiled, noting that our mugs were almost empty. "You guys really are cops. You drink gallons of coffee and never use the bathroom."

Straightening up, she added, "Do you need anything more than coffee refills?"

Jamie lifted a squeeze bottle of ketchup from behind the salt and pepper shakers. "Other than coffee, I'm all set."

Holly paused, distracted by Jamie's shoulder patch. "You're from the Navajo police?"

Jamie nodded as he squirted ketchup on his hash browns. "Yup. I'm here assisting my Park Service friends. Are you Paiute?"

Holly glanced at the Navajo Nation Police badge pinned to Jamie's uniform shirt, then nodded and said, "The tribe might not appreciate you poking around on their turf."

"Someone threw a rock through my window. I don't suppose you'd know if a Paiute threw it?"

Holly studied Jamie's face for a moment then replied, "You look like a half-breed, like me."

"I grew up on the Navajo reservation with my mom."

Holly snorted. "Yeah, white men are willing to bed a Native woman, but not hang around to deal with their kid." She glanced at me. "I suppose you hung around to raise all your kids."

"I don't have any children."

Jill leaned forward. "That love 'em and leave 'em attitude isn't unique to white men and Native women. There are a lot of single moms."

After assessing Jill, Holly replied, "I'll bet your husband stuck around to help you raise your kids."

Jill smiled and avoided the question. "I'm still married to the same guy who swept me off my feet."

Jamie, who knew our backstory of meeting in mid-life, becoming friends, then marrying, choked on his coffee. Wiping his mouth with a napkin, he asked, "Do you think anyone from the tribe might've been involved in the ranger's death?"

Holly shrugged. "That's where the cops will look if they don't make a drug connection. They're sure there's always an Indian behind every crime...if they look hard enough."

"Do you know the *Si-Te-Cah* legend?"

"I'm not into tribal lore. You've got to ask the folks who are into that stuff." Seeing another customer standing at the cash register, Holly hurried away.

"She's a little bitter," Jill said.

"No," Jamie replied. "Holly is a realist. Life is different for us, Jill. You've never been a minority."

"I was a female park superintendent in a man's world."

Jamie put forty dollars on the table.

Jill dug in her pocket for her charge card. "I've got breakfast."

Jamie stood and stepped toward the restrooms. Nodding toward the money he said, "That's the tip."

Tones sounded on Deputy Kellen's radio, and he stood while listening to the dispatcher's announcement. He threw some bills on the table, then turned and took a step toward us as Jamie returned from the bathroom. "Is that your squad in the parking lot?"

"What's up?" Jamie asked.

"The California Highway Patrol is chasing a suspected drug smuggler toward town. The CHP trooper has requested backup and asked if someone could deploy stop sticks." Deputy Kellen nodded toward the door. "Consider this a formal request for an agency assist." Looking at Jill and me, he said, "This might be your murderer returning from Mexico."

We followed Kellen as he jogged out of the restaurant. I got in the front passenger seat of Jamie's patrol car, with Jill buckling herself into the rear. Pulling onto the street, Jamie turned on his flashers and siren, then followed Kellen out of town. A mile south of Lone Pine, Kellen stopped on the shoulder and Jamie pulled up alongside him as I rolled down my window.

"Have you ever qualified with a shotgun?" Kellen asked me.

"Annually for the past twenty years."

"Get in with me." When I was seated, he reached down and released the lock on the shotgun mounted between us. "There's a round in the chamber and four rounds in the magazine. It's #3 buckshot."

"Okay," I replied as I pulled the shotgun next to my knee. "What's your plan?"

Speaking to Jamie and Jill, he said, "I'm going to set up just south of town before this guy can turn off on any of the city streets. I'll park partially blocking the northbound lane and throw out stop sticks in the other lane as he passes."

"What do you want us to do?" I asked.

The deputy glanced at me. "Do you think you could put a load of buckshot into his radiator? That might end this chase faster than the stop sticks." He turned to Jamie and said, "Stop the southbound traffic so no civilians get hurt."

The highway was nearly empty, and we were on the outskirts of town within two minutes. We met one northbound car before Deputy Kellen parked, blocking the northbound lane. Jamie parked his squad on the southbound road shoulder fifty yards away, his lightbar flashing. He and Jill prepared to flag down any cars who were following us. I took cover behind the deputy's car as Kellen pulled a case containing the stop sticks from his trunk.

The whine of a distant siren signaled the approaching CHP chase. Within moments, I saw a nondescript pickup racing toward us, with a CHP squad following.

Kellen spoke into his radio, announcing our set up. Then he looked at me, leaning on a fender. "Do the feds have rules against shooting at moving vehicles?"

"Not that I recall," I replied.

"Our policy says we can't, so it's good that you have the shotgun."

"Great. I'm your loophole."

The gap between us and the approaching chase closed quickly. The pickup was dust-covered, masking whatever color it was painted. I could make out a topper covering the pickup bed, and I saw two heads in the cab.

Glancing at the landscape around us, I quickly realized the flaw in our setup. The squad was blocking the northbound lane. Kellen was ready to throw the stop sticks into the other lane. Farther behind him, Jill and Jamie had stopped three vehicles that were idling on the shoulder fifty yards beyond the roadblock. To my left, lay flat open land.

The pickup slowed slightly as it approached us, its passenger gesturing toward the open shoulder to my left. At the last second, the driver jerked the steering wheel. For a fraction of a second, the pickup was careening directly at me. I fired the shotgun at the pickup's grille, then jumped to my right hoping to avoid the impact by being behind Kellen's vehicle. The pickup missed Kellen's squad by inches and as it sped past, I fired a shot ahead of the back tire as it passed, hoping I'd led the vehicle far enough to put the shot into the tire.

A cloud of dust and steam engulfed us as I pumped the shotgun and fired a third shot at the opposite rear tire as the pickup pulled back onto the highway. A second later, the CHP patrol car sped past.

"Get in the car!" Kellen yelled as the trooper passed.

I dove into the passenger seat and was buckling my seatbelt as Kellen shifted the squad and slammed his door. "What's your name?" he asked as we accelerated past Jill and Jamie.

"Fletcher."

"I think you connected with all three shots," he replied. "There are chunks of tire flying off the back wheels and I can smell the stink of boiling antifreeze as it's steaming out of his radiator."

"Remind me of your name."

"Kellen."

"Where are the rest of the Inyo County cars?"

"They had something up in Bishop. It's us and the CHP trooper who'll be doing this."

"I've got two rounds left in the shotgun."

"There are shells in the glovebox."

I fed three more shells into the tube magazine. When I looked up, the pickup was racing down the right lane just ahead of the CHP trooper. Both of the pickup's rear tires were shredded, sparks flying off the metal rims as they spun on the road surface.

"Without antifreeze, that engine is going to overheat and lock up," I said. "Are you prepared for a footrace?"

Kellen glanced at me. "It's so flat here, I can chase them in the squad until they fall down or give up."

"Good plan. My knees aren't what they used to be."

"Were you really a city cop?"

"For twenty years."

"Shit. I bet you saw a lot more excitement than we get in this county."

I laughed. "We had weekly stolen car chases and domestic calls."

The words were hardly out of my mouth when the pickup's engine blew, spewing oil on the road and locking up the vehicle's four wheels. It slewed to the right until the broadside momentum caused the pickup to flip and roll. One of the occupants was flung out of a window. He put out his hands to break his fall, but his tumbling motion spun him onto his back, followed by a roll, with his arms and legs flailing like a rag doll.

Kellen jammed the brakes and veered left to avoid rear-ending the CHP squad. We skidded to a stop alongside the steaming pickup. Kellen was ready to jump out, but I stopped him. "Call for an ambulance."

"Huh?"

"The kid who was thrown out of the pickup is going to need an ambulance. Call!"

I left the shotgun in the county squad, guessing that the pickup's occupants were in no condition to put up a fight. Rushing toward the pickup, I fell in step behind the female CHP trooper who had her gun drawn.

She was intently focused on the pickup's cab, which had come to rest on the driver's door.

With her pistol gripped in two hands and safely pointed at the ground she yelled, "Get out!"

Leaving my pistol holstered, I edged past her and knelt down to look into the cab through the cab's spiderwebbed windshield. Assuming that the occupant was either badly injured, unconscious, or dead, I was surprised to see blue denim squirming against the window.

"Hey! Are you okay?"

The response was a string of expletives in Spanish. The pickup's occupant cried out, "*¿Paco, Está bien?*"

Kellen ran past me and climbed up the pickup's undercarriage until he was kneeling on the passenger's door, looking in the window. The trooper kept her pistol aimed down but was ready to fire past me. From the perch atop the pickup, Kellen drew his pistol and yelled, "Fletcher, get back! There's a gun!"

I heard cars stop on the other side of the overturned pickup. Jamie called out, "Jill, dial 911. We need an ambulance and fire truck."

Responding to Kellen's warning, I stepped aside, trying to get out of the line of fire from either the occupant or the trooper behind me.

"Get away from the gun!" Kellen yelled. I looked up, seeing him perched on top of the pickup. He pointed his pistol into the passenger window. "Don't touch the gun!"

Before I could pull my pistol, there was an exchange of gunfire between Kellen and the man in the cab. The pickup's windshield disintegrated. A man struggled through the shattered glass, a gun in his left hand. Seeing the trooper, he raised his pistol. The trooper moved to her right and fired repeatedly at the person in the pickup, most of her shots missing the man and hitting the pickup or pavement. With the victim's gun still pointed at the trooper, and his finger on the trigger, I took aim and fired two shots that hit the man's torso. Kellen shifted to look over the pickup's hood and took a shot nearly straight down. The driver collapsed, his body spasmed, and the pistol fell onto the pavement.

Jamie flew around the pickup with his pistol drawn, ready to fire at whatever threat he found. Jill a step behind him.

"Stand down," I said, as much for the trooper and Kellen, who both had their pistols pointed at the now dead pickup driver. I holstered my pistol and walked over to the driver, kicking his pistol aside, so it was well out of his reach, not that a man who'd been shot nearly a half dozen times was going to reach out and start firing at us.

The trooper, who had probably never fired her weapon anywhere but on a practice range, stood stunned, staring at the driver's body, her pistol still gripped in both hands.

Lowering her gun, she looked to me for direction as I was apparently the most senior person at the scene. "Shouldn't we do CPR until the ambulance arrives? I was taught to always render medical aid after a shooting incident."

I looked at the lifeless driver. One of Kellen's last shots had hit his head. "Do what you have to do," I replied. "But this guy isn't going to an ER. His next trip is to the morgue."

"But..."

"Like I said, you do what you have to do. I'm not doing CPR on a corpse."

Kellen holstered his gun and jumped down from the truck. Almost as an afterthought, he spoke into his radio mic, reporting shots fired and a dead victim.

Almost immediately, the dispatcher relayed the information and asked for all available units to respond.

The trooper looked toward Jill, who had joined me in front of the pickup's windshield. "Ma'am, have you been through this before?"

Jill nodded. "Holster your gun, trooper. The shooting is over."

The young trooper looked down at her pistol, almost as if she'd forgotten it was in her hand. She slipped the pistol into her holster and stood still, apparently in shock. Jill moved to her side and gestured toward the CHP squad car. I heard her say, "Call your sergeant. Tell him what's happened."

"Yeah. Good idea," the trooper said, pulling a cell phone from her pocket. She sat inside her car and had a conversation we couldn't hear.

Kellen seemed exhilarated. "Wow! That was nuts. I wonder what they've got in the back of the pickup? I bet they were hauling drugs."

Jamie nodded for me to follow him. We walked behind the pickup to where the passenger had been ejected from the rolling vehicle. The passenger was young, maybe in his late teens. It was hard to tell because he'd probably been moving sixty mph when his body hit the pavement. The scene reminded me of motorcycle accidents I'd seen where the rider hadn't worn a helmet or leather clothing.

The boy's t-shirt was shredded and covered with blood. His head and face were scraped raw by the pavement, and all of his limbs were extended in unnatural angles. I looked at Jamie and whispered, "Dead?"

He nodded. "If he was lucky, the impact knocked him unconscious before his skin was scraped off. I suspect he bled out internally."

An ambulance rolled to a stop at the rear of the crowd that was gathering. A male EMT pushed through the people, carrying a nylon pouch. Jamie stopped him before reaching the body. They had a quiet discussion and the EMT set the bag aside. He took out a stethoscope, knelt, then gently placed it on the passenger's chest. After a few seconds, the EMT nodded to Jamie and stood. The silent exchange confirmed that the victim was no longer in need of medical aid.

I gestured for the EMT to follow me. He repeated the process with the driver, reaching the same determination. "We'll secure the scene," I said. "Do you have sheets or screens you can put up to cover the bodies until the crime scene people get here?"

After draping the stethoscope around his neck, the EMT nodded. "Yeah, we've got sheets in the ambulance. We'll pull ahead to block the street view, then I'll cover the victims."

Jill and Deputy Kellen were talking when I left the EMT. Kellen's adrenaline was wearing off and he was more subdued. In the distance, I heard several approaching sirens, slightly out of sync. Taking a deep breath to help clear my thoughts, I inhaled the smell of burnt gunpowder, blood, antifreeze, gas, and sweat. They were the odors that would return later in my recurring nightmares.

I joined Jill and the trooper, who stood talking near the front fender of the CHP squad vehicle. "Are we okay?" I asked.

Jill nodded. "We're getting there. Sadie, the trooper, spoke with her sergeant. He contacted the California Bureau of Investigation. They'll dispatch a CBI team to work the crime scene."

I walked over to the young trooper who was staring at the driver's body as the EMTs spread a blue sheet over him. "Sadie, are you okay?"

She nodded. "I'm fine." After a pause she asked, "Was my shot the one that killed him? I was kind of aiming, but...wow...it's not like the firing range at all."

"The CBI will make that determination." As soon as I'd said that I realized she was asking a different, personal question. "We all killed him. It wasn't just you. At least three of us fired shots. Keep in mind, you were firing in self-defense. He was shooting at you."

"Yeah, he was getting ready to..." Then she turned and looked at her squad vehicle. She bent down and ran her finger over a bullet hole in the front fender. Looking up at me, she asked, "How close was this to hitting me?"

"I don't know exactly where you were standing. I was focused on his gun."

"Was I almost killed?"

Jill moved closer to Sadie. "You are wearing a vest. You'd have been sore, but you wouldn't have had a life-threatening injury."

"How can you know that?"

Jill patted her ribs. "I once took a pistol shot to the vest. It hurts like hell, but I'm still here to talk about it."

Sadie looked at Jill. "I have kids at home..."

"This is an aberration. You'll probably never fire your gun outside of the range for the rest of your career."

Sadie shuddered, then removed her pistol from the holster.

"What's up?" Jill asked.

"I have to look at the magazine. I don't even know how many shots I fired."

After ejecting the Glock's magazine, she looked at the back where the remaining unfired cartridges were visible through small holes. "I shot five times. I could've sworn I'd only shot twice."

"We're often surprised by the details after we recover from the heat of the moment," I said.

"How many shots did you take?" Sadie asked.

"Three."

"Did your shots hit him? I'm not sure whether I did or didn't."

"All three of my shots hit the driver," I replied. "I think a couple of Deputy Kellen's shots also hit home."

"Okay, so I might not have been the one who killed him. Right?"

Sensing her need to feel innocent of taking another person's life, I nodded. "I doubt your shots killed him."

"My son is nine. He'll ask me."

"Tell him you're not the killer."

She stared into my eyes. "You're sure."

"I took the killing shot. It wasn't you."

Sadie returned her pistol to its holster and nodded. "Okay. Thank you." After a moment of consideration, she walked toward me and put out her hand. "In that case, thanks for saving my life."

"It's what one cop does for another. You're part of a law enforcement family. We all look out for each other."

"That's it, isn't it. Thanks."

Jill walked past me and nodded toward the shoulder of the road. "That was good. You said what she needed to hear."

"I hope she'll be able to sleep tonight."

Jill looked into my eyes. "We both know she's going to have nightmares."

"Yep."

Chapter 14

After talking to the sheriff, his lead investigator, and a CBI investigator, Jill and I were excused from the scene of the shooting. Deputy Kellen pulled me aside as Jill walked away and Jamie spoke with the CHP sergeant. I was ready to surrender my pistol for forensics, but Kellen surprised me. "As far as the sheriff knows, you never fired a weapon here. Understood?"

"Why?"

"He's got a burr under his saddle about you Park Service guys. No one's going to look too closely at which bullet killed that Mexican drug runner. Since there won't be a trial, no one's going to question you or even ask about your involvement."

"That's fine with me."

After walking away from Kellen, Jill called our boss to inform him that we'd been involved in another shooting incident. "What did Kellen want?"

"He says we weren't involved in the shooting. The sheriff wants the whole incident to be neat and tidy with his deputy and the CHP the only agencies involved."

I sighed. "I don't see it. It would've been nice to have at least one of the smugglers to interrogate about the Manzanar murder."

Jill watched as the CHP sergeant questioned Jamie. "The sheriff's department will probably close the Manzanar case now."

"Their minds were made up before we arrived."

Jill punched our boss' phone number into her phone, then she motioned for me to join her. She held the phone away from her ear so I could hear Jack. "Since you already know that you two have been involved in more shooting incidents than the entire rest of the entire Park Service Investigative Branch, I've stopped counting. You know the drill. Submit an online incident report. Jill, cut and paste your report into Doug's form. We both know I'd die from the shock if he ever filled out his own report."

"I just spoke with the senior deputy. They're going to minimize any references to Park Service involvement in this incident. They're focusing on the role of their deputy and the CHP trooper."

"That's fine. Fill out a report for our records and try not to ruffle their feathers."

Grimacing, I replied, "No, I think you'd laugh at the lengthy and painful report filled with typos and grammatical errors."

"You're probably right. Cut and paste Jill's report into yours. What's your plan now? Are you through with the Manzanar investigation?"

"The sheriff's department is probably closing their Manzanar case. The sheriff thinks the drug smugglers were probably Erik's killers. We've still got a few leads. One of them involves a nearby Paiute-Shoshone reservation in Bishop. We were planning to drive there when a local deputy grabbed us for backup."

"Keep me posted."

I smiled at Jill as she ended the call. "Jack really appreciates all you do for us."

"What choice do I have? The reports would never be completed on time, and they'd be unreadable. You step on toes and irritate people. And..." Jill stopped before completing that thought.

"And, what?"

"You're often hopeless and clueless about social things. Your mother would never know what's happening in your life if not for me."

"Mom doesn't need to know what's happening to me. I make her crazy."

Jill reached out and squeezed my hand. "She's getting older, and you are her only child. You two need to stay connected."

"You do a wonderful job of keeping her informed."

"I shouldn't be the only one keeping her informed. She'd appreciate a call from you occasionally."

"Nah, she'd rather talk to you about aches and pains, and bodily functions. I don't deal with those discussions well."

Jamie and Deputy Kellen approached us. Kellen offered his hand. "Thanks for the backup. This could've been a real mess without you guys."

Sensing that I wasn't going to say anything, Jill smiled and said, "I'm pleased we could lend a hand. This wasn't the ending we would've preferred, but we were in it with you."

"As I told Doug, we've got this. If you guys want to clear the scene, go. Oh shit. Your rental car is still at the café."

Jamie nodded to his car. "I'll give them a ride."

As Kellen walked away, I asked Jamie and Jill, "Are we still going to Bishop today?"

Jill looked at me, hopefully. "I think that would be a nice diversion."

Jamie shrugged rather than voicing an opinion.

"Okay, let's go."

* * *

Jamie was characteristically silent on our drive to Bishop, staring out of the side window. As usual, his silence made me uncomfortable. After ten minutes of silence, I asked, "How are Liz and my godson?"

"Good."

"Would you like to expand on that?" I asked. Glancing at the rear-view mirror I saw Jill smiling, reveling in my discomfort.

"No."

Hoping to get a rise out of Jamie, I asked, "Is Liz the park superintendent yet?"

"No."

"Have you made a decision about moving from the Navajo Nation Police to the Park Service?"

"No."

"Are you still considering it?"

"Yes."

I looked at Jill in the mirror. She smiled and shrugged, unwilling to take up the discussion. "Are you thinking about having more children?"

Still looking out the side window at the scenery, Jamie replied, "Yes."

"Dozens more?" I asked, hoping to get a rise out of him.

"One, maybe two."

"Is there anything new on the rez?"

"Nope."

Trying to compose an open-ended question, I thought for a moment. "What are your plans for Noah's education?"

That seemed to stump Jamie. He thought so long I suspected he wasn't going to answer. Finally, he said, "Public school."

"You can give more than a one-word answer."

"I just did."

Jill leaned forward and put her hand on Jamie's shoulder, causing him to turn and look at her. "Are you and Liz happy with your situation?"

"Mostly."

"What isn't working?" she asked.

"Life with one foot on the rez and the other in Flagstaff."

"How are you planning to deal with that?"

After staring at me for a second, Jamie turned his head and looked at Jill. "There is no plan."

"How does Liz feel about that?"

Jamie turned to look out the side window. "She wants me to resign from the Navajo Police and take a job with either the Flagstaff PD or the Park Service."

"Are you considering those options?"

"Not really."

Jill glanced at the mirror, checking to see if I was waiting for her to continue the questioning. I shook my head, so she went on. "I assume that decision will be critical to your happy marriage."

"Liz thinks so."

"Do you disagree?"

"She tells me what she thinks. When I don't argue, she thinks the discussion is settled."

"Not arguing is not a sign of your acceptance, right?"

"I don't argue."

"That's not what I asked."

Jamie sighed, then twisted in his seat so he could look directly at Jill. "Your marriage counseling skills suck."

I saw Jill's smile in the mirror. "I think they're quite effective. I've apparently got you to speak about a topic you're avoiding with your wife."

"The people on the reservation need me."

"So do your wife and son. Liz needs to be part of the decision about your future with the reservation. At a minimum, she needs to understand that you're not going to leave the Navajo Nation Police, and why, so she can deal with that plan."

"She knows."

"So, you've discussed it?"

"I haven't resigned or followed up on the Flagstaff PD job offer. She must know."

Jill leaned back. "The FPD offered you a job?"

"Yeah."

"Did you tell them you're not taking the job?"

"Not yet."

I glanced at Jamie and asked, "How long ago did they make the offer?"

"A couple of months ago."

"And you haven't answered them?" I asked.

Jamie stared out of the window without replying.

"Jamie," Jill said, "you have to tell them one way or the other."

"Yeah." Jamie seemed to be considering that until he said, "Tell me about the ranger who was killed. Is there something in his life that bugs out as a motive?"

Knowing that Jamie's marital conversation was over, I said, "Not really. By all reports, he was a quiet, nice guy."

"I'm on Erik Petersen's Facebook page," Jill said from the back seat. "His posts are mostly the reposting of things he's read elsewhere. His most recent post was about the release of black-footed ferrets in South Dakota. Before that, he reposted some Park Service information about taking only pictures and leaving only footprints when you visit the parks."

"Has he posted anything personal?" I asked.

Jill continued to move her finger on the cell phone screen. "I have to page back through a couple months of pictures. Here's a selfie of him and some people in a bar. I recognize Tonya and Casey. The other people aren't named."

"He did socialize at some point," I mused.

"Here are some posts from when he visited Minnesota last summer. He went with his parents to the Minneapolis Swedish Institute for a dinner with the Swedish ambassador. It appears his parents own a furniture store with lots of Scandinavian themes. Here's a selfie with his parents standing in front of their store."

"Are there any with his girlfriend?" Jamie asked.

"Yes, there are a few with Hailey. He's smiling. She's not. Here's a picture of them at the Death Valley National Park entrance sign. Again, he's smiling, she's not."

"They broke up after that, right?" Jamie asked.

"Yeah," Jill replied. "He was more into her than she was into him. He liked camping and environmental stuff. I think she was more of a city girl who preferred creature comforts."

Jamie watched as Jill paged through Facebook posts. "What about the other rangers? Are any of them likely suspects?"

I shook my head. "They seemed like a mostly quiet bunch."

From the back seat, Jill said, "I'm on Grace Watanabe's Facebook page. All her posts are about grandchildren."

For Jamie's benefit, I explained, "She discovered Erik's body. I think she was genuinely disturbed by the find. She is either the coolest, cold-hearted killer I've ever met, or she is just a quiet, pleasant ranger who was thrown into a bad situation."

"Okay," Jill said from the back. "I'm on Becky Stipe's page. According to her profile, she's divorced. All her posts are about her cats."

Jamie smiled. "You can't trust cat ladies."

"She has no life outside of work and her cats," Jill said. "Alright, I'm moving on to Casey. Those are his initials. His name is Krispin Charles O'Brien. He's only been a ranger for a year. He's a purported narcissist from a rich Denver family."

"How rich?" Jamie asked.

"There's a picture of his family *compound* in the mountains outside of Denver. He's got pictures of himself skiing with a bunch of friends. There are lots of selfies with him and people who appear to be drunk. He's always wearing stylishly frumpy clothes. Oh, here's a picture of him wearing a tux in a wedding party. Here's a picture taken outside of a frat house somewhere. Everyone looks drunk."

"It doesn't sound like he needs to work," Jamie said.

"We heard that he's learning the value of money after totaling his daddy's Maserati," I replied. "I don't see any motive that Casey might have. Certainly not money."

"Rich people can afford drugs," Jamie replied. "Maybe Erik was his supplier."

"It appears Casey likes liquor and partying with his friends. From what we heard, that's not where his life would crossover with Erik."

"Who is the next potential suspect?" Jamie asked.

"We know about Erik's roommate, Todd. And Todd's girlfriend, Lexi. Of the people so far, I'd say their only motive might be moving Erik out of the apartment so Lexi can move in."

"That's pretty thin," Jamie said. "One of them would have to be a psychopath to kill over an apartment."

"As I said before, whoever killed Erik is a psychopath."

Jamie considered that comment. "Probably. If that's the case, it's going to be really hard to uncover his killer. Psychopaths often have an obscure motive and are usually really adept at hiding themselves. At least until something tips them over the edge."

"Tonya Marshal is one of the seasonal rangers. From her posts, I'd say she put the 'social' in social media. She appears to be a party girl. She's from Kansas City and had lots of posts with a guy named Steve, until a month before she took the job in Manzanar. All her recent posts are selfies or with the Manzanar rangers."

"Does it look like she was running away from a painful breakup?" I asked.

"Steve is in every one of her pictures until he wasn't. Then, there are pages of quotes about what jerks men are."

"Is Steve still alive?" Jamie asked.

It took Jill a few moments to answer. "It appears Steve is engaged. Uh oh."

"Uh oh?" I asked.

"Steve's fiancé was Tonya's best friend, at least a close friend at an earlier point in her Facebook history."

"Ouch," Jamie said. "We know that Tonya can suffer through one of life's most painful events and not kill the person who hurt her. Is there something Erik might've done to her worse than that?"

"Not that I can see," Jill replied. "Erik isn't in any of Tonya's selfies, so I think he was irrelevant to her."

"Next potential murderer," Jamie said.

"Kevin Roberts is the seasonal ranger we interviewed earlier. He doesn't have much social media presence. Nothing on Facebook. On Twitter, he's got a lot of angry posts about illegal aliens committing crimes in the US. Here's one about racial purity, morality, and old-Testament justice."

"Kevin sounds like he'd be a suspect if we were looking at the murder of an illegal alien. Do any of his Twitter comments target Erik?"

"None that I have seen," Jill replied. "He seems to be focused on racial purity and right-wing conspiracy theories. Here's a comment about a militia group."

"It sounds like he's at the opposite end of the political spectrum from Erik," Jamie opined.

"He seems like an unlikely Park Service ranger," I said. "The USPS tends to hire environmentalists, historians, and forestry majors."

"You're social profiling," Jill said. "We hire a lot of people from a variety of backgrounds."

I looked at Jill in the mirror. "But the people who hang around for their entire careers are folks concerned about maintaining the parks and teaching about natural history."

Jamie chuckled. "They certainly don't join the Park Service to get rich. When Liz was a seasonal ranger in the Flagstaff parks, she qualified for food stamps."

"It's a lifestyle choice," Jill replied. "Most of us do it because we love the job."

"Who's left on your list of suspects?" Jamie asked.

"Seth Cline is another seasonal ranger. Other than the murderer, he was the last person to see the victim alive."

"What does his social media look like?" I asked.

"Seth doesn't post much. Until a year ago, he was attending a small liberal arts college in Ohio. He posted a graduation picture with his parents. There are a few pictures of him playing Frisbee golf."

"Frisbee golf is a thing?" Jamie asked.

Jill held out her phone so Jamie could see several guys gathered around a post draped with chains. "He took pictures of a series of *holes* where you throw your Frisbee until you hit the post and it falls into the chains. He has a picture of the variety of Frisbees he uses."

"Is his picture next to the dictionary definition of nerd?" Jamie asked.

Jill chuckled. "He hasn't had a lot of posts since moving to Manzanar. He's got pictures of the entrance and the monument, with a few comments about how moving visits here are for the families of former internees. Here's one picture of him in a bar with the other rangers. It appears that's the only social thing he's done since he gave up Frisbee golf."

"Unless Erik was dissing him over his nerdiness, I don't see Seth as a suspect," I said.

Jamie shrugged. "Maybe he uses his nerdiness to cover his psychopathic tendencies."

"The only other person from Manzanar is Superintendent Ed Richardson," Jill said. "He's a married father of three grown children. Manzanar is his first position as a superintendent, so he's probably still learning to be a people manager."

"What's interesting about him?" Jamie asked.

Jill silently paged through her phone. "Well..."

"Well, what?" I asked.

"Well, he's absolutely bland. He works, is a Boy Scout leader, and spends time with his wife and family. His wife's the one who has a Facebook page, and he shows up in her holiday and vacation pictures."

"Do you think he's living a hidden life?" Jamie asked. "Maybe he's got a secret marriage to a biker chick in Oakland or something."

Jill snorted. "I'd be surprised if Ed's ever had a speeding ticket."

"Who else works at the park?" Jamie asked.

"I guess there are a couple of retirees who volunteer on weekends and contract maintenance people. That's it!"

"You'd better check out the retirees," Jamie said, smiling. "They're notorious for killing people in fits of rage."

"Yeah, I pulled over a little old woman who was speeding in Walnut Canyon," I said. "When I asked for her driver's license, she handed me her concealed carry permit and told me she had a pistol in her purse."

"Yeah," Jamie replied. "You never know when you're going to need a pistol to deal with something in the middle of Arizona."

Sighing, Jill said, "I don't see one of the retired volunteers stringing Red up on the fence and slashing his throat."

"We're back to the psychopath thing," Jamie said. "You need to find someone whose brain is messed up enough to commit a crime like that. The problem is they live among us, yet we don't see them until they're arrested."

Having vetted the rangers, the rest of our drive to Bishop was silent. I thought about a past St. Paul murder case. It was unusual because all of the people associated with the victim had alibis. *A murder by a stranger is unusual. Ninety-nine percent of the premeditated murders I'd investigated were committed by spouses or people close to the victim. The other cases were second-degree murders, a person killed during another crime, or in a fit of rage. In those cases, the murderer fled the scene immediately.*

"What's going through your mind?" Jill asked.

"We're missing something. Erik's killer was sending a message."

"Like a drug cartel," Jamie suggested.

"The sheriff's department is all over that aspect, and this doesn't feel like a drug hit. This feels personal. The killer was angry."

Jill shook her head. "Erik was a puppy. Who would kill a puppy?"

"Maybe the puppy peed on the carpeting too many times," Jamie suggested. "People who are breeding show dogs sometimes euthanize the runts and puppies with genetic deformities, like hip dysplasia. Eric was an outcast anomaly with red hair."

Jill turned to look at Jamie. "Dairy farmers sell their bull calves for veal. It's not worth feeding them because they're not valuable for beef."

"I doubt Erik was culled from the gene pool."

Chuckling, Jill said, "Who doesn't want a blue-eyed redhead in their gene pool?"

After a moment, Jamie replied, "Most of the world's population has brown eyes and dark hair. Erik was an extreme minority. Think about the reverse of the Ku Klux Klan."

Chapter 15

Highway 395 entered Bishop from the south. The mapping feature on Jill's phone navigated the route to the Paiute Tribal Headquarters, a computer voice telling me to turn left in one hundred feet.

"We're turning toward the Bishop Hospital," Jill announced from the back seat.

Jamie commented, "I wouldn't think a town this size would have a hospital."

"Bishop is the largest Inyo County town," Jill commented as we passed the small hospital.

"Turn right in one hundred feet on Tu Su Lane," Jill's phone directed. "Your destination will be on your right."

We passed the Paiute Cultural Center as I slowed to take the turn. As promised, the one-story white Paiute Headquarters parking lot was the first driveway past the turn.

"The Bishop Paiute tribe operates a casino, so they're relatively prosperous," Jamie commented as I parked in a spot reserved for visitors.

Inside the entrance, Jamie led us to the receptionist's desk. "We have an appointment with the chairwoman," he said.

The young Native woman smiled and nodded. "Mary is expecting you. Her office is the first door on the left."

Mary Peacham sat reading at her desk when Jamie knocked on the doorframe of her open doorway. Smiling, she removed her glasses and said, "Please come in."

Expecting to meet with an elder, I was surprised to see that the tribal chairwoman appeared to be in her thirties. She gestured for us to take chairs surrounding a small conference table near the door. She closed the door as we sat. "How can I assist the Navajo Nation Police and US Park Service?"

Jamie looked at me. "I'm Doug Fletcher, and this is my partner, Jill. We're from the National Park Service Investigative Services Branch, and we're being assisted by Jamie Ballard, who is an officer with the Navajo Nation Police. We're investigating the murder of a ranger at Manzanar National Historic Site."

Continuing to smile politely, Mary nodded. "How is that connected to us, here in Bishop?"

I nodded to Jamie, hoping he'd explain our visit. After composing his thoughts, he said, "We spoke with a tribal historian, in Lone Pine, and he suggested that we speak with you. The Bishop Paiute reservation is considerably larger than the Lone Pine reservation, and he felt that you might have a better perspective on people who might be irrationally concerned about *Si-Te-Cah*, the red-haired tribe."

Mary cocked her head. "You feel that someone killed the ranger because of the *Si-Te-Cah*?"

Jill leaned on the table. "We really don't have a lot of leads in this case. It was suggested the red-haired victim may have triggered a response from someone who is knowledgeable about the *Si-Te-Cah*."

Mary leaned back. "As I recall, and to be honest my memory of that history is incomplete, the *Si-Te-Cah* were a legendary tribe of red-haired giants who were driven into a cave and killed. I can't imagine why any modern tribal member would attack a redheaded ranger because of a thousand-year-old legend."

"We understand your skepticism," Jill replied. "As I said, we're tracking down remote leads, and this is one line of inquiry."

Mary looked at Jamie and asked, "Does this seem like a reasonable possibility, Officer Ballard?"

Jamie drew a breath and nodded. "To put your mind at ease, we're not here because we want to pin this crime on a Paiute. The person who committed this murder is probably psychotic and not dealing well with reality. The possible link to *Si-Te-Cah* was suggested by the Lone Pine Historian."

"So, you'd like me to identify a psychotic Paiute historian who might have killed a redheaded ranger?"

I chuckled. "In a perfect world, that would be the answer. Having spent a quarter century in law enforcement, I know that identifying a murderer who isn't the victim's spouse or relative is rarely that simple."

Mary leaned back and steepled her fingers as she considered what I'd said. "First of all, I can't identify any crazy man who's hung up on the *Si-Te-Cah*. Secondly, I think it's highly unlikely that there is anyone on this, or any other Paiute reservation, who thinks of the *Si-Te-Cah* as anything but a legend."

"The red-haired bodies recovered from Lovelock Cave put some reality to that legend," Jill replied.

Mary raised her eyebrows. "The archaeologists think the hair of those people may have been colored by the minerals leached from the rocks in the cave."

"Your archaeological knowledge hints that you have more than a schoolgirl's recollection of a history lesson," Jill said. "Where did you go to college?"

Mary nodded toward a framed diploma hung over her desk. "I suspect you saw my BA in Native Studies. I graduated from Cal Poly Humboldt."

Smiling, Jill replied, "You must've been a star student. Your memory of the Lovelock Cave excavation is extraordinary." Leaning back so she could study the diploma, Jill added, "You graduated Summa Cum Laude. That's very impressive."

Mary smiled. "I felt it was my duty to take my classes seriously."

"You're an outstanding representative of the Paiute," Jamie said. "I can see why you were elected chairwoman."

"You're very well-read yourself, Officer Ballard. I assume your position is well-earned and highly respected."

I put my hand on Jamie's shoulder. "Officer Ballard is well-respected by the Navajo Nation. That's why we rely on him. He's consulted on several Park Service cases where there have been Native culture issues."

"Do you think a Paiute killed the ranger, Officer Ballard?"

"We're exploring the possibility that someone is irrationally hung up on the *Si-Te-Cah* legend. Perhaps, someone who is dabbling in psychotic drugs."

The chairwoman nodded and said, "I can't be of any further assistance, but the Tribal Police chief's office is at the end of the hallway." Standing, she said, "Let me introduce you to him."

The chairwoman walked into the police chief's office without knocking. A stocky white-haired man wearing casual clothing was leaning on the corner of the only desk and talking to a young, uniformed officer. They both looked surprised to see us.

After introductions, Mary said, "These folks are investigating a murder and would like to consult with you." After that, Mary excused herself.

Mike Allen, the white-haired police chief frowned as he looked at his watch. "I don't know about you folks, but I don't think well on an empty stomach. Would you be willing to take this discussion to a café instead of standing around my office?"

Jamie's face lit up. "Great suggestion!"

The chief locked his desk and file cabinet, then gestured for us to move into the hallway. "Take Tu Su Lane north to the T, then turn left. The Wanaaha Casino is a few blocks away on the left-hand side of the highway."

"We're eating at the casino?" I asked.

Allen smiled as he removed a key ring from his pocket. "The food is good, the prices are reasonable, and it keeps the money on the reservation."

"It works for me," Jamie replied.

Allen led us to the front door, then paused. "Officer Ballard, why don't you ride with me?"

"We'll follow you," I replied.

"Why do I suspect that our interview with the chief will be concluded before we get to the casino?" Jill asked.

"Are you kidding? Do you think the chief will find Jamie more talkative than we do?"

Getting into the rental car, Jill buckled her seatbelt. "I think they're more comfortable with each other than either of them is alone with us."

"I suppose we'll see," I replied, following the chief's unmarked Dodge Charger out of the parking lot.

Compared to Las Vegas casinos, the Wanaaha Casino was modest. We turned off the highway at the casino sign, then bypassed the main entrance, parking near the back.

Standing with Jamie, the chief unlocked a side door and explained, "I thought you'd probably want to bypass the gaming area and go directly to the restaurant."

Walking past the police chief, who held the small door open for us, Jill said, "I didn't think bypassing the slots was possible. The casinos I've seen all want you to walk past the gaming area to access any of the other interior areas."

"That's generally true," the chief said. "However, the casino manager thinks bringing officers through the middle of the casino upsets the guests. He gave me a key so I could use the side entrance."

Following the chief down the hallway, I could hear the clinking and dinging of the slots. We emerged near the restaurant entrance. The hostess smiled at the chief and led us to a small alcove near the back of the dining area. She handed us menus, then smiled and said, "Let me guess; black coffee for all of you."

"This goes on my tab, Kaleena."

The hostess nodded her understanding and left.

Before I could say anything, the chief nodded to Jamie, then leaned forward. "Officer Ballard explained your murder and the rumor about *Si-Te-Cah*." Allen paused, then pursed his lips. "I appreciate your cultural sensitivity. Bringing your friend, the Navajo cop along, was a nice gesture."

"Jamie actually spoke to you?" I asked, looking shocked.

The chief chuckled and nodded. "He's a real chatterbox compared to several of my officers."

"Do you have any thoughts about our murder case?" Jill asked.

"I understand the Inyo County Sheriff's Department has already determined the murder is drug related."

"With all due respect," I said, hoping to not insult the local department, "I think they may have reached that conclusion before all the facts were in."

The chief's look of mock surprise was priceless. "What? A cop jumping to a conclusion without evidence? What is this world coming to?" he said with a laugh.

The hostess returned with coffee mugs. After setting them out, she stood and looked at the chief. "I suggest the open-faced prime rib sandwich with au jus. It comes with a side salad and your choice of potato."

The chief nodded. "I'll have the special with fries and a Caesar salad, Kaleena." Then he looked at us. "It's usually the best item on the menu."

We all accepted his recommendation, pausing our discussion until after the hostess left.

"Kaleena is my granddaughter. It's nice to see the young people on the reservation working. Jobs haven't always been available to them."

Jill nodded. "I grew up in western South Dakota, on the edge of a Lakota reservation. There was a lot of prejudice among the white ranchers."

"There's an issue of culture clash," the chief explained. "There was little on the reservation that prepared any of us for a forty-hour a week job. On the other hand, the white people showed little patience for teaching us and accommodating our cultural differences."

"Nothing has changed for the Navajo," Jamie said. "My people tend to shun city jobs and the structure of living as whites. I think we've reached an uneasy acceptance of each other's cultures."

Jill looked pained.

Chief Allen clasped his hands and leaned on the table. "How can I help with your investigation?"

"If you could point us to a sociopath who is hung up on red-haired people, we'd be appreciative," I said.

The chief smiled, then looked at Jill. "What's your second choice?"

"How well known is the *Si-Te-Cah* legend?"

"It's one of the many historical stories told to our school children. I'm not sure what your experience was with history classes, but I've forgotten ninety-nine percent of what I was taught."

Kaleena returned with a young man carrying a tray of sandwiches and salads. After setting out our meals, she stepped back. "Is there anything else I can get for you right now?"

"What do you remember about *Si-Te-Cah*?" Jill asked.

Obviously unprepared for the question, Kaleena frowned. "He was a red-haired giant, right?"

Chief Allen smiled at us, then at her. "Close enough. Thanks."

As Kaleena left, I watched people through the narrow opening to the main dining area. Most seemed cheerful and chatted with the waitstaff. I noticed one guy who pushed his food around. I thought, *there's a guy who's lost too much.*

"You look distracted, Doug," the chief said.

"I'm wrestling with this case. The drug motive seems off."

"What else do you have left to investigate?"

"Someone mentioned water rights issues. Do you think that could be a motive, chief?"

It was apparent I'd struck a nerve with that question. "The Bishop Paiute Reservation was originally several thousand acres. When the Los Angeles mayor discovered there was water here, within his reach, the size of the reservation was reduced to the current few hundred acres and the water was diverted to LA."

"So, that could be a motive," I said.

"It's painful, but it's ancient history. Those water rights were stolen over a century ago. No one is going to restore them." The police chief leaned back. "Maybe you're overthinking this. Sometimes, we find that the first motive we consider is the real thing."

Jill nodded. "A very wise detective once said, 'Once you eliminate the impossible, whatever remains must be the truth, no matter how improbable.'"

Chief Allen smiled. "I think Sherlock Holmes was brilliant."

Grimacing, I said, "As I've told my partner, Sherlock Holmes is fictional. No matter how many times Jill quotes him, he's still a figment of Arthur Conan Doyle's imagination."

Jamie couldn't let that pass without comment. "Too bad Sherlock is smarter than most of the cops I've met."

"It's easy to be smart when you know how the story ends," I replied.

"Jamie, how would you feel about taking a job in Bishop? I could use another smart cop."

Smirking, Jill said, "Gee, Jamie, now you've got two job offers to consider."

"Chief, is there someone we could talk to about the *Si-Te-Cah* angle? Do you have a Bishop tribal historian?"

"You don't need a historian, Doug. You already know the history. What you need is someone who can point you to a sociopath. Sadly, there are too many of them in both the Native and white communities. And throwing drugs or alcohol into the mix only lowers people's inhibitions."

Kaleena returned with a black folio. The chief wrote in a generous tip, then signed the slip. Nodding her thanks Kaleena looked at Jill and me. "If you're in town Saturday, the *Sierra Vistas* are playing in the lounge. They're really good."

Jill smiled but shook her head. "I doubt we'll still be around on Saturday."

After checking his watch, the chief looked at me. "Is there something else I can do for you?"

The unhappy diner caught my eye again. He'd started to fidget and sweat. Standing, I nodded toward the dining room. "Chief, I think you need to talk to a guy who's having a meltdown in the dining room."

As the chief stood, the angry man confronted his young male waiter. Chief

Allen tapped Jill's shoulder as he passed. "Have Kaleena call security."

Jamie and I were a step behind the chief when he reached the lone diner's table. Inserting himself between the angry man and the waiter, Allen stood over the man with his badge at the diner's eye level. "Is there a problem, sir?"

"The pit boss pulled the blackjack dealer while I was on a hot streak. By the time the new guy got new cards and shuffled them, I got colder than the mountains. When I complained, the pit boss handed me a chit for a free lunch, thinking that would buy me off." Suddenly aware of Jamie and me, the man glanced at our badges and guns. "I see the cavalry has arrived."

"It appears you've finished your meal, sir," the chief said. "I'll have one of the security guards escort you to your car, just to be safe."

While the man glowered, two security guards rushed into the dining room with Jill a step behind them. Seeing the chief, they approached slowly and stood on either side of the diner. "Sir, why don't you come with us."

The man reluctantly stood and walked away, flanked by the two beefy security guards.

"Does that happen often?" I asked as waiters and waitresses rushed to their tables, reassuring diners the show was over, and offering free desserts.

Allen gestured to the hallway where we'd walked in. Once away from the dining room, he said, "There are always people who are unhappy with their losses. Anyone who understands the odds knows that the house usually wins. These places aren't built because they're handing out charity."

Once outside, the chief stood by his car, deep in thought. "Talk to my nephew, Rufus. He's a counselor with an office at the community center. If there's anyone crazy enough to attack a ranger because he had red hair, Rufus will know about it." The chief offered his hand to Jamie. "I was serious about that job offer."

"I'm flattered, but I'm not ready to leave Arizona."

Shaking Jill's hand, Allen smiled. "If you ever want to discuss Sherlock Holmes philosophy, I'd be happy to buy you and your partner cups of coffee."

Grinning at me, Jill said, "I think a discussion about a fictional detective who solved every case in three hundred pages would irritate my partner."

Shaking my hand, Allen tilted his head toward Jill and Jamie. "You're lucky, Doug. You've got damned fine people working with you. I hope you find the killer."

Jill got in the back seat of the rental car, leaving the front seat for Jamie. "What did we learn from Chief Allen?" she asked.

Jamie frowned. "He thinks the Inyo County Sheriff's Office might be right about the drug angle."

"Do you agree with him?" I asked.

After briefly considering the question, Jamie replied, "If there was a drug angle, someone would've thrown a Molotov cocktail through my window, not a rock. It's not drugs."

"What do you think about the chief's suggestion that we talk with Rufus, the counselor?" Jill asked.

Jamie wrinkled his nose as if he'd bitten into a lemon. "He can't reveal anything specific to us because he's bound by patient confidentiality rules." He paused. "On the other hand, he might be willing to offer his general thoughts about radical tribal elements."

We followed the chief back to the tribal headquarters building and I spoke to him in the parking lot. "Where is Rufus' office?"

"His office is at the other end of the building from mine. Let's see if he's in."

Chapter 16

At the opposite end of the building, we entered an anteroom furnished with two comfortable chairs and a children's play area featuring a small table with coloring books and crayons. The chief paused outside the inner door, then knocked. "The blue light isn't on, so he's not with a client right now."

From behind a closed door, we heard a chair scrape. A young man, dressed in a t-shirt featuring an unfamiliar rock band, jeans, and boots appeared. "Uncle Mike, what's up?"

The chief gestured toward us. "My friends from the Park Service and the Navajo Nation Police are investigating the murder of a ranger at Manzanar. They'd like to talk to you about the possibility that a tribal member was the assailant."

Rufus smiled at Jill and me, then stared at Jamie. "Why are the Navajo Nation Police investigating a murder at Manzanar?"

"The Fletchers asked for my Native perspective on the Manzanar crime scene," Jamie replied. "They'd heard about *Si-Te-Cah* and asked if there might be a link to the red-haired ranger's murder."

Turning to Jill, Rufus asked, "Why didn't you ask one of the Paiute tribal members?"

"We spoke with John Standing Bear, the Lone Pine Reservation historian. He suggested talking to someone on the Bishop Reservation. He thought there might be someone more volatile here, closer to Lovelock Cave and the *Se-Ti-Cah* massacre."

Rufus looked at the chief. I sensed, more than saw, an eyeroll. "You brought them to me because of something Standing Bear told them?" Returning his focus to us, Rufus said, "I can't comment on anything I've heard in counseling sessions."

"I take it you don't have much time for John Standing Bear," I said. "He's recording Paiute oral history."

The chief cleared his throat. "If John was only recording what he's heard, he'd be doing us a great service."

"Don't you think he's doing a credible job?" Jamie asked.

After glancing at Rufus, the chief said, "I've heard he's embellished the history as much as any of the elders who've spoken to him."

Growing impatient, Rufus kept glancing at the clock. "Are we done?"

"I thought you might be able to answer their general questions about hotheads and irrational people."

Rufus looked down and stared at his boots. "You think a crazy Indian might've killed that guy?"

"We're exploring a number of possible motives," I replied. "The ranger had red hair. The historical *Si-Te-Cah* angle was mentioned to us, so we're following that thread."

The chief checked his watch. "I've got to run. I hope Rufus can answer your questions."

With the chief gone, Rufus was less deferential. "Listen, I'm a licensed psychologist. My patient conversations are confidential. Uncle Mike knows that. I don't know why he dragged you down here."

Jamie surprised me by answering, "There are Navajo tribal members with psychological issues. Our reservation is huge, so most of those people are too far from a clinic to see a counselor. I keep an eye on them and sometimes I'm able to talk them back from doing something stupid. I do it because they're my people, not because I'm a cop trying to enforce the law."

Rufus shrugged. "I'm sorry. I can't comment on my patients."

"Whoever killed the ranger was a psychopath," I replied. "Are there people on the Bishop Reservation capable of that kind of violence?"

Leaning against the doorframe, Rufus considered my question. "I went to school at UCLA and did my clinical training with the LA County Public Health Bureau. We saw a lot of people from the courts. I quite literally interviewed a psychotic killer every week.

Some had already killed a person. Others were only one confrontation away from murder. Based on my experience there and here, I can tell you there are people suffering from psychotic problems everywhere. Like your Navajo friend said, there are people on the fringes here and in every society, who will act inappropriately when confronted with social, economic, and perceived problems. The Bishop Reservation is not an exception."

"Have you ever spoken with someone who was hung up on the *Si-Te-Cah*," Jill asked.

Rufus weighed his response, then replied, "I've heard of the *Si-Te-Cah*."

Smiling, Jill said, "That's not exactly what I asked."

Returning Jill's smile, Rufus said, "I told you; I can't comment on what my clients have discussed with me."

Trying to clarify Rufus' answer, Jamie asked, "Have you heard about the red-haired giants in either an educational setting or in your office?"

"Learning about them is part of our history lessons."

"And..." Jamie prompted.

"I can't comment on what people have said during their sessions."

"Someone *has* commented on the *Si-Te-Cah* in a session?"

Remaining stone-faced, Rufus replied, "I've said too much." He checked the clock, then gestured toward the hallway, signaling for us to leave. "I have a client arriving in a few minutes."

We shook his hand and walked out. Rufus stopped Jamie, who was trailing Jill and me, whispering something to him. Jamie nodded but said nothing.

In the car, I looked at Jamie and asked, "Can you tell us what Rufus said?"

"More story is told by what is unsaid than what's said."

"A riddle?" I replied.

Tipping her head back, Jill thought for a moment. "Peter, Paul, and Mary had a lyric, 'I think I could really say somethin' if you know what I mean. But if I really say it, the radio won't play it, unless I lay it between the lines.'"

Jamie looked toward Jill. "He can't answer the question we've asked him. By not saying it, he's told us something."

"Ahh," Jill replied, "One of *his* patients has mentioned the *Si-Te-Cah*, so he can't tell us that except by not denying it."

"Aren't therapists required to report a crime they learn about during a session?" Jill asked.

Jamie shook his head. "On the reservation, you're facing the trifecta of confidentiality: He's a therapist, but he's also a shaman and a tribal member."

"He's a shaman?" I asked.

"His bone necklace had a morning star. That signifies that he's a healer."

"I'm sorry, but isn't that what psychologists do?" I asked.

"It's more than that, Doug. Rufus has healing powers beyond his psychological therapy." Jamie paused. "He's deeply committed to protecting the privacy of his tribal patients. He won't tell us anything directly."

"But he left the door ajar," Jill said. "He hinted that he might know the person who killed Red Petersen."

Jamie looked toward the community center, deep in thought. "I don't think Rufus knows who killed your ranger."

"He could've said that."

"That would've been telling us something," Jamie replied.

"Rufus told us that John Standing Bear was embellishing the oral history. That must mean the historian isn't one of his patients," Jill observed.

"And, by not commenting, Rufus implied that he doesn't think John Standing Bear is our killer," Jamie added.

I backed away from the community center and turned toward Lone Pine. "I hate these confidentiality arrangements. Priests can't point out murderers. Neither can doctors, psychiatrists, or ministers. You'd think people like that would want to get those people out of their communities."

"Doug," Jill said, "your cop bias is showing."

"You'd think Rufus' conscience would bother him if he's shielding a killer."

"Perhaps it is," Jamie replied. "He didn't lie to us and said he doesn't know who the killer is. He's done as much as his conscience allows."

"How many people belong to the Bishop Paiute tribe?" I asked,

Jill took out her phone and entered the question. "There are 2,000 members of the Bishop Paiute-Shoshone tribe. Most live on their reservation."

I looked at Jamie and asked, "What are the chances that someone from the tribe will tell us there's a crazy Paiute who's capable of killing a park ranger?"

"I'd say the odds of that happening are the same as you walking out of their casino with a million dollars in slot machine winnings."

"That bad?" I asked.

Jamie thought for a second. "There's a chance of that happening but I wouldn't bet my house on it."

Apparently ignoring our discussion, Jill was tapping on her phone. "What are you up to?" I asked.

"Lovelock, Nevada is a six-and-a-half-hour drive from here. The online guide suggests stopping at the Marzen House Museum before setting out to visit the cave."

"Is there a visitor center at the cave?" Jamie asked.

"It doesn't appear so. The guide recommends picking up maps at the museum in Lovelock."

Jill continued tapping on her phone, then held it to her ear.

"What are you up to?" I asked.

She raised one finger to silence me. "Hello! My name is Jill Fletcher and I'm an investigator from the National Park Service. How many of the people who visit you are interested in visiting Lovelock Cave?"

Turning on the speaker, Jill set her phone on the seatback so we could all hear the conversation.

The voice who answered sounded like an elderly female volunteer. "We have a few people a week who ask about the cave. I'm not sure how many of them actually drive out there to look at it."

"Who controls access and charges visitors?"

"There's no access control. The site is on a Bureau of Land Management tract. The BLM erected signs at the entrance and built stairs inside the cave. The site is open 24/7 without controlled access. Anyone can walk in and look around."

"Do you think most visitors stop at the museum before driving to the cave?"

The woman chuckled. "I doubt it. Local school groups go out there, and there are websites with maps and information beyond what we offer."

"Do many Paiute visitors stop off to see you before going to the cave?"

"We've had a few Native visitors making a pilgrimage to the site of the battle. I wouldn't say there have been many. Keep in mind that we only see a percentage of the cave's visitors."

"Have you had any recent Paiute visitors who seemed agitated about the battle at the cave?"

The woman chuckled. "Agitated? No. I can't recall a single person who's shown anything more than passing curiosity about the cave."

"Has there been a young Paiute man, or group of men, who've visited recently?"

"Other than school children, most of our visitors are senior citizens or history buffs. I don't recall any young Native visitors in the past few weeks."

"Thank you, ma'am."

"It's been my pleasure. You've provided a nice diversion during a quiet day. Please stop by and introduce yourself if you come to visit the cave."

"I will," Jill promised. Looking up, she shrugged as she disconnected the call. "Another dead end."

"Not at all," I replied. "We know there are no restrictions on access to the site, and no suspicious characters have stopped at the museum recently."

Jamie nodded. "Exclusionary information is important."

"I don't see how we've excluded anyone," Jill replied. "Anyone could've driven to the Lovelock Cave site without stopping at the museum. The site has no entrance control, no electronic monitoring, and no ranger presence."

Understanding swept over me. "True, but the site is remote and nearly unknown to anyone who wasn't taught about it in school. If our killer was there, it's because he visited the site with his school or learned about it in class or from tribal elders."

Jamie tapped my shoulder. "Turn around. Go back to the community center."

I looped around the block in the reverse direction. "What are you thinking?"

"I'm going to ask the receptionist about Bishop Paiute elders."

I parked in the same spot we'd previously occupied and Jamie got out of the car as it rolled to a stop. He was only gone a minute before returning with an understated smile. Handing Jill a piece of paper, he asked, "Can your phone find this address?"

After tapping on her phone screen, she waited. "This address is only a few blocks away. It's the Bishop Care Center."

"Pauline Goad lives in room 118," Jamie replied. "She's the oldest member of the Bishop Paiute tribe."

I parked near the front entrance, and we walked into what could've been a retirement home anywhere in the United States. A young Paiute woman seated behind a desk in the entryway looked up and smiled as we approached. An ID card hanging from a yellow lanyard indicated that her name was Trish "How can I help you?"

Taking the lead, Jamie said, "We'd like to visit Pauline Goad. I believe she lives in room 118."

Nodding toward a group of women watching television in a nearby alcove, Trish said, "Pauline is the white-haired woman in the wheelchair."

Jamie led us to the alcove and knelt next to the white-haired woman. "*Maik'w*, Aunt Pauline."

The woman, who'd watched us walk in, turned to Jamie and cocked her head. "You call me your aunt, but I don't know you."

"In my Navajo culture, we address all of our female elders as 'Aunt.'"

After a moment of consideration, the woman nodded. "Why do you need counsel, my nephew?"

Nodding toward Jill and me, Jamie said, "My friends are trying to find the person who killed a US Park Service ranger at Manzanar. A Paiute historian in Lone Pine suggested that a Bishop Paiute may have mistaken him for a member of the *Si-Te-Cah*."

Frowning, the woman asked, "Did the ranger have red hair?"

"He did, Aunt Pauline."

"I once went to Lovelock Cave where my people defeated the *Si-Te-Cah* many years ago. I don't believe that any of their tribe survived the battle."

"Are there those who think there were survivors?"

"I've sometimes seen red-haired people. I've never thought they were the red-haired giants, the *Si-Te-Cah*."

Jamie looked up at us, making sure we could hear the conversation. I nodded, then he asked, "You are wise in the ways of the world. Are there young people who are less wise, and who feel the need to earn their feathers?"

"There are always spirited young men who hear the stories of glory. They find life on the reservation tiresome and often look for ways to relive the past."

"Can you think of anyone who might mistake a red-haired ranger for a member of the *Si-Te-Cah*?"

Pauline looked away from Jamie and closed her eyes. "I am old. Young men don't seek the guidance of female elders. They listen to the stories told by the old men and take them to heart. The unwise among them sometimes wish to relive past Paiute glory as a way to escape reservation life."

"Is there someone who is most likely to try to find that glory?"

"There are many young men who have not yet discovered the wisdom of age. I imagine there are several who might try to earn their feathers in a number of ways."

"We think the killer might not know the boundaries provided by wisdom and age. Do you know of someone like that?"

Pauline's eyes opened and she looked at me, then at Jill. "Who is this woman traveling with you? Is she your wife?"

"Jill is the wife of my friend. She works for the Park Service and is helping us search for the ranger's killer."

Pauline lifted her left hand and motioned for Jill to approach. When Jill knelt beside Pauline's wheelchair, the old woman put out her hand. "Let me touch your fingers, niece."

Jill cupped the old woman's hand in both of hers and spoke softly. "I'm humbled by your wisdom."

"Your hands are soft, not like those of a woman who works the land."

"I grew up on a ranch, riding horses and mending broken fences. Now I work with my head, not my hands. I catch thieves and murderers."

Looking into Jill's eyes, Pauline said, "You have killed people, but that memory haunts you. The dead visit your dreams as demons and interrupt your sleep."

Pauline's words rattled Jill. She glanced at me, then looked at Pauline. "You can see my soul. I take no pride in the lives I have taken. They were no more than rabid dogs who'd bitten kind people."

"Will you kill the man who attacked the person he thought was a *Si-Te-Cah*?"

"I never plan to kill anyone, Aunt Pauline. I've only drawn my gun to protect the lives of the innocent."

"What is your name, child?"

"I'm Jill Fletcher."

"I will call you *Kuh'eyokomp*, the flower that heals."

Jill looked at Jamie, who smiled and mouthed, "You've been honored."

Smiling, Jill replied, "Thank you. What shall I do to deserve that kind name?"

"You put off your personal life to serve others. Now you've found the happiness that escaped you. Those choices show wisdom and kindness beyond your years. You will find the man who killed the red-haired ranger. That search may put you in danger, but you were sent by a greater power to remove the stain caused by that careless act."

"Thank you. Where will I find that man?"

"I don't know his name. His spirit is troubled, and he tries to escape his demons by using smoke that blinds his eyes."

"I don't understand," Jill replied.

"He doesn't see things clearly, which makes him dangerous to himself and others. Be careful."

"Where do I find him?"

"You've already crossed his path, *Kuh'eyokomp*." Pauline looked away and drew a breath. "I must rest now. Thank you for visiting."

Jill and Jamie stood, having been dismissed. We walked out of the building and stood under the portico. "What did we learn?" I asked.

Jamie smiled and said, "Jill has been honored with a Paiute name. *Kuh'eyokomp* means Desert Globemallow. It's an orange flower known for its healing powers."

Smiling, I said, "You've been given superpowers."

"Yeah, which superpowers have I been given, Jamie?"

"The Globemallow was ancestrally used to treat cuts, stomach aches, infections and colds."

Looking unimpressed, Jill replied, "I don't know how any of those healing powers will help with our investigation."

After a moment of contemplation, Jamie replied, "Perhaps Aunt Pauline bestowed that name on you because you'll be able to heal a broader infection by removing the killer."

"She mentioned that I've already crossed the killer's path." Jill looked at Jamie. "Is she just a slightly demented elderly woman happy to have company or do you think she actually has a vision of what's happening?"

Jamie shrugged. "It's hard to say. She seems sane. Experience has taught me to treasure information I receive from my elders. They seem to have a sixth sense about the world and see things with their minds that I can't see with my eyes."

Jill stared into the distance. "If that's true, we've crossed paths with the killer. The most recent people we've spoken with are Chief Allen and his nephew, Rufus. Neither of them seems like a killer."

"Normalcy is the disguise killers use to their advantage," I replied. "Think of the legendary serial killers; they all appeared very normal and were able to approach their victims without arousing suspicion." I started walking to the car.

Trailing behind, Jill said, "I'm trying to list all the people whose paths we've crossed since our arrival. We started with the rangers and deputies at Manzanar, who I think we can rule out. Next was the motel manager, a couple of waitresses, a hairdresser, a historian, the receptionist at the Bishop Paiute Tribal Center, the tribal president, and his nephew."

As we got into our rental car, Jamie added, "You've forgotten the people at the casino. There was a waitress, an angry gambler, a couple of security guards, and whomever you spoke with to alert security about the commotion in the restaurant."

Starting the engine, I said, "My money is on the roommate's girlfriend. She's shady and there's something off about her."

I glanced at Jamie in the rear-view mirror. He seemed deep in thought. He looked at me in the mirror. "You skipped over the cops. Is there something going on with them? You said they were totally focused on the drug business. Are they trying to divert your attention from them?"

"To what end?" I asked. "What motive would they have?"

Jamie shrugged. "What motive would anyone have to kill what appears to be a nice ranger who never irritated anyone?"

Jill shifted in her seat. "There is *no one* who has ever gone through life without irritating family or co-workers or friends. Maybe someone is pretending to be okay with Red but is really simmering under the surface." She paused, then added, "If the cops showed up at your place of work investigating the murder of a co-worker, would you say, 'Gee, he was a real jerk, and the world is a better place now that he's dead?'"

"The roommate and his girlfriend both said he was a wonderful guy."

"Seriously?" Jamie asked. "I mean, everyone gets irritated with their roommates over something. If it's not about paying their half of the rent on time, it's over who ate what out of the refrigerator or cupboard."

"With women, it's who borrowed whose clothes, jewelry, or feminine supplies."

"Feminine supplies are a big issue?" I asked,

"They are if your roommate uses up the last of your supply and doesn't replace them before your next period."

Jamie chuckled. "I think we can rule out that motive."

Jill waved off his comment. "That's just an example of how silly or stupid things get out of hand."

"Money, sex, and drugs," Jamie said from the backseat. "Those are the biggies. Is there someone on Jill's list who would have those motives?"

"By all accounts, Red wasn't into the drug or alcohol scenes," Jill replied. "It doesn't sound like he's had a recent romantic relationship."

"Has anyone mentioned money?" Jamie asked.

"Not to us," I replied.

"Most rangers don't earn enough money for it to be an issue," Jill said. "There's always some tension about paying bills, but it's not a murder motive. When you're all broke, everyone is in the same boat and you all row together."

"That's true for everyone but Casey. He was rich, now he's working his way back into his family's good graces. Maybe he's unable to get by on a ranger's salary," I suggested.

"He's a narcissist," Jill replied. "I think people like him are above getting their hands dirty by killing someone. I think they get their joy from feeling superior."

"Was the victim a gambler?" Jamie asked. "Maybe he was losing big at the Bishop casino."

Jill dug in her pocket and pulled out a business card. "I got a card from the head of casino security. I'll ask him if Red's ever been a customer."

Jamie pulled out his cell phone and looked at the screen. "It's too late to call him today."

"Let me guess," I said, glancing at Jamie in the mirror. "It's time for supper."

Nodding, Jamie replied, "Good suggestion. A steak would taste good."

Chapter 17

Hearing Jamie's voice outside our motel room, I put on a jacket and stepped out to check on Jamie while Jill showered. He was staring toward the Sierra Nevada mountains while talking on his phone.

"...but I think it's best if..." Being interrupted, he threw his left hand up in response. "I know staying with the tribal police will be tougher. On the other hand..."

After being cut off again, he rolled his head in frustration. Hearing my door close he turned toward me, his look pleading.

I assumed he was having a conversation with Liz, his wife, and shook my head. I wasn't going to get between them.

"It's fine? What does that mean? You don't sound like this decision is fine." He took the phone away from his ear and stared at it as if it had done something on its own.

"Liz doesn't like your decision to stay with the Navajo Nation Police?"

Jamie looked disgusted as he slipped the phone in his pocket. "She said it was 'fine,' but it didn't sound like she meant it."

I chuckled. "You need a primer on wife vocabulary."

"Like what?"

"Fine does not mean okay. Fine means that you're wrong and she's not going to argue with you anymore."

Jamie squinted at me. "That's not the definition from *Merriam's Dictionary*."

"Try the *Urban Dictionary*. Their definitions are more in line with modern marital arguments."

Not accepting my input, he asked, "Are there other words that have different meanings when used by my wife?"

"'Go ahead' is a dare, not permission." While Jamie mulled that thought, I added, "'Nothing' means 'something' when used in the context of discussing what's bothering her. 'Whatever' means she's given up the argument despite you being wrong. 'It's okay' means you need to think hard about what you're about to do because whatever happens is going to cost you."

"Where do you dream up this stuff?"

"This lesson is brought to you from the school of hard knocks. I have messed up so many marital arguments that those words and phrases have been burnt into my mind." I paused, then asked, "How many of those lines did Liz use during your discussion?"

Jamie stared at me as he flashed back to whatever Liz had said before I walked out of the room. Without answering me, he took out his phone and walked down the sidewalk away from me. I heard only the first part of the discussion. "I thought about what you said…"

The door opened behind me, and Jill walked out. "Who is Jamie talking to?" she asked, hearing his voice, but not the whole conversation.

"Jamie told Liz he wasn't taking the Flagstaff PD job. She told him it was 'fine.'"

Jill closed her eyes. "Uh oh. Fine isn't good."

"I explained that to him, along with hints about other marital discussion landmines."

"There are marital landmines?" Jill asked as Jamie walked farther away so we couldn't hear his conversation. "Give me an example."

"I told him that 'go ahead' wasn't permission, but more of a dare."

"Have I ever said that to you?"

"The incident that sticks in my mind is a discussion I had with my ex-wife about going to a cop's retirement instead of accompanying her to a lecture on global warming."

"Ah," Jill replied. "When you two were drifting apart."

Jamie ended his call and walked back toward us with hands stuffed in his jean's pockets. Something about his appearance made me think of a puppy that had been scolded for peeing on the floor. "Let's go," he said, walking to the back door of our rental car.

Jill turned to him as I drove out of the parking lot. "Did you and Liz come to a decision?"

"What did blabbermouth tell you?" he asked.

"Doug said you were discussing your job choices with Liz."

Jamie glared at me in the rear-view mirror. "Can we talk about the murder? It'd be less painful."

"Did you come to an agreement?" I asked.

Jamie shook his head.

* * *

Our waitress recognized us and delivered black coffee as soon as we were seated. "The breakfast special is still an English muffin sandwich with an egg and bacon. Otherwise, we have all the usual menu items."

After taking our orders, she disappeared into the kitchen. Jill seemed distracted as our server walked away. "Our waitress is another person whose path we've crossed."

Jamie glanced at the door leading to the kitchen. "Nah. She's not a psychopathic killer. She's too gregarious and is holding down a regular job."

Jill leaned on her elbows feigning deep interest. "Just what does a psychopathic killer look like, Jamie?"

"They're people who don't play well with others. They can put up a façade for a few minutes, but acting drains their energy, and they eventually drift away.”

“But they can look like any other normal person, right?” Jill asked.

“At first blush, yes. I’ve found that psychopaths can’t maintain a conversation. Their world is very self-centered, and they’re unwilling to acknowledge the wishes or needs of others. They can bluff their way through a short interview, but if you engage them in a longer interrogation, they eventually break.”

“Break?”

“They lash out and become defensive. Every sentence will contain *I, me,* or *my.*”

“That sounds like a narcissist,” Jill replied.

“Narcissism is a psychological disorder. Take that to the extreme and you may have a psychopathic killer who is willing to end the life of anyone getting between them and what he wants.”

When the conversation lulled, I added, “Jamie’s mostly right. I’ve found that psychopaths are generally loners because they’ve offended or cast aside anyone who disagrees with them or fails to enable their psychosis. They’re manipulative, and most of the people they interact with become aware of the manipulation and walk away.”

“Do you mean financially manipulative?” Jill asked.

"That can be part of it. I think they enjoy being the puppeteer and relish seeing people acting as they want."

Our breakfast arrived, ending the conversation. We ate in silence, Jamie focused on consuming his trucker's special. Jill was deep in thought. Pushing her empty bowl away, she removed a notebook and pen from her pocket. She flipped the notebook open to a page filled with names. "I think this is everyone we've spoken with since we arrived in Lone Pine." She turned the notebook so we could read the two columns. Several notations were job titles: sporting goods store manager, stylist, receptionist, etc.

I slid the notebook closer to Jamie and apparently sighed too emphatically.

"What?" Jill asked, responding to my sigh.

"How much credence do we place in an old woman's comment that our paths have crossed that of the killer?"

Jamie passed the notebook back to Jill and said, "*Halne'ii.*"

"What?" I asked.

"We Navajo believe that our elders have become *Halne'ii,* prophets. I'm sure it's the same with the Paiute Nation. Don't discount the words of a wise woman."

I signaled the waitress for a coffee refill, then turned to Jamie. "At some point, we're going to need a search warrant for someone's house, apartment, office, or car. I won't approach a federal magistrate for a search warrant based on the vision of a Paiute prophet."

We sat quietly while the waitress topped off our coffee and then cleared our plates. "Will there be anything else?"

Jamie smiled and said, "I'll take the bill."

With the bill in hand, Jamie pulled out his wallet and counted out enough cash to cover the bill and leave a substantial tip. He leaned the bill and cash against the napkin holder and walked to the restroom.

Jill thought for a moment, then pushed her chair back. "Not all of us have a bladder that will hold a full gallon of coffee."

When Jamie returned with Jill a step behind, he asked, "What's the plan?"

I gestured toward the door and didn't speak until we were inside the car. "Let's walk through Jill's list, chronologically. If we think any of the unnamed people are possible suspects, we find their names and check their background."

Jamie cracked a smile. "See, Jill, sometimes he *does* listen to us."

"I listen to what you say all the time," I replied as I started the car. "I may not act on your suggestions, but I weigh them."

Pulling out her list, Jill slid her finger down the names. "Do we agree to eliminate the park staff and deputies?"

Jamie leaned back and stared at the ceiling. "I have a hard time seeing a cop or ranger slashing a guy's throat."

"Slashing someone's throat is a very personal attack; almost vengeful," I said while thinking out loud.

"Like a crazy ex-girlfriend," Jill suggested.

"That would be off-the-scale crazy for a woman," Jamie opined. "Like that Glenn Close movie with the pet rabbit in the stewpot."

I glanced at Jamie in the mirror. "That was fiction. I've never heard of anyone actually doing something like that."

"You're measuring crazy by city standards," Jamie replied. "When you get out into the country, there's a whole new level of crazy."

Jill nodded. "You deal with people who are living off the grid and they sometimes do things differently from city folks."

"Maybe we shouldn't discount the county deputies or park staff," I said. "The only people we've spoken with at length were Red's roommate and his girlfriend. The girlfriend is goofy, but she doesn't seem like a psychopath. We should spend some time with the rest of the rangers."

Jill seemed uneasy with that comment. "Rangers are..."

"Are what?" I asked. "Tree hugging passivists who don't kill flies? Do they just shoo bugs out of the house without harming them?"

"Ed, Grace, and Becky have been with the Park Service for decades. If they had some deep-seated psychiatric problem, it would've come out before now. If we were going to spend time checking out the rangers, I'd focus on the seasonal people."

Jamie leaned forward. "Jill's right. Goofballs can hide their craziness for a while, but not decades. If you're looking at the staff, check out the new people first." He paused, then asked, "What about the volunteers? Have we even met any of them? Maybe one of them has a screw loose."

Jill grimaced. "*Has a screw loose?* Really? That's the most technical term you could use?"

"You both knew what I meant."

Jill looked over her shoulder at Jamie. "Practice talking to us like we're law enforcement professionals you've never met before. You'll be less likely to blurt out something like that when you're around people who don't know you, or when you're being cross-examined by a shrewd lawyer who's pulling your strings, trying to get you rattled."

"I think a jury would laugh if I said something like that during a trial."

"In this case," I said, "Jill's probably right. You don't want to let a pejorative like that slip out in the wrong setting."

"I should work with you two more often," Jamie said as he leaned back. "I get marital and linguistic advice. I'm sure I'll become a better person because of your guidance."

"So, you think one of the volunteers might be a slasher?" I asked.

Jill shook her head. "Most of the volunteers are retirees. I don't see a septuagenarian slashing a ranger's throat."

"Maybe Red made a derogatory remark about their frequent bathroom breaks," Jamie said. "Or made fun of someone's Buick."

"That's nearly as politically incorrect as your comment about having a loose screw."

"One brick short of a load. Is that better?" Jamie asked.

Jill crossed her arms and refused to answer.

"Did you notice the MAGA bumper sticker on that seasonal ranger's pickup? He's definitely not a tree hugger," Jamie said. "What's his name? Kevin?"

"Maybe he bought the truck with the bumper stickers already there," I opined.

Jamie's look showed his skepticism. "People don't buy trucks with slogans they dislike. Even if they did, the paint scraper would be out the next day and the bumper stickers would be gone."

Chapter 18

A rental car was parked in the Manzanar parking lot when we arrived. From inside, I heard a man speaking in Swedish-accented English. A very blonde, blue-eyed man was standing next to a woman with strawberry blonde hair. They were middle-aged and looked haggard. Ed Richardson gestured for us to join them.

"Jill and Doug Fletcher, these are Red's parents, Ilsa and Vigo Petersen. Jill and Doug are the investigators I told you about."

Ilsa grabbed my hand as if it was a lifeline. "You're the investigators who were sent from Texas?"

"That's right," I replied. "I'm terribly sorry about your son."

Vigo fixed his gaze on Jill's pistol. "I have a hard time dealing with the American police carrying pistols. In Sweden, the police aren't as heavily armed as the officers here."

"I take it you don't think women should carry guns?" Jill stated as much as asked.

"It's not that at all. Women are as capable as men. In Sweden, there's no sexual prejudice. As a matter of fact, I could see how an armed female police officer could be more effective than her male partner in many situations."

Smiling, I said, "My partner is known for her diplomacy and negotiating skills."

Vigo shook my hand. "That's part of my message. Men tend to react with fists when women react with reason."

"Your accents make me feel like I'm back in Minnesota," I said. "I grew up in a St. Paul suburb. There are a lot of people with Swedish roots there."

"We own a furniture store outside of Minneapolis. A lot of our customers like the clean lines of Scandinavian designers and the light-colored woods."

"That's part of IKEA's draw," I said, which made the Petersens cringe.

Ilsa patted my hand. "We're not fans of IKEA."

"Why did Erik take a job in California?" Jill asked. "Didn't he want to be part of the furniture business?"

Ilsa shook her head. "He wanted to strike out on his own. You know how young men are."

Jill nodded, expressing her understanding. "I think we all want to make our own way. My parents weren't pleased when I joined the Park Service. They were even less pleased when I made it my career."

Tears formed in Ilsa's eyes, and she sniffled. "We hoped he'd come back and take over the furniture store."

I looked at the superintendent and asked, "Do you have a coffee pot in the back room?"

Looking embarrassed, Richardson nodded. "Where are my manners?" He gestured toward a door in the rear of the visitor center.

The room was obviously not intended for guests. Furnished with four scarred wooden chairs set haphazardly around an equally scarred wooden table that looked like it might've been left over from the days Manzanar was a camp. Jill guided Ilsa to a chair as I held coffee mugs while Richardson poured from a carafe.

"Have they revealed anything about Red's life?" I whispered.

"Not really. I didn't know what to say to them, so we haven't had a conversation."

After carrying the mugs to the table and setting them in front of Ilsa and Vigo, I asked, "Is there anyone or anything from Erik's Minnesota life that would point to someone being angry enough to kill him?"

Ilsa looked shocked. "No!"

Vigo looked up with vacant eyes. Apparently unable to speak, he shook his head.

Jill accepted a mug of coffee from Richardson who stepped back, looking like an uneasy servant awaiting direction. She put her arm around Ilsa's shoulders. "I'm sorry to ask these questions, but we're trying to find a motive for Erik's death."

"He was a quiet boy," Ilsa replied. She took a sip of coffee, then grimaced. "Do you have any cream?"

The superintendent scurried to a small refrigerator in the corner and returned with a small carton of coffee creamer. "I hope hazelnut is okay," he said as he set the container in front of Ilsa. I retrieved a plastic spoon from a box near the coffee pot and set it on the table.

Stirring creamer into her coffee, Ilsa sniffled. "I don't think Erik was happy here."

"Why was he unhappy?" Jill asked.

Ilsa sipped her coffee and appeared to be happier with it after adding the creamer. "He had a girlfriend. We thought they were serious. But you know how young people don't talk about their romantic situation with their parents." Ilsa took another sip of coffee, then added, "They'd broken up. Erik didn't talk about her much after that."

"Did he get along with his co-workers?" Jill asked.

I glanced at the superintendent, who shrugged.

"I think most of them were nice. Erik said one person was unhappy with him."

When Ilsa failed to expand on that comment, I asked, "Did he say who that was, or why they were unhappy with him?"

Vigo surprised me by saying, "It was one of the other young men. Erik thought it was strange that someone would be angry about him being the son of Swedish immigrants."

I looked at Richardson, and again he shrugged.

"Did he tell you that person's name?" Jill asked.

Ilsa looked at Vigo, who shook his head. "I don't recall the person's name, but it was a young man."

A thought apparently struck Ilsa. "Erik said that person was a right-wing jerk. He and Erik had an argument about what another ranger was telling visitors about this place. Erik thought of this camp as a symbol of oppression. The other ranger was telling visitors that the Japanese people here were being given food and housing so they wouldn't be persecuted. In his mind, the Japanese people got government protection and welfare."

I stood, looked at Richardson, and then nodded toward the door. After closing the door behind us, I made sure the public area of the visitor center was empty before asking, "What did you know about this?"

Unable to look me in the eye, Richardson stared at a rack of books. "Kevin has an alternative view from our official Park Service history of Manzanar."

"He's telling visitors Manzanar was government welfare? That we were giving the internees free food and housing, not that they were imprisoned?"

"I've never heard Kevin say those things."

"Other rangers have complained about his view of the camp, correct?"

"I may have heard some rumblings."

"Have you ever confronted Kevin about what he's telling the visitors?"

Richardson blinked and looked away. "Listen, we all have different views about history. Kevin gives visitors an alternative viewpoint."

I stepped into the superintendent's personal space and pointed a finger at his chest. "You are in charge of this historic site. It's your responsibility to make sure the rangers are sharing the Park Service's official view of the camp's history."

Taking a step backward, Richardson replied, "I'm not going to get into Kevin's face over his view of history. He's a seasonal ranger. He's only here half of the year."

"How heated were the exchanges between Kevin and the other rangers?"

Richardson wrinkled his nose. "I overheard Grace giving him an earful one time."

"What did you do?"

"I told them it was inappropriate for the rangers to argue."

Rolling my eyes, I asked, "Did you correct Kevin's view of the camp?"

"Um, no. I didn't think..."

"Did you know Kevin was giving Erik a hard time about being a first-generation immigrant?"

"Um, no. I mean, Kevin is pretty open about his views on maintaining ethnic purity."

"Erik was a Swede! He was white. How does Kevin deal with minorities like Grace?"

"I don't think he's ever said anything to Grace about her ethnicity."

"Call her."

Richardson recoiled. "She's off. I don't want to bother her at home."

"Get out your cell phone and call her right now. I want to know if she and Kevin have ever had a confrontation about her ethnicity."

"I don't have her number in my phone. I'd have to look it up."

"Do it!"

I waited while Richardson unlocked a cabinet and removed a file. Finding what he wanted, he punched numbers into his cell phone. When he started talking, I gestured for him to hand me the phone.

"Grace, this is Doug Fletcher, the investigator. Can you join us at Manzanar?"

"Can this wait? It's my day off."

"I'd appreciate it if you could give us a couple of hours of your time."

Overhearing us, Jill took the phone from me and used her diplomatic skills, ones I'd never learned. "If we could steal a couple of hours from your day off, we'd like you to give us a tour of Manzanar. We heard that you're the site's historical expert."

After a brief conversation, Jill handed the phone back to me. "She's on her way."

Richardson rolled his eyes. "You know that she'll be on overtime, or I'll have to comp her other time off."

I glared at the Superintendent. "Grace has information that's invaluable. A few hours of overtime will be well worthwhile."

"Fine," Richardson replied, waving us off.

Jill and I walked outside of the visitor center and waited on the sidewalk. "What's our plan?" Jill asked.

"We're going to ask Grace to give us a Manzanar tour. While we're touring, you're going to charm her into revealing all the staff secrets."

"I really hate manipulating people."

I smiled. "But you're so good at it."

"That doesn't make it any easier or more palatable."

* * *

It took Grace nearly half an hour to drive to Manzanar. She stepped out of her car and met us alongside our rental. Her demeanor said she wasn't pleased with us.

Jill stepped forward and shook Grace's hand. "I'm so glad you agreed to take us on a tour. It's obvious that you're the historical expert on the staff."

Grace clearly knew she was being manipulated but smiled at Jill's attempted praise. "What would you like to know?"

"Tell us about the site," Jill suggested.

"The barracks site is one square mile that was taken from the Owens Valley Paiute tribe. The location was far enough from the West Coast that it was unlikely any of the relocated people could act as spies or saboteurs of coastal facilities. The water rights associated with the site made it self-sufficient for farming, gardening, cooking, and toilet facilities."

"How many people were relocated here?"

"At its peak, there were ten thousand people here in housing blocks." Grace paused and looked at us. "If you're serious about getting a tour, let's take a drive."

I drove and Grace directed me around the site.

"Manzanar had all the facilities of a small town. In addition to the barracks, there were dining rooms and recreational facilities. The biggest adjustment for the internees was the total lack of privacy. The barracks didn't have interior walls, and the toilets and showers were communal. Over time, the families hung sheets between each other's sleeping areas to provide a bit of privacy, but the toilets and showers offered no modesty." Grace turned her head and nodded to an open area with a basketball backboard. "To our right is a replica basketball court and there was a baseball field beyond the fence."

"How were the internees relocated?" I asked. "Were they arrested and taken away in handcuffs?"

"It was less formal. They were ordered to pack up and go to the train depot on a specific date with no more than one bag per person."

Jill looked shocked. "They must've had more than one bag of belongings wherever they lived before the relocation."

"Many of them owned homes and businesses in California, Oregon, and Washington. They were forced to lock up or sell their businesses, sell their household goods, and bring only what they could carry. The American public was told the relocation was for the safety of the internees. In reality, the Pearl Harbor attacks caused so much xenophobia that the safety of the internees was a consideration. However, the main goal of the relocation was preventing the Japanese, who were easily identifiable, from spying or sabotaging the war effort."

"We heard that Kevin might've had some problems with your ethnicity. Is that true?" I asked.

There was a pause before Grace replied, "There is no love lost between Kevin and me, if that's what you're asking."

"Did he ever make a derogatory statement about you?"

"Kevin is more oblique. He mostly avoids me. I overheard him telling visitors that the government relocated the Manzanar detainees for their protection, and that they should've been charged room and board for their government-supplied housing. I confronted him and corrected what he'd told the visitors. Kevin didn't argue with me, but I wonder how many other groups of visitors were misled by his comments."

Grace directed me to a building featuring the silhouette of a cook in the door. "This was one of the dining halls. Each dining hall fed three hundred people. Much of the food served here was grown by Manzanar internees on nearby orchards and farm plots."

Jill looked around. "This is desolate and there was no produce grown here in the winter months."

Grace paused, composing her thoughts. "Manzanar is a miserable place in the winter. It's cold here in the foothills, and the buildings were poorly insulated. The air blew through the cracks and around the doors. The residents made the most of it. But life wasn't pleasant. One internee commented that after an overnight dust storm, the only white parts of his sheets were where his head and body had been."

Jill grimaced. "And the next morning they went to the communal shower where they watched each other scrub off the dirt."

"Kevin told visitors this was a protective camp?" I asked.

Grace nodded.

"Did you tell the superintendent about Kevin's misstatements?" Jill asked.

"Ed doesn't like to deal with conflict. I told him but he waved it off without confronting Kevin. He asked me not to file a formal complaint because it would be a stain on my record."

"Thank you for your candor."

"Mr. Fletcher, Ed Richardson should never have been appointed superintendent. He has no supervisory skills. He ignores things that need to be addressed. People arrive late for their shifts and leave early. Red shouldn't have been working alone the night he died. I shouldn't have been opening the park alone when I found his body."

We drove on to an area marked as a park. "This area was called Merritt Park. The residents created a pond and Japanese garden here. Something pretty and tranquil can make the unbearable tolerable."

"A little Garden of Eden in the middle of hell," I observed.

"Kevin likes to point this out as an example of the good life the Manzanar residents had."

I looked at the desolate area with the now rickety bridge built over what had been a pond. "Grace, I'll make sure that information gets to the right people."

Grace paused, staring at her shoes. She looked at Jill. "Have you always been a Park Service investigator?"

"I started as a seasonal ranger and moved around a lot. I was the superintendent of the Flagstaff parks before I became an investigator."

"So, you've been in my shoes?"

"I have."

Grace turned to me. "What's your history?"

"I was a city cop, then a detective. After retirement, I started as a seasonal ranger and moved into the law enforcement side of the Park Service a few years ago."

"You probably don't get the social aspects of a ranger's job, Doug." Turning back to Jill, she asked, "Can you address my issues with Ed without ruining my career?"

"As far as I'm concerned, your information came from an anonymous source. However, if this information is passed on and the inspector general shows up, you need to share your concerns if you want the situation to change."

Grace nodded. "Think about what my grandparents went through here. I suppose standing up for myself should be part of my DNA."

We drove to the white memorial obelisk in the cemetery. "What do the Japanese characters on the monument mean?" Jill asked.

"The characters say, 'soul consoling tower,'" Grace replied. "During an annual pilgrimage, visitors set memorials on the monument or tied ribbons on the fence. I've seen thousands of origami cranes arranged on the posts."

Jill reached out and touched Grace's arm. "You are the perfect ranger for this posting."

"Thank you." Stepping back, Grace looked toward the Sierra Nevada mountains in the distance. "This seems like such a desolate place, but the people who were interned here brought it to life. In addition to the barracks, there were orchards, gardens, sports fields, and churches. Children went to school and played games between the barracks. There were high school baseball and basketball teams that played against the other area schools. Of course, all of their games were played here, inside the wire, so they were always the home team. Looking at this place now, it's hard to imagine, isn't it?"

"You and the other rangers are keeping those memories alive," Jill replied.

Grace smiled. "When the first people were brought here, one of the men asked why there were soldiers. One of the MPs said they were there to protect the internees. The old man cocked his head and asked, 'If you're here to protect us, why are your bayonets pointed inward?'"

Somewhat at a loss for words, I observed, "I hope this serves as a reminder that this should never happen again."

"People are already forgetting about this phase of American history. Kevin telling visitors that this was a relocation camp intended for the protection of the internees is counterproductive." Turning to look at the mountains again, Grace added, "I wish there was a way to either change his mind or move him to a different park."

Jill nodded. "I still have a friend who works for the US Park Service Human Resources Department. She might be able to find a different posting for Kevin."

"Can that happen so it doesn't appear to be a promotion or a move to a nicer post?"

"There are a couple of really remote parks in Nebraska," Jill replied.

Looking around, Grace said, "They can't be any more remote than this."

"Yeah, four hours from the nearest airport makes this a long way from anything," Jill agreed.

Grace said goodbye to us in the parking lot and then drove away.

Emerging from the visitor center, Richardson watched with apprehension as I approached. Jill walked past the superintendent without acknowledging him. "Well?" he asked me.

"Grace has had problems with Kevin. Have you ever confronted him?"

Richardson looked away. "There's always some level of conflict among the rangers. I suspect Grace's quiet demeanor set her up for some horseplay and kidding."

"It sounds like Grace has a bounty of information about Manzanar's history."

"There's no question she's smart and well-versed in that history." Richardson paused a moment and then said, "It's just that she's kind of confrontational about it.

Kevin talked about this place from a different perspective. I thought it was nice to present an alternative view of history.”

“Even if that perspective is wrong?” I asked.

Richardson frowned. “I thought you were here to investigate Red’s murder. Why are you asking me about the friction between Grace and Kevin?”

“Was there friction between Kevin and Erik?”

“Although we try to present an unbiased view of the park, most of the rangers tend to lean toward the political left. Kevin’s views are further to the political right. That puts him at odds with the others.” Richardson froze. “Oh, no. Red’s murder isn’t about politics. We may vote differently, but we’re not killing each other over conflicting political views.”

“Are you sure?” I asked.

“Get serious. The country is polarized right now, but Republicans aren’t shooting Democrats. And no one here is going to kill someone over their political views. Nope. I can’t accept that.”

“If that’s not the motive, why do *you* think Erik was killed?”

Richardson opened his mouth to speak, then stopped.

“What were you going to say?” I asked.

“I don’t know why Erik was killed.”

“You’re uncomfortable about something.”

Richardson looked away and stared into the distance. "What do you think of Todd Overland's girlfriend?"

"Do you think Lexi had something to do with Erik's murder?"

"She's rather odd. I mean, she's older and manages a sporting goods store. She has access to guns, and she sticks to Todd like glue."

"Erik wasn't shot. What does Lexi's access to guns have to do with the murder?"

Richardson waved off my comment. "Guns are just a symbol of her attitude. She's into violent things, and I think her relationship with Todd is unhealthy. I think she views Todd as her ticket out of Lone Pine. Erik was in her way."

I looked at Richardson skeptically.

"You asked what I thought. Now, I've told you."

After the superintendent returned to the visitor center, I met Jill in the driveway. "This sucks," she said.

"Yeah."

"What did Richardson have to say?"

"He hasn't been dealing with any of the friction between the rangers."

"You're kidding. He admitted being ineffective?"

"Richardson says Kevin's politics are different, and that's okay. On the other hand, he pointed out that it wasn't Grace who was killed. He thinks we should be looking at

Lexi. He views her as a gold digger who saw Erik as a barrier to her relationship."

Jill's grimace told me she was struggling with that as a motive. "I didn't get the impression Lexi was violent."

"Maybe we need to talk to her again. Richardson thinks her access to firearms is indicative of her violent tendencies."

"Really?" Jill asked. "Ed needs to take a drive to South Dakota and Wyoming where every pickup has a gun rack in the back window."

I snorted and said, "Let's take a trip to the sporting goods store. I'd like to speak to Lexi again, just to put my mind at ease about her violent tendencies."

Chapter 19

The three customers in the sporting goods store were checking out the camouflage clothing options. Spying Todd Overland's girlfriend behind the rear counter, I wound through the aisles, then skirted around an end display that featured a pyramidal stack of shotgun shells as high as my shoulders. Lexi, who had been focused on the threesome trying on jackets, looked annoyed.

"Do you have a second?" I asked.

After glancing toward Jill, then at me, Lexi's attention returned to the customers. "Not really," she replied, nodding toward the aisle.

"Shoplifters?" Jill asked.

"Not so far, but they've been trying on a lot of stuff and haven't put anything in their basket."

"I'll keep an eye on them while you and Doug talk." Jill moved to the end of the aisle with the customers and paused.

Lexi sighed and glared at me. "What is it this time?"

"Did Erik have a problem with you and Todd?"

"We didn't kill Erik. Next question."

"How about your neighbors, his co-workers, or park visitors? Was there friction between Erik and any of them?"

"We really don't see much of the neighbors. We say hi when we bump into them in the hallway or on the stairs. I don't even know their names."

"How about co-workers?"

Lexi sighed and looked past me, watching Jill and the shoppers. "I've never gotten to know most of the rangers, except to be introduced at the bar. The two old women aren't social. I mean, they go home after work and don't interact with the younger rangers."

"No issues with Grace or Becky," I reiterated.

Shaking her head, Lexi replied, "I couldn't have even come up with their names."

"How about the younger rangers? You said they sometimes socialize together. Tell me about them."

"There's the cute rich guy who goes by his initials," Lexi paused, trying to recall the name. "Casey. He's a stuck-up rich narcissist whose shit doesn't stink."

"Is he a problem for the other rangers?"

"Naw. He just shows up, tries to impress everyone, then wanders off to pick up local women."

"How about Seth, Tonya, and Kevin?"

"Seth is even more of an introvert than Erik. He just sits and smiles. Tonya is a party girl. She's a little touchy about being Black in an area where the only other minority people are Native, but she's never in anyone's face about it."

When Lexi paused, I asked, "Tell me about Kevin Roberts and Ed Richardson, the superintendent."

"Kevin is a piece of work. He's way out there on the political right and isn't afraid to tell the others why their views are wrong. He doesn't mesh well with the rest of the rangers, so I didn't see him often." Lexi paused, and then continued, "Well, he was here in the store. I sold him a Chinese-made AK-47 rifle."

"He didn't have a problem passing the background check?"

I saw Lexi's expression change. "Oh yeah. Kevin bitched about government intrusion into our lives as I made the call, but he passed the check and walked out with his rifle."

"Tell me about Ed Richardson."

"He's a wuss. He doesn't know how to manage people—makes suggestions but never gives orders. He lets all the rangers push the rules. He's kind of like the cartoon of the three monkeys. You know, the one is covering his eyes. The second is covering his ears. The third is covering his mouth. He pretends to not see or hear anything, then doesn't say anything about the stuff he does see and hear."

"Tell me about Erik's breakup with Hailey."

Lexi looked past me, watching Jill, who was keeping an eye on the customers. "There's nothing to tell. She dumped him. He was sad. End of story."

"What do you know about Hailey's brother Tanner?"

"Tanner Qualls?"

"Hailey said her brother ran Erik off one night."

"I've never heard that story before. On the other hand, Erik would probably have been embarrassed and wouldn't have told us."

"What do you know about Tanner Qualls?"

"Lone Pine is a small town, so I'm sure we've run into him. He's not part of my social circle, so I don't know him personally." Lexi looked past me at the customers, then paused. "You know, I did run across someone named Qualls. He came in to buy a gun. I ran him through the federal background check, and it came back 'transfer denied'."

"I assume he had a felony conviction," I replied, thinking back on the few times I'd been called to a gun shop because an irate customer had failed a background check.

Lexi frowned. "I think he had some mental thing. You know, like a sticky-sock vacay in a psych ward."

My mind raced as I processed this tidbit of information. "Do you remember where Tanner Qualls lived?"

Lexi shrugged. "I assume his address was somewhere in Lone Pine. Our gun customers are all local, as opposed to the tourists who buy logo clothing and hiking gear."

The three customers found something they liked and were approaching Lexi and me with their selections. "I think your shoplifters just turned into buyers."

"It happens," Lexi replied as she stepped aside and smiled at the approaching customers.

Jill followed along behind them until I nodded toward the door. Outside of the store, I said, "We need to look at Tanner Qualls. Lexi said he failed a federal gun background check."

"Refresh my memory, who is Tanner Qualls?"

"He was the brother of Erik's girlfriend; the one who escorted Red away from her apartment."

"He's not someone we've run across," Jill said, hinting at the Paiute woman's advice that we'd spoken to the killer.

I sighed. "Maybe Jack can track down information about Tanner for us."

Jill punched a number into her cell phone as we walked to our rental car. "Hi,

Jack, this is Jill Fletcher. We have a person of interest in the Manzanar case who failed a federal gun purchase background check. Do you have a contact at the Bureau of Alcohol Tobacco and Firearms?" After listening for a moment, she disconnected the call. "Jack is texting me a name and phone number for his ATF contact."

"As I recall, there's a federal database of all people disqualified from owning a firearm," I said as I drove away from the store.

The chiming of Jill's phone announced the arrival of a text. After a quick glance at the screen, she touched the provided phone number and switched her phone over to speaker as the call connected. A woman's voice answered, "ATF, Special Agent Kroger."

"This is Jill Fletcher, from the USPSISB. We're investigating a homicide at Manzanar National Historic Site and were advised that a person of interest failed a federal background check. Can you tell us why?"

After a slight pause, the woman replied, "Please give me your Park Service badge number." After Jill supplied her Park Service ID information, I could hear computer keys clicking. "Your ID matches the phone number you're calling from. What's the name of your person of interest?"

"He's Tanner Qualls. I believe that he lives in Lone Pine, California."

After another pause, the woman replied, "Tanner Ashton Qualls was denied a gun transfer on August 10, 2023."

"Can you tell us why the transfer was denied?"

"He has a 922 (d) exclusion."

"I'm unfamiliar with that terminology. What does that mean?"

"According to 18 U.S.C. § 922 (d), it is illegal to sell or dispose of any firearm or ammunition to any person knowing or having reasonable cause to believe that such person 'has been adjudicated as a mental defective or has been committed to any mental institution.'"

I pulled to the side of the road and said, "This is Doug Fletcher, also of the Park Service. Why, specifically, was Mr. Qualls disqualified?"

"There's a notation that he'd been adjudicated under the California OMHD statute." When we didn't respond, she added, "Under the California penal code, there are six criteria that must be met: 'The offender has a severe mental disorder. The offender used force or violence or caused serious bodily injury in one of their committed crimes. The severe mental disorder was one of the causes of, or was, an aggravating factor in the commission of the crime for which the offender was sentenced to prison. The offender's severe mental disorder is not in remission or cannot be kept in remission without treatment. The offender had been in treatment for the severe mental disorder for ninety days or more within the year prior to the offender's parole or release. As a result of the severe mental disorder, the offender represents a substantial danger of physical harm to others.'"

"What crime was Mr. Qualls charged with?" I asked.

"His file says he was charged with felony assault under California Penal Code § 240 PC which defines an assault as 'the unlawful attempt, along with the present ability, to cause a violent injury to another person.'"

"Does his file show where the assault occurred?"

"He was tried in Inyo County and confined in the Patton State Hospital after being convicted of criminal behavior due to mental illness. Is there anything else I can do for you?"

"Do you have his address?" I asked.

The ATF agent read a Lone Pine address, then added, "That location appears to be a halfway house for paroled offenders."

"Thank you," Jill replied before disconnecting the call. She turned to me and asked, "Are you planning to drive up and knock on the front door, or are we going to request backup from the sheriff's department?"

"Let's find Jamie. I think the two of you can knock on the front door while I watch the back."

Jill snorted. "I think Jamie would be a better choice for the back door. If someone runs away, he'd be better suited for a foot chase."

Pulling back onto the street, I replied, "Sometimes age, experience, and treachery are better tools than being prepared to chase down a suspect."

"Really? What would you plan?"

"I'd trip him, then pounce on his back."

"That worked so well on the rodeo bull rider."

"He sucker-punched me. I didn't have time to prepare for him."

"I think it would be better if you and I were the door knockers and Jamie dealt with anyone sneaking out of the back."

"Whatever," I replied. "Call Jamie and have him meet us for lunch."

* * *

Jamie suggested a fast-food restaurant with outdoor seating. After collecting our orders, we sat at a table away from the only other outdoor diners, a group of noisy teens who eyed us suspiciously. Jamie stuffed half a dozen fries in his mouth while unwrapping one of the two burgers he'd ordered. "You found a suspect?"

Jill explained while I unwrapped my burger. "The ex-girlfriend's brother tried to buy a gun but failed the background check.

He was committed to a state mental hospital for treatment after an assault."

Jamie nodded as he chewed his first bite of burger. "It sounds like he fits the psychopath profile, and he may have had a problem with his sister's breakup."

Sensing Jamie's distraction, I asked, "What did you find out?"

"John Standing Bear, the Paiute historian, isn't as upstanding as he'd like us to believe. I asked around among some elders. They feel like he's rewriting the oral history being collected from them."

"Why would he do that?"

Jamie thought for a moment. "He's going to write a book. One sure way to get a history book to sell is to propose a premise contrary to popular beliefs. He'll probably make a few bucks and get his face on television."

"That doesn't make him a killer," I replied.

"No. But it makes him less than the stellar, upstanding member of the community that he'd like us to believe he is. It also brings into question his motive for sending us to Bishop to find someone who would be upset about the *Si-Te-Cah*."

"Do you think Standing Bear threw us a red herring?" Jill asked.

"At this point, I don't know what to think."

"Why would he send us on a wild goose chase?" Jill asked.

"I don't know," Jamie replied as he unwrapped his second burger.

Irritated that he hadn't expanded on his response, I asked, "Would you care to guess?"

"Not really," he replied as he rearranged his pickles and tomato slice.

"Humor me," I said.

"I have relatives who enjoy irritating people. They take personal pride in creating chaos and proving they are smarter than others."

"That sounds like they're manipulating people," Jill observed.

"For them, it's a game."

"Do you think that's what the historian was doing?" I asked.

"That's a possibility."

As I ate my burger, I mulled Jamie's comments. "I'm inclined to believe he sent us off to focus on something away from what he didn't want seen."

"Could be," Jamie replied as he chewed.

"Do we need to follow up on him?" Jill asked.

"Probably not if you've got a more promising suspect," Jamie replied. "I think he was just yanking our chains."

"Where did you find the elders who cast doubt on John Standing Bear's veracity?"

With a slight grin, Jamie replied, "Where any good cop finds elders who want to talk; they were drinking coffee at the Totem Café."

Intrigued, I asked, "What else did the elders have to say?"

"They laughed when I told them John Standing Bear sent us to Bishop. They thought the idea of a Paiute killing a red-haired ranger because they thought he was one of the *Si-Te-Cah* was funny." Jamie asked, "What's your plan?"

"I thought we'd find Tanner Qualls and ask him about Erik Petersen."

"Without getting an okay from the sheriff's department?" Jamie asked.

"They're busy chasing their drug angle. I thought we'd talk to Tanner and see where that leads."

Jamie grimaced, obviously uneasy about something.

"Spit it out. What's bothering you?"

Jill watched in amusement as Jamie wrinkled his nose, like he'd smelled a skunk.

"I haven't had much luck interviewing crazy people. They tend to do stupid things and sometimes react badly to a cop showing up unannounced at their door."

"Do you have a better suggestion?" I asked.

"Let's ask the elders in the Totem Café about him. They might have some interesting insights."

Jill laughed. "Don't tell me you're still hungry."

"My eating is a variation of Doug's admonition to sit when you can and sleep when you can. I eat when I can because I never know when I'll get another meal."

"Really?" I asked. "We're not lost on the Navajo reservation. There are restaurants every few blocks."

Jamie glanced at Jill and replied, "You two have a way of finding trouble. I wouldn't want something like a runaway suspect and subsequent arrest to keep me tied up over mealtime."

"Fine," I sighed. "The Totem Café is our next stop."

* * *

Now after the lunch rush, the café was nearly empty. The few remaining patrons were finishing off the last of their meals or at the cash register paying. The exception to that was a round table in the center of the dining room. Five of the eight chairs were occupied by gray-haired Paiute men, each with a coffee cup close at hand. One of the men saw us walk in and waved. He pulled out the chair next to him and gestured for Jill to take it.

"To what do we owe the honor of a visit from a pretty woman?"

Jill smiled, showing her dimples as she sat at the scarred wooden table that reflected the ambiance of the knotty pine paneling and the historic black and white pictures dotting the walls. "I always appreciate flattery."

The man, whose face was lined by years in the sun, smiled. "If only I were forty years younger and unmarried."

That comment brought a round of laughter from the other men seated around the table. Jamie and I sat in two open chairs, then signaled the waitress for coffee.

Jamie nodded to the men. *"Maik'w,* Uncles. If any of you are hungry for a piece of pie, my friend Doug has a government charge card and will be happy to buy."

The oldest man continued to smile but shook his head. "I'd love a piece of pie paid for by the government. However, I suspect there is a price to be paid."

The waitress arrived with our coffee, and I gestured toward the men seated around the table. "Bring my new friends whichever variety of pie or cake they would like."

After glancing at each other with huge smiles, they each ordered a slice of pie. The oldest man, sitting next to Jill, asked her, "What is your partner looking for in return for a slice of pie?"

"We've heard that Tanner Qualls has a reputation. Is that true?"

The old man's smile faded as he considered Jill's question. Gesturing to another of the men who was missing several teeth, he said, "We all have reputations. Roger is known as a great lover. The truth is seldom as good as the rumor."

"What rumors have you heard about Tanner?" Jill asked.

"Do you know that he's crazy?"

"We've heard that rumor."

"It's not a rumor."

Waiting for an expansion of that comment brought a full minute of silence. Jamie finally asked, "What crazy things has he done?"

Roger leaned forward as if preparing to whisper a secret. "He doesn't understand boundaries."

"Like trespassing?" Jill asked.

"No, he doesn't know when to stop. He's out of control."

The man next to Jill nodded. "He nearly beat a guy to death over a game of pool. His buddies pulled him off the poor kid, but not until Tanner had cracked his skull." The speaker paused when the plates of pie arrived and were passed around the table. I handed my charge card to the waitress who smiled and walked away to ring up our orders.

"Is this a rumor or a true story?" I asked.

"We weren't there," Roger replied. "But Tanner was arrested and sent to the state hospital instead of jail."

The old man who'd spoken earlier nodded. "It's probably for the best. Either he would've killed someone there, or he would've been killed in prison. He doesn't take kindly to being corrected, bullied, or even looked at crosswise."

"We heard that he's back in town," Jamie said as the men dug into their slices of pie.

Roger nodded. "I heard he acts like a normal person when he's taking his medicine. The only problem is that he sometimes forgets a dose."

"Does he have a job in town?" I asked.

"I think he mows grass for the city and picks up garbage from the ditches. You know, things he can do without interacting with anyone else."

"Where does he spend his evenings?"

"I think he's under house arrest. He lives with a bunch of other idiots in a house over on Union Street. I don't think they allow him to go out in the evenings because he'd be drinking, and that's when his real problems start."

Roger nodded toward the door. "I'd start with the Lone Pine City Works Foreman. He'll know where Tanner is working."

"How do he and his boss get along?" I asked.

The men looked among themselves as the waitress delivered the receipt with a pen. "Maggie, how do Tanner and your brother-in-law get along?"

The middle-aged waitress paused, looking at Jamie, Jill, and me. "I guess they do okay. I mean, Steve doesn't get in Tanner's face over things. Tanner does things like he thinks they should be done, and Steve keeps his criticism to himself."

"That doesn't sound like a comfortable arrangement," I said.

Maggie shook her head and accepted the signed receipt. "It's not."

"Why does Steve put up with it?" Jill asked.

"Because Tanner is paid by the state, he gets slightly more done than if no one was doing the work." I was about to ask her another question when she put up her hand to stop me. "I can't say any more. The guys have already probably told you more than you should've heard."

"It sounds like Tanner is the town bully," I said to the guys.

They all shrugged or looked away. Roger finally broke the silence. "No one crosses Tanner. He's as likely to smash our heads as he would be to say hello if we greeted him. So mostly, we stay away from him. I've been known to cross the street if I see him walking toward me."

"Did he have a problem with the ranger who was killed?" Jamie asked.

The men stiffened and stared at each other. Finally, Roger drew a deep breath and let it out slowly. "That's the guy who was dating Tanner's sister?"

Jamie nodded, "Yes, him."

"His sister is that tiny thing who works at the realty office. Tanner is protective of her. Their parents died a few years ago, and I think Tanner keeps an eye on her."

"Have you ever seen Tanner pull a knife on anyone?" I asked.

"He uses whatever is handy. His fists, a knife, a pool cue, a beer bottle. He's not picky. He just likes to be up close and personal with the people he's hurting. I think he likes to see their pain."

Chapter 20

After thanking the elders, Jamie, Jill, and I walked to the rental car. "Tanner Qualls sounds like a piece of work."

Jamie nodded but said nothing.

Jill looked worried. "I think we should tell the sheriff's office what we've heard. We don't need to confront Tanner ourselves."

I looked toward Jamie, who'd stopped alongside the rear door of our rental car. "What do you think?"

After climbing in the back seat, Jamie buckled the seatbelt and looked at me in the rear-view mirror. "I think someone will get hurt if we try to question Tanner."

"I'd like to minimize the chance of that happening," I replied.

Jamie looked at Jill. "Men underestimate you."

Confused by that comment, Jill replied, "I don't know if I should be flattered or insulted by that comment."

"It's an observation, not a judgment."

"Are you suggesting that I should be the one to question Tanner?" Jill asked.

With a straight face, Jamie said, "He might not hit a woman."

Turning my head, I looked over the seat at Jamie. "He might not hit a woman? Really? The man is crazy. I mean literally, crazy. I don't think gender is a barrier for him."

"It might be," Jamie replied. "Maybe he loves his mother and sister."

"And maybe his mother beat him and that's why he's messed up," I replied.

"It sounds like his fury is usually directed at men," Jamie countered.

Jill put her left hand between us. "Do I get a vote in this election?"

Irritated at the interruption, I replied, "Sure. What's your vote? Do you want to take a chance that the crazy man isn't going to punch you, or would you prefer to wait until there's a plan B?"

"It's the middle of the afternoon. Let's drive over to the halfway house and ask to see his room."

Jamie nodded. "That plan has merit. Tanner's on parole, so I'm sure law enforcement can enter his room anytime without notice, to check for liquor, drugs, and contraband."

"And if he's there?" I asked.

"Jill will use her superior negotiating skills to defuse whatever situation arises."

"Thank you, Jamie," Jill said after lowering her hand.

Shifting the car into gear, I mulled the potential situations we might encounter. *What if he's got a gun? What if he pulls a knife? What if he overpowers Jill and takes her hostage?*

"You're too quiet and you gave up too easily," Jill said.

"There are a hundred ways this could go wrong."

"Doug, he might not be Erik's killer. He might have an alibi and we'll be able to move on to other suspects."

From the back seat, Jamie said, "There's something about the Paiute historian that bothers me."

"You mean, beyond the fact that he's rewriting their oral history?"

"There's a problem with oral history. Everyone who retells it shapes it from their personal perspective. It becomes something akin to rumors where there's a thread of truth, but it's hard to discern that truth from the embellishment. The farther we get from the events, the thinner the thread of truth."

"So, the elders who are relating the stories to John Standing Bear are telling them as they recall but may be putting their own spin on them. Correct?"

"Yes."

"How is Standing Bear's recording of the stories with *his* personal spin any different from what the elders are telling him?"

"John's an academic. He should be writing the stories as they're told, citing the sources as is done with all academic, historic, and scientific papers."

Surprising both of us, Jill asked, "How is what he's doing different from what was done with the Bible? I mean, aside from translating the words incorrectly and deleting any stories that made women look important or powerful."

Jamie snorted. "My father was a missionary. In his words, 'the Bible is a prayerful recording of ancient stories and papers.'"

Jill cocked her head and said, "The difference being that the Bible was transcribed by a rabbi or priest, someone who prayed for God's guidance while making the transcription?"

"That's what made it a Holy Bible," Jamie replied before changing the topic. "I think Union Street is the next turn. Take a right."

With our theological conversation ended, I slowed so we could read address numbers on the houses as we passed. That proved unnecessary because the halfway house was the largest building on the block, looking more like an apartment building than the surrounding homes.

"I wonder how the neighbors feel about living next door to a halfway house full of people in transition to a *normal* life?" Jill asked.

Parking in front of the building, I replied, "I assume the property values reflect the houses' proximity to the building full of people in transition." I opened the car door, preparing to step out.

Jamie stopped me. "I think it would be best if Jill approached the house on her own. Seeing you and me might precipitate an unwanted response."

"I don't think it matters," I replied. "Based on my experience, there will be someone there who is like a house mother, making sure people behave, don't party, and don't bring in prostitutes."

Jill stepped out of the car. "Oh, good. I won't have to deal with any drunks or hookers. That's an upside."

Jamie and I stood on the sidewalk while Jill pushed the doorbell. The woman who answered the door weighed close to 400 pounds, had tattoos on her arms and neck, and appeared to be close to sixty years old.

"Yes?" she asked.

"Is Tanner Qualls here?"

"Do you mean, does he live here? Or are you asking if he's home?"

"Both," Jill replied.

Leaning past Jill to see Jamie and me, the woman seemed in no rush. "Are you all cops?"

"Yes," Jill replied.

"Tanner is at his job. He'll be back at about 3:30."

"We'd like to see his room."

The woman paused. "Show me some ID."

Jill removed her credentials from her pocket and handed them to the woman who examined them closely.

Handing them back, the woman asked, "Are you all Park Service cops?"

"One of my partners is from the Navajo Nation Police."

"Having three strangers who are cops walking around inside might stir some people up. Can I show you Tanner's room while the boys stay outside?"

Jill glanced at Jamie and me, who hadn't heard the woman's request. "Stay out here. I'll be back shortly."

Jill disappeared through the door, and the housemother looked up and down the street before closing the door behind her.

"The woman who answered the door looks suspicious," Jamie said. "Like she killed off the real manager and is waiting for the cops to show up and arrest her."

"I think that look is a better fit with this environment than having some guy in a suit or white coat. She's probably a drug and alcohol counselor, too."

Jamie studied the second-story windows which displayed a variety of window coverings running from threadbare sheets to expensive accordion blinds. A couple of the rooms had potted plants set on the sill. "That plant in the far-right window looks like marijuana."

"It's not our problem."

"I'm just saying..."

"It's probably hemp. They grow it for therapeutic CBD oil."

Jamie stared at the window for another moment, then turned to me. "Are you always a smartass, or do you save up until you're around me?"

I smiled. "You're my favorite smartass target. But I stay in practice by tormenting others when you're not around."

"Thanks."

A car turned the corner toward us, slowing as it drew near the halfway house. "I think one of the residents feels uneasy about seeing cops standing outside of his apartment building," Jamie observed. "Maybe we should wait in the rental car until Jill returns, just in case Tanner shows up."

"I feel like we should stay nearby in case someone goes crazy about a cop searching Tanner's room," I replied.

"I've been thinking about the guy with the MAGA bumper stickers."

"Huh?" I asked.

"The seasonal ranger with the attitude. Kevin. Something's wrong with that guy."

"Wrong, as in his politics, or wrong as in mentally disturbed?" I asked.

"I picked up a vibe that your *white suburbanite* radar might've missed. He wasn't impressed that I'm a Navajo cop. He looked right past me and addressed you the first time I met him."

I drew a breath and blew it out. "I don't often sense that when we're together."

"I'm used to benign prejudice. Kevin's attitude had more of an edge to it. You know, like he'd like to have a private discussion with me in an alley."

"Really?"

Jamie stared into the distance as he weighed his words. "I think he's probably more bluster than a bully. However, I have no jurisdiction here and I could create a problem for you and Jill if he took a swing at me and I responded."

"If he's really Red's killer, there's more to him than his bluster. Let's see what Jill finds in Tanner's room. If she comes up empty, I think we'll take a drive over to Kevin's apartment and knock on his door. He *did* give Grace a bad time."

"If Kevin's part of a militia group, or has had some form of right-wing legal orientation, he's not going to let three cops search his place without a warrant."

"How do you think he'd react if Jill showed up alone?"

Jamie stared at me as if I'd lost my mind. "I think you either hate your wife, or you're planning to illegally entrap Kevin by using Jill as bait."

"If he invites her in, there's no entrapment."

"And we'll be hiding around the corner waiting for her to call for backup when she sees a bloody knife sitting on his coffee table?"

"We had a code phrase during a Spearfish prostitution bust. I yelled 'Mickey Mouse' as soon as the hooker discussed the price with me. The cavalry rushed in and arrested her."

Jamie's sly grin told me he remembered the story. "I heard she had you naked on the floor before your backup rushed in."

"Well, there was a problem with our communications, but things never got that far."

"No, but her crazy pimp broke in from the next room and nearly killed two cops before he was shot."

I sighed, "There's always an unknown factor to any operation."

"Let's tell the Inyo County deputies about our suspicions. They can get a warrant and bring in a SWAT team."

"They're still focused on the drug cartel. I doubt there's anything I could do short of delivering a handwritten confession that would change their point of view."

Jill appeared on the front steps of the halfway house and apparently thanked her guide. Once she was seated in the car, I asked, "Did you find anything incriminating?"

"Take me to the motel. I want to take a shower."

"Tanner's room was that bad?" Jamie asked.

"I think a rat would be embarrassed to live in filth like that."

"I assume you didn't find anything to connect him with Red's murder," I said as I started the car.

"There was so much stinky crap in his room that I had to breathe through my mouth. All of it was disheveled, dirty, and disgusting. But I didn't find anything bloody, nor did I find anything that would be a parole violation. No guns, no alcohol, no drugs." Jill paused, then said, "Augusta, or Gusty as the guys call her, said all the guys were here for supper the night Erik was killed. She did a headcount that evening, and Tanner was playing cribbage with three of the other residents until lights out, at ten. He's got an alibi."

"She remembered that Tanner was playing cribbage on that specific evening?" I asked.

"Apparently, there is a routine. The same guys play cribbage every evening."

"She's sure he didn't sneak out for an hour?" Jamie asked.

"The door and windows have sensors that alarm if they're opened. Gusty runs a tight ship."

Chapter 21

After driving away from the halfway house, I summarized my discussion with Jamie about Kevin while Jill was gone.

Jill listened, then stared out the window. After a couple of blocks, she pulled out her phone and typed in a search for Kevin's information. "There's no address or phone listed for Kevin Roberts in Inyo County. He's either living in a campground or somewhere off the grid."

"I can see that," Jamie said. "If he's a conspiracy theorist, he may be paranoid enough to keep his personal information hidden from the government."

"When I was a park superintendent, I had everyone's phone numbers and addresses."

Nodding, I said, "Call Ed Richardson and ask him for Kevin's home address."

Jill punched in Richardson's number and put the phone in speaker mode. "Hi, Ed. This is Jill Fletcher. We'd like Kevin Roberts' home address."

"I have his cell phone number but don't know his street address. He lives in an apartment in the Lone Pine Funeral Home. I think he gets free rent for answering their phone during non-business hours."

After consulting the internet, Jill said, "The only funeral home in Lone Pine is where we met with the coroner. If you make a U-turn, we'll be back there in a few blocks."

Jamie leaned on the seat back. "If he's living in a funeral home, we don't need a search warrant if the owner lets us in."

I felt hopeful. "Aaron was a nice guy. I'm sure he'd let us peek in the apartment."

"We might have a different problem," Jill said as she flipped through her phone search. "I think Kevin belongs to the East Slope Militia. He's in a picture on their website."

"A militia group has a website?" Jamie asked. "I'd think they'd want to stay off the web."

"It's not a Facebook page," Jill said, holding up her phone so Jamie could see the picture. "I'm on the dark web."

"How did you get access to that?" Jamie asked.

"The feds have tapped into most all these fringe groups. I went to a training course on using FBI and US Marshals' databases. Kevin is tagged in a few of their pictures."

"Huh," Jamie nudged my shoulder. "Did you go to that class, too? Or did you sleep through that part of the instruction?"

"I must've been busy chasing down bad guys."

"Oh, I forgot. You're computer illiterate," Jamie replied.

"I'm not illiterate, I choose to defer the computer work to people who are more skilled."

Coughing into this hand, Jamie said, "Dinosaur. We just passed a café with a homemade rolls sign. I think we should have a plan before we show up unannounced at the funeral home."

"Right. This has nothing to do with you being hungry." I turned at the corner and circled the block, rather than making a U-turn. I found an open parking spot in front of the café.

The mid-afternoon crowd was nearly non-existent. I noticed a table in the back and was preparing to lead the way when I heard someone call Jill's name. Turning, I saw Grace Watanabe seated in a booth across from a middle-aged man wearing jeans and a plaid shirt. Like Grace, he had oriental facial features, and his dark hair had a touch of gray.

Jill led us to the booth and introduced Jamie.

Grace smiled politely and said, "This is my husband, Louis."

The man slid out of the booth and shook hands with all of us. "Grace has told me a lot about you, Doug and Jill."

"Don't believe everything you hear," I joked.

Jamie looked at me, then back to Louis. "In Doug's case, believe the bad half and forget the good half."

Nodding toward a table set for six, Louis suggested that we sit at the larger table with them. "I don't often get to meet Grace's co-workers," Louis said as we sat. "She didn't mention a Navajo Nation Police Officer. Is there a Native aspect to your investigation?"

"Doug and Jill thought there might be," Jamie replied. "I think we've moved past that."

Our conversation stopped when the server arrived with coffee cups and a carafe. Smiling at Louis, she asked, "Do you have a local gig coming up?"

"We're playing at the Bishop casino Saturday night."

"I may have to make the trip up there," she replied.

"Your sign says homemade rolls," Jamie mentioned as he looked toward an empty glass case built into the counter.

"Yup. Every morning, we have fresh cinnamon and caramel rolls. They usually sell out by ten o'clock."

Jamie feigned extreme sadness. "Dang it."

"There might be a few slices of apple pie and some chocolate cake in the kitchen."

After sighing dramatically, Jamie said, "I'll drown my sorrow in coffee and console myself with a piece of cake."

"How about the rest of you?" the server asked.

We all shook our heads, so she turned to leave.

"Wait!" Jamie called out. "I don't want to eat alone. Bring all of my Park Service friends slices of pie. If they don't eat them, I may have to clean their plates for them."

Jill nodded toward Grace. "My friend works for the Park Service too. If Jamie's buying, you should bring pie for everyone."

Grace, who was small and trim, tried to refuse. "I don't eat many sweets," she said.

"If the Navajo Nation Police offer to buy you a slice of pie, you should take it," I said.

Louis grinned as our server left. "You three must know each other very well."

"Doug and I are married to each other," Jill explained, "and Jamie has helped us on several investigations."

Louis glanced at his wife. "I don't think Grace's rangers have the camaraderie you three have."

Grace blushed. "We don't socialize with the seasonal rangers. They sometimes get together in the evening for drinks and I'm not into the bar scene."

Jamie nodded emphatically. "Yeah, old folks like Doug don't get out much after dark."

Louis waited for me to respond. When I didn't say anything, he asked, "Are you just going to sit there and take it?"

"There's no point in arguing with him." To change the subject, I asked, "You play in a band?"

"There's a small group of us who play a few gigs a year. I play guitar and sing backup."

Smiling, Grace said, "He's very humble. Louis used to be in a band that played all up and down the west coast. Now, they practice in our garage every Saturday."

"I got tired of living out of a suitcase, so I finished my degree," Louis explained.

"Do you have a day job?" Jill asked.

"I'm a freelance computer geek. I've been programming full-time for Allegiant Airlines for the last year. I'm trying to smooth out glitches in their staffing program."

"As a programmer, I suppose you can work from anywhere that has high-speed internet," I said.

"I love the flexibility. Do you know what they call a freelancer between jobs?"

We all shook our heads.

"Unemployed."

We chuckled until Louis's smile faded and he looked at Grace. "Did you tell them about the arguments?"

Grace picked up her coffee cup and shook her head.

"Arguments?" Jill asked.

When Grace didn't answer, Louis frowned. "All is not peaceful among the Manzanar rangers."

"Tell us more, Grace," Jill prompted. "Are you having problems with someone besides Kevin?"

"No. Just Kevin," Grace replied without expanding.

"Tell them about..." Before Louis finished the sentence, Grace put her hand on his arm and shook her head.

"Tell us about what?" I asked.

"It's just dirty laundry," Grace said softly as our server arrived with a tray of desserts.

"Your Navajo friend wanted the chocolate cake. I brought the last two slices of pie and cut cake for the rest of you." After setting the deserts around randomly, our server straightened up. "I'll be back in a minute to warm up your coffee. Is there anything else you want?"

Jamie stopped with a forkful of cake halfway to his mouth. "Do you have any ice cream?"

Grinning broadly, the server asked, "Vanilla, chocolate, strawberry, or chocolate chip?"

"I think vanilla would go well with my cake. How about the rest of you?"

We all refused ice cream and the server left.

Pushing her piece of cake in front of me, Jill leaned forward and asked, "What dirty laundry?"

Louis ate a forkful of cake and waited for Grace. "Go on. Tell them."

"Kevin belongs to some paramilitary group. He goes into the hills with them. They shoot their guns, drink beer, and talk smart."

"And?" Jill asked.

"And nothing. He's just a stupid kid."

Louis shook his head. "Tell them."

Glaring at Louis, Grace hesitated while stirring the apple pie with her fork. "Kevin said I should move back to Japan." She paused. "My family has been here for three generations. I don't even speak Japanese."

"Does the superintendent know this?" Jill asked.

"There's no point. Kevin would deny it. Just like he denied..." Grace froze.

"What did he deny?" I asked.

Grace put an apple slice in her mouth and shook her head without looking at me.

Jill reached out and put her hand on Grace's arm. "Does this have something to do with Erik?"

Obviously irritated by his wife's silence, Louis spoke up. "Kevin and Erik had an argument."

"What did they argue about?" Jill asked Grace.

"The same stupid stuff. Erik was a first-generation immigrant. Kevin told him to move back to Sweden with the rest of the communists."

"Kevin called Erik a communist?" Jill asked.

"Erik was talking about the great social programs in Sweden, and how the US really needed to step up and provide nationalized healthcare and employment protections like the Scandinavian countries. Kevin said those were *communist* benefits."

Louis shook his head. "Kevin's not smart enough to know the difference between socialism and communism."

"When did this argument occur?" I asked.

"About a week ago. Just after Kevin came back from his militia retreat."

"A few days before Erik's murder?" I asked.

Louis leaned forward. "I told her to say something to Ed Richardson."

"It's none of my business!" Grace protested as the server brought Jamie a heaping bowl with three scoops of ice cream in it.

"Are you guys talking about those militia nuts?" Our server asked as she set the bowl in front of Jamie.

"Have they been a problem for you?" I asked.

"The sign says we reserve the right to refuse service to anyone. The militia guys aren't welcome here. They spout off right-wing shit and alienate our customers. Mac ran them all out the last time they were here and told them not to come back."

With the waitress gone, I slid my plate to Jamie. He spooned a scoop of ice cream on top of my pie. "You guys go ahead and solve this murder while I finish off Doug's desert."

"Who else overheard this argument?" Jill asked.

"I think Ed heard it. But he walked away."

Jill looked at Jamie as he wolfed down my pie and the ice cream. "When you finish eating, we're going to have a talk with Kevin."

Jamie waved a forkful of pie. "Give me one more minute."

Jill shook her head while Jamie shoveled food in. "Grace, we may need you to make a formal statement about your interactions with Kevin and the argument he had with Erik."

"I don't think I can do that."

Reflecting on one of Grace's earlier comments, Jill said, "Your grandparents would expect no less of you."

Louis nodded. "She's right, dear. You need to speak up."

"I think we need to visit Kevin at his apartment," I said.

Jamie waved at our server. "Can I get our check and a box for the last piece of cake?"

Jill and Grace walked to the bathroom while Louis, Jamie, and I waited for the check and a takeout box. Watching the women walk away, Louis said, "Grace has been really upset by the friction at the park. Erik's murder was the icing on that ongoing mess. I don't think she's slept in days."

"People are unprepared to deal with the discovery of a murder victim," I replied.

"What else has Grace said about the workplace friction?"

"There are always issues between the full-time rangers and the seasonal people. Grace tries to teach the new rangers the site's history. She expends a lot of energy teaching them the park history and how to be *proper* rangers. Then, they leave and she's mentoring a new group a few months later. The turnover is tedious."

"She doesn't have much respect for Ed Richardson," I said.

"This is his first supervisory position. He's too concerned about being everyone's buddy and not concerned enough about being a supervisor. I suppose he'll learn the job. For now, Grace finds him frustrating."

Jamie slid the last piece of cake into a Styrofoam clamshell as Jill and Grace returned to the table. We shook hands with Grace and Louis, then walked to our car.

"The funeral home isn't too far from here, is it?" I asked.

"It's just a few blocks away," Jill replied.

Chapter 22

I parked in the lot adjoining the Lone Pine Funeral Home. Kevin's jacked-up pickup truck, sporting offroad tires and right-wing bumper stickers, was parked in the back corner. A gray Infiniti was parked next to the sidewalk leading to the entrance. There was no sign of the coroner's Toyota Landcruiser.

Strapping on her bulletproof vest, Jill said, "I suppose an Infiniti is an acceptable upscale car in a small town. It's not as ostentatious as a Lexus or Cadillac, but nicer than a Camry or Chevy." Chiding me for not pulling my vest out of the trunk, she said, "Put on your vest. Kevin's a nut."

"Yeah," I conceded.

Jamie stopped us before we stepped away from the rental car. "You two go in and talk to Kevin without me. There's no need to inflame him by having a minority officer on scene. I'll look in the windows of his pickup to see if he left a bloody knife or drug paraphernalia on the seat."

"You're not planning to poke around inside the truck, even if the doors are unlocked. Right?" I asked.

Taking a pair of surgical gloves from his pocket, Jamie smiled and said, "That thought never crossed my mind."

The funeral home's front door was unlocked, the carpeted entryway dimly lit and empty. A light shone through a door halfway down the hall, so I led Jill to the open room opposite the coroner's closed office. Knocking on the doorframe, I startled the stocky man with salt and pepper hair who was apparently looking at a casket catalog on his desktop computer.

The man's surprise quickly turned to a well-practiced reassuring smile. "Can I help you?"

The man glanced at the Park Service logo on our body armor and our badges as we walked into the office. "I'm Doug Fletcher, a US Park Service investigator. This is my partner, Jill."

The man stood and walked from behind the desk, extending his hand. "I'm Jon Hawes, the funeral director." As we shook hands he added, "Are you the rangers who met with my brother, the coroner?"

"We are," I replied. "Something else has come up."

"Is this about Erik Petersen's funeral arrangements?"

"Indirectly," I replied.

The funeral director gestured toward chairs set around a small table. "Can I get you a cup of coffee or an iced tea?"

"No, thanks. We just had coffee in town," I replied as I sat.

"Erik's parents were here earlier. We reviewed the plans to transport his remains to Minnesota."

"Tell us about Kevin Roberts," Jill said.

Hawes frowned as he sat. "There's not much to tell. Kevin lives in a spartan apartment above our embalming room. He's quiet and polite, answers the phones on weekends and at night, then relays messages to me in a timely manner. That's all I ask of him. Is there a problem?"

"We heard he's a bigot," I said.

Looking troubled by the comment, Hawes said, "I haven't had any specific conversations with Kevin that would lead me to that conclusion. Not that we mix socially."

"We understand he's a member of a local militia group known to go shooting in the foothills."

"I have no idea what Kevin does on his weekends. Like I said, he's quiet and does all that I require of him."

"Do you know if he's in his apartment right now?" I asked.

"If his pickup is parked outside, I imagine he's here."

"Is he alone?"

"I haven't seen him today, so I don't know."

"Does he entertain often?" Jill asked.

"Like I said, he's quiet. I rarely see him bring guests to the apartment because he uses the back entrance rather than walking past my office."

"Does he have a girlfriend?"

Hawes smiled. "I've seen him with a young woman. I don't know the nature of their relationship."

"Would you take us to the apartment and give us permission to search it?"

The funeral director leaned back. "My father is a US marshal and has indoctrinated me in the Fourth Amendment rules about unreasonable search and seizure. I need more information before I'd be comfortable allowing you to search the apartment."

Jill put on her most disarming smile. "We think Kevin might've been involved in Erik Petersen's death. We'd like to talk with him and see if there's anything incriminating in his possession."

"I assume you'd have a search warrant if you had probable cause tying Kevin to Erik's murder."

Continuing to smile, Jill said, "We'd prefer to keep things low key for the time being. Since you own the premises, you can give us permission to search."

Hawes leaned back and steepled his fingers. "I'm Kevin's landlord. Dad never discussed the laws pertaining to a police search of a renter's apartment."

"Does Kevin pay rent?" I asked.

"Not in cash. I give him the apartment in lieu of his phone messaging services."

"Does he have a lease?"

"Not a written lease."

I stood. "Then you're just taking us to one room of your business and allowing us to look around."

Jon stayed seated. "I haven't given my permission."

Jill took out her phone and started paging through screens. "Kevin belongs to the East Slope Militia. How do you feel about him keeping firearms in your apartment?"

"I'm a hunter. I'm not opposed to people exercising their Second Amendment rights."

"What if he had an assault rifle—or two—and a few thousand rounds of ammunition?" I asked.

Hawes frowned and shifted in his chair. "I'd be uncomfortable with that scenario."

Jill found the screen she'd been seeking and handed her phone to the funeral director. "Isn't Kevin the second person from the right? Isn't he the one with the linked machine gun cartridges draped over his shoulders?"

After viewing the picture, the funeral director stood and returned Jill's phone. "I guess I'd like to know if Kevin has a machine gun in the apartment." He reached for a keyring and led us down the hallway.

At the last door, I stopped Hawes before he inserted the key. "Unless you're wearing a bulletproof vest under your shirt, I suggest that you let Jill and me enter first."

Hawes glanced at Jill, who was pulling her Glock from its holster. Then he looked at my body armor as I removed my pistol. "I see the wisdom in your suggestion," he said, stepping back from the door and standing behind me.

Television sounds coming through the door made me think Kevin was probably distracted. I slipped the key into the lock and slowly twisted it until I felt the deadbolt ease back. Gripping the doorknob, I nodded to Jill, who nodded back.

"Police!" I shouted as I pushed open the door. Stepping to the right as I entered, I swung my pistol toward the figure seated in a recliner, his back to the door. Jill stepped to the left and moved toward an open doorway apparently leading to a bedroom in the studio apartment. The open area to my right was a small kitchenette and living room.

Kevin's head lurched forward as he lowered the recliner's footrest. Releasing the handle, his hand reached for something buried among the game controllers and food wrappers on the end table to his right. "Gun!" I yelled to Jill, who kept moving to her left. Seeing nothing to provide cover between me and the kitchen counter, I opted to keep moving, hoping to make myself a more difficult moving target. "Put the gun down!"

The top of Kevin's head appeared as he rolled off the chair. A pistol barrel came into view as he dropped to the floor. Moving my finger from the guard to the trigger, I jerked a quick shot toward Kevin's gun.

The muzzle of Kevin's pistol flashed and the plaster over my head exploded. To my left, I glimpsed the silhouette of a person in the bedroom doorframe before the door slammed shut.

"Watch the door!" I yelled to Jill as I moved to my right, trying to monitor Kevin, who had taken cover behind the recliner. Seeing Kevin's pistol moving, I fired two more shots into the arm of the overstuffed recliner. I heard Jill also fire two shots toward the recliner. That was followed by another of Kevin's unaimed shots which also hit the ceiling above me.

"Watch the bedroom!" I yelled to Jill while I tried to position myself where I'd be hard to hit but would have a shot at Kevin if he popped up. I focused on Kevin, the known threat, leaving Jill to deal with whatever was going on in the bedroom.

My ears were ringing from the shots fired in the enclosed apartment. In my peripheral vision, I saw Jill move toward the bedroom door. While taking cover alongside the door, she reached out with her left hand and tried the doorknob.

The muzzle of Kevin's gun poked over the arm of the recliner. He fired two unaimed shots that hit many feet away from me. Focusing on where I thought his hand was, I fired two shots and Kevin's gun disappeared from view.

"Something's happening in the bedroom!" Jill yelled. She pounded on the door with her left hand. "Open up! Federal officers!"

I was unaware of any activity in the bedroom, hoping anyone there was sheltering behind the mattress. Then, the door flew open. A young woman yelled, "Damned socialist feds! Go to hell!"

Glancing in that direction, I saw a woman dressed only in a t-shirt holding a rifle against their hip. I jumped to my left, away from the direction the rifle was aiming. The shooter swung the gun toward me. That move was followed by the deafening sound of the AK-47 fired on fully automatic.

The first shot hit where I had been standing. Luckily, the shooter's aim didn't catch up with my move. Bullets stitched a row up the kitchen wall and onto the ceiling as the shooter failed to control the gun's recoil, the muzzle jumping higher and more erratically with each following shot.

I dove to my left and fired at the muzzle flashes coming from the darkened bedroom. Pistol shots rang out to my right as Jill took shelter behind a row of cabinets while offering covering fire to distract the shooter.

The firing stopped when I assumed the AK's magazine was empty. My ears were ringing, and the apartment ceiling looked like Swiss cheese. Not hearing the shooter reloading, I edged toward the apartment's entry door, while keeping my pistol aimed at the bedroom. A second later, I heard the rifle clatter to the floor followed by a thump and moan that made me think someone had been hit and had collapsed to the floor.

"Jill?"

"Yeah?"

"Are you okay?" I yelled, trying to be heard over the ringing in my ears.

"Other than being deaf, yeah."

"What do you see in the bedroom?"

"She's hit. Her gun is down."

"Cover her. I'll check on Kevin."

I moved around the recliner and found Kevin clutching his knees in a fetal position with the pistol near his feet. I kicked his pistol toward the door and held my aim at him. "Can you get up?" I asked as Jill approached the bedroom.

Not uncurling, Kevin said, "Holy shit. Was that Edie shooting?"

"Who's Edie?"

"I think she's his girlfriend," Jill replied. "It appears she was asleep in the bedroom."

"Jill, how is Edie?" I asked.

Instead of answering, Jill yelled toward the hallway, "Mr. Hawes! Dial 911. We need an ambulance."

I heard the funeral director speaking into his phone as he moved away from us down the hallway. "There's been a shooting at the funeral home. There are cops here who say they need an ambulance. No, I don't know who was shot. I don't think it was a cop."

I heard the woman sobbing in the bedroom, followed by the clink of spent rifle cartridges being kicked aside in the bedroom. "Jill?"

"Edie has an abdominal wound. I have her rifle."

I looked at Kevin. "Are you hit?"

Kevin shook his head. "How about you? Did I hit you?" His question sounded hopeful.

"Not even close," I replied as I took handcuffs off my belt.

"Damn, hitting a moving cop is a lot harder than shooting paper targets."

"Lucky for you," I said. "Roll onto your stomach and put your hands behind your back."

Running footsteps in the hallway preceded Jamie's arrival. Breathless, he stepped into the apartment, leading with his pistol. His uniform shirt and pants were stained with chocolate cake and his fingers appeared to be sticky with frosting.

"We're clear," I said as I snapped Kevin's wrists in handcuffs.

"Where's Jill?" he asked as sirens whined in the distance.

"She's in the bedroom with Kevin's girlfriend."

"Are you two okay?" Jamie asked Jill as he stepped toward the bedroom door.

"We are. The girlfriend is hit."

Looking at the bullet holes in the walls and ceiling, and the shell casing on the floor, he said, "It sounded like a damned war in here."

"We must've interrupted your snack," I said, looking at the cake smeared on Jamie's hands and uniform.

"It was very inconsiderate of you to start shooting when I had a piece of chocolate cake in my hand." Jamie holstered his pistol and wiped his dirty hand on his pants as he stepped into the bedroom. I heard Jill's voice as she spoke to Jamie.

"So, Kevin, how did it feel to slit Erik's throat?" I asked as I lifted him to his feet.

"I don't know what you're talking about."

"No? Then why did you shoot at us?"

"I was protecting my domicile against an illegal search by the socialist police."

"I should've known you didn't have the courage to actually cut someone's throat. That takes more guts than the average militia member has."

"I've got plenty of guts. I'm ready to defend the constitution and the rights of US citizens."

"That's militia bullshit. All you guys do is drink beer, talk tough, and shoot up a bunch of ammo. It takes discipline and toughness to pull the trigger when the gun is aimed at a person."

"I shot at you," Kevin protested.

"You fired your weapon blindly while cowering behind a chair. That's hardly heroic. It's more like the gang bangers and drug dealers."

"You don't know shit about me."

"I know that you were willing to let your girlfriend take on two cops while you hid out of the line of fire. Is there something I've missed?"

"My other actions speak for themselves."

"Yeah? What would they be? Were you in charge of grilling the burgers at the last cookout?"

Kevin finally realized that I was baiting him. "I want a lawyer."

I led Kevin toward the door, then paused next to the tiny kitchen table. A soiled, Army-style camouflage jacket hung over the back of a chair. Sniffing the air, I got a hint of woodsmoke odor. "Is this the coat you wear to militia outings?" I asked, recalling Grace's comment about smelling woodsmoke when she found Erik's body.

"Why do you care?"

"It smells like you were roasting marshmallows over an open fire. Does the militia make S'mores?"

"You don't know shit about us. Outdoor cooking is a part of our survival training."

"I'll bet you were wearing this coat when you strung Erik up on the fence."

"Huh?"

"Grace smelled wood smoke when she found Erik's body. I'll bet the pine smoke on your jacket will match whatever traces the forensics team found on Erik's clothing. You left traces behind when you were stringing him up."

Edie wailed from the bedroom as Jamie carried the AK-47 into the living room in a gloved hand. Jamie nodded toward the bedroom. "There's an arsenal in there."

Chapter 23

We turned our pistols over to the Inyo County deputies and drove the rental car to their law enforcement center to make formal statements. Jill and I were thankful to be interviewed in offices rather than interrogation rooms with two-way glass. The deputies who took our statements treated us with the professional courtesy offered by fellow law enforcement officers.

* * *

After the interviewer left, I checked out the family pictures, certificates, and framed awards in the office where I'd been left waiting. I determined the office's occupant was Detective Gloria Menendez. Based on the pictures, I saw she had three kids, all in their teens, and she was proud of their athletic and academic accomplishments. There was a framed award for bravery, presented when she was still in uniform. Having discerned all that, I was going to discover about Detective Menendez, I was trying to find the score of the Minnesota

Twins game on my smartphone when the office door opened and a trim, middle-aged woman with a folder tucked under her arm and carrying two Styrofoam cups walked in. She set a cup on the table in front of me and set her own cup and the folder down before making eye contact. The picture ID on her lanyard confirmed that she was Detective Menendez.

Looking at me as she took a sip of coffee, Menendez seemed to be waiting for me to say something. When I remained silent, she opened the folder and passed it to me. "You're Doug Fletcher, right?"

"Yep."

"The same Doug Fletcher who assisted Deputy Kellen during the drug stop?"

"Yeah. How did that turn out? What did the CBI find in the back of the truck?"

"They recovered twelve kilos of methamphetamine, twenty thousand dollars in cash, and a garbage bag of fentanyl-laced oxycontin pills."

"That's quite a haul. I'm sure the CBI, sheriff, and CHP are all doing a happy dance. Did anyone mention the contribution of the Park Service or Navajo Nation Police?"

Shaking her head like I'd asked a very stupid question, Menendez handed me a pen. "Here's a transcript of your statement about the events at the funeral home. If it's correct, sign and date it."

I read the transcription of my interview. Noting no typos or errors, I signed and dated the last line and passed it back to her. "Am I free to leave?"

Menedez leaned back in her chair and stared at me. "You are one lucky sonofabitch. If the woman in the funeral home had ever fired that AK-47 before, she would've shredded you."

"My old sergeant used to call me Lucky Fletcher."

"Really?"

I snorted. "Hell, no. He used to ream my butt for doing stupid shit. That's what sergeants are good at."

"Since the bullet that passed through the female assailant was a .45, and your partner was shooting a 9mm, I assume the shot that hit the woman was fired from your pistol. Our ballistics people will verify that. Considering she was firing a machine gun at you; I assume the district attorney won't file charges against you or your partner."

"That's mighty kind of him to think we might be justified in returning fire at someone who was trying to kill us."

Detective Menendez leaned on the table. "What the hell were you two thinking? I assume you knew that Kevin was a member of a crazy militia group. Why would you walk into a situation like that without backup?"

"Your deputies made it clear we were unwelcome guests who were to stay out of their way. I had the impression that they might not respond to anything less than a 'shots fired' call from us."

A tiny smirk appeared on Menendez's mouth and disappeared as fast as it showed up. "The boys can be a little parochial. They generally loosen up once they get to know you."

"I'd like to know what you find on the cell phones recovered from the funeral home apartment."

"That information won't be publicized until the trial."

"What trial?"

"The district attorney hasn't seen the cell phone video and pictures yet. Once he does, I imagine we'll have the whole alphabet of state and federal agencies lined up here to investigate and charge a number of people in the militia."

I leaned my elbows on the table. "The militia is involved?"

"It appears the fully automatic AK-47 from the apartment was customized by a militia gunsmith. In addition to that illegal weapon, we found explosives and other military hardware reported stolen from a Nevada National Guard armory in the apartment. Like I said, we're going to have a regular convention of law enforcement people here. The sheriff is fuming that people will be trampling all over his turf now that you messed up our surveillance of the militia." Seeing my surprise at that statement, she added, "Yeah, you stepped into the middle of an undercover operation. Our guy, who's been inside the militia for the past eighteen months, has been pulled out and will have to testify in the upcoming trials."

"Ah," I said, leaning back in the chair. "We messed up your surveillance, so we're being rushed out the door."

"I was wondering what your wife saw in you. You're smarter than you look, Fletcher."

"Where is my wife?"

"Your Navajo Nation cop friend drove her back to your motel to clean up and change clothing after I reviewed her statement. She was a mess after doing first aid on the girl you wounded."

"How is Edie?"

"HIPAA laws don't allow us to pass on medical information. From a legal perspective, she's got a belly wound that punched through her guts in a couple of places. Being a cop, you understand how much tissue damage a .45 slug does. It makes a little hole going in," Menedez held up her little finger to indicate the size of the entry hole, then made a fist, "and leaves a softball-sized hole when it exits. She's been surgically patched up and they're pumping her full of antibiotics to keep her from going septic."

"I'm glad you're not sharing any confidential medical information, Detective. I wouldn't want you to get in trouble."

Menendez smiled. "We all know medical confidentiality is a dance. We learn the steps and hope they don't change the tune."

"Back to the cell phones."

"As I told you, the content of the phones will remain confidential." After glancing over her shoulder to verify that the door was closed, she said, "Let's just say there were videos that will keep a bunch of officers and lawyers busy for months."

"I'm most curious about the slashing murder of a Park Service ranger."

"I was told not to comment about the video showing Kevin Roberts and Edie Boxer beating your ranger and stringing him up on the fence. Kevin was ready to leave him there, but Edie urged him on, pointing out that the ranger was an immigrant stealing American jobs and blocking Kevin from getting a permanent position."

"Really? Erik was white. I thought the militia was concerned about Mexican immigrants."

"They're usually complaining about Hispanics, Blacks, Asians, and Arabs, but they're apparently willing to confront first-generation European immigrants, too."

"Kevin did the slashing, but only after Edie egged him on?"

Menedez considered her reply. "If Edie hadn't called Kevin a dickless wimp, Erik would probably still be alive. She's a piece of work with a real blood lust."

"Does Edie Boxer have a criminal history?"

"You're really pushing the limits of what I'm not going to tell you." Menedez ran her tongue around the inside of her lips as if she'd eaten something distasteful. "Let's say we know Edie and leave it there. I won't mention her shoplifting, drug possession, or domestic assault arrests."

"Thanks for sharing that."

"I didn't share anything. And, if you say I did, I'll deny it." Menendez put my signed statement into the folder and closed it. She stood and nodded toward the door. "If you, Jill, and Jamie aren't busy, a couple of us are going to the Long Branch. I'd let you buy me a beer."

Walking to the door I joked, "I'm buying you a beer because...?"

"I solved your murder case."

"*You* solved *my* murder case?"

Holding the door for me, Menendez smiled. "If there's any question about that, just ask my sheriff. He'll tell you exactly how his people solved the murder despite the bumbling incompetent rangers sent by the Park Service."

"Can you at least give partial credit to Jamie Ballard from the Navajo Nation Police?"

"The sheriff might go along with that. He likes to stay on the good side of the Paiute voters." She paused momentarily and then said, "If you stop by tomorrow before you drive to the airport, you'll be able to pick up your weapons."

"Will the testing be completed that quickly?"

"The sooner you're gone, the fewer questions there will be about who gets credit for solving the murder."

"To be clear, Detective..."

"Call me Gloria."

"To be clear, Gloria. I don't give a rat's ass about who gets credit for solving the crime, as long as the bad guys are arrested and sent to prison."

"I find that hard to believe, Fletcher."

"I'm Doug. My partner is Jill. We're just working cops like you. The only difference is that Park Service investigators don't usually get involved in arrests. Our role is advisory, in support of the local agencies."

Looking skeptical, Gloria replied, "If that's true, do you have any openings?"

"If you give me one of your business cards, I'll pass your name along to our boss."

Gloria's cell vibrated as we reached the front door of the law enforcement center. She stopped me while she had a short conversation. "Change of plans. Jamie and Jill ordered pizzas. I'm picking up beer. I'll meet you at the hotel in fifteen minutes."

"Gloria."

She stopped and turned. "What?"

"You're okay."

"I've had my chain yanked so many times by so many people, I can't tell if you're serious or not."

"I'm deadly serious. I appreciate the professional courtesy you've extended to us. Thank you."

Menendez smiled. "I'll see you in fifteen minutes. I might even buy expensive beer instead of that cheap swill I was planning to get. After all, we're celebrating the first murder I've solved this year."

Epilogue

After sleeping in until 7:00, we showered, packed our bags, and put the remnants of the pizza boxes, napkins, and beer bottles in wastebaskets. We loaded our suitcases into the car. Jamie stepped out of his room when he heard us slamming car doors. "Do you have a second?" he asked.

"Sure," I replied as we followed him into his motel room.

Like us, he'd packed his backpack and was ready to depart. I could see he was building up to something important. His aversion to conversation made it difficult for him to begin.

"What's on your mind?" Jill asked, hoping to break the ice.

"I have to call Liz."

"About your career plans?" she asked.

He nodded.

"What are you planning to say to her?" Jill asked.

Tipping his head back, Jamie stared at a water stain on the ceiling. "I still have to make a decision."

"And that decision is?" I asked.

"It's complicated. I feel a tie to my Navajo roots."

"You have a family, your own clan. Don't they take precedence over your mixed feelings about being Navajo?" I asked.

Jamie looked at me. "I've never had a nuclear family. Everyone on the rez was part of my extended family, an aunt or an uncle who looked out for me."

I nodded. "That was because your white, missionary father was called to a different parish. He left you and your mother behind."

Jamie shook his head. "That's not entirely true. My mother wouldn't leave the reservation. My father wanted us to move with him to Oklahoma, but Mom refused to leave. I don't think he abandoned us as much as Mom..." Jamie paused, looking for words. "Mom had never been farther from home than Shiprock. The Navajo nation was her entire world."

"You've seen a lot more of the outside world than she ever did," Jill said. "Does that make you want to stay or leave?"

Jamie shrugged. "It depends on the day. Some days I want to flee poverty and tribal issues. Other days I want to stay and make things better."

I empathized with Jamie's dilemma. "Every time I arrest some scumbag, I hope

I've made the world a better place. Then, the attorneys work out a plea deal and the scumbags are back on the streets before I've finished the paperwork."

Jill's mouth curled into a smile. "Most people complete the paperwork faster than Doug does."

With the tension broken, Jamie chuckled. "The reservation is getting better. There are more jobs. They're installing solar panels for water pumps and household power. There's better healthcare and schooling."

"Does that mean they need you more, or less?" I asked.

Jamie looked at Jill. "You worked near the reservation for a decade. What do you think?"

After glancing at me, Jill said, "I know you have a loving wife who would like to raise a growing family. They're your clan, and they need you."

"Yeah, and Liz wouldn't do well on the rez."

"You could continue to live in Flagstaff and also stay on the Navajo Nation Police force," I suggested.

Jamie shook his head. "The reservation is huge, and I get called all over. It's often impractical to get back to Flagstaff at the end of a shift."

"If you took a job with the Flagstaff PD, you'd be working rotating shifts. You'd be around, but a lot of the time you'd be trying to sleep during the day. That's not easy when you live alone. With kids in the house, it'd be nearly impossible," I said.

I heard Jamie's stomach growl. He smiled and said, "Can we continue this discussion at the café?"

* * *

Jill took out her phone and punched in a number as I pulled out of the motel parking lot with Jamie following behind in the Navajo Nation Police car. "Who are you calling?" I asked.

She motioned for me to be quiet. "Hi Jack, we've wrapped up the Manzanar case and will be driving to Las Vegas shortly after getting our weapons back from the county cops."

She listened for a moment, then switched on the speakerphone and said, "I wanted to communicate how helpful it was to have Jamie Ballard with us to sort out the tribal issues. There are situations where two white investigators just can't delve into the Native American issues that we face in some investigations. Jamie really came through for us."

"It was fortunate that you were able to tap him as a resource," Jack replied.

"He's been a crucial link in a couple of our investigations," Jill said. "It would be nice if Jamie was a resource available to all of the Park Service investigators."

Jack chuckled. "You make it sound as if I should hire him."

Jill looked at me and shrugged. "I'm not sure he'd take the job, but he's definitely got valuable and unique skills. Do you have any openings?"

Jack sighed. "I never know what my budget will look like. Most of the NPS is cutting headcount, so it'd be hard to justify adding a person."

"I understand," Jill replied. "It was just a thought."

"It's a good thought, and he'd add diversity to our workforce," Jack replied. "I'm afraid it's just not feasible right now."

After disconnecting, Jill put the phone in her pocket. "It was worth a shot."

I found a street parking spot near the café and pulled into it. "I'm not sure Jamie would take a Park Service job if it was offered to him."

We walked to the café in silence, meeting Jamie near the front door. "Have you made a decision?" I asked as we walked into the café.

"The spirits haven't spoken to me," he replied.

We sat at a table near the kitchen. "Do you often wait for divine inspiration before making decisions?" I asked.

Jamie waited until our server had delivered menus and poured coffee before answering. "Sometimes the answers come to us indirectly."

"Indirectly?" Jill asked.

"Like Jill being fired from the Flagstaff superintendent's job. Don't you think that was divine intervention, allowing you to make a life change and marry Doug?" Jamie asked.

Jill grimaced at the thought of that unfortunate turn of events. "I think it was more serendipity than divine intervention."

Having made his selection, Jamie set his menu aside. "Isn't that the same thing?"

Jill didn't have an answer, so I interjected, "I don't think the great spirit, or whatever you call your deity, cared about Jill's personal situation."

"I do," Jamie replied. "You and Jill were meant to be together."

Jill's phone vibrated and she reached into her pocket, hoping to answer the call before it went to voicemail. I smiled and said to Jamie, "I'll give you odds it's one of our mothers calling with information about a medical issue."

Shaking his head, Jamie replied, "I won't take that bet."

Jill wrinkled her nose at us as she struggled to answer the call. "Hi Jack," she said as she left the table.

Our waitress arrived while Jill was outside. I ordered oatmeal with fresh strawberries for Jill. Jamie ordered the rancher's special, again. I ordered eggs, whole wheat toast, and bacon.

Having apparently finished her conversation with our boss, Jill returned and sat, smiling. She leaned toward Jamie. "Divine intervention has occurred."

"Huh?"

"That call was from Jack Pardee, our boss. He has an opening for an investigator, and he feels that it would be advantageous to have an experienced Navajo cop in that position."

Jamie stared at Jill, then looked at me. "You two have been conspiring behind the scenes."

Ignoring Jamie's comment, Jill added, "Jack says he'd like you to relocate to Denver, but he's open to letting you live wherever you want, as long as you're near an airport. The job involves flying to crime scenes throughout the US and may require you to be away from home a week or two a month."

"Why does he want a Navajo investigator?" Jamie asked as our breakfasts were delivered.

"Many of our investigations, like this one and the one involving effigy mounds in Iowa, benefited from having a Native perspective. You bring something none of his other investigators have the perspective of life on a reservation. You understand Native culture and traditions."

Jamie dove into his meal as Jill spoke. I was beginning to think he was ignoring Jill's comments until he wiped his mouth. "You're serious?"

Jill picked up her phone and called Jack. After a brief conversation, she handed her phone to Jamie.

Accepting Jill's phone, Jamie walked outside. Jill ate oatmeal as we watched Jamie pace back and forth outside the windows while talking to our boss. After a few moments, he stopped pacing and looked at us through the windows. He nodded, apparently agreeing with something Jack was saying.

We'd finished our meals when he returned and handed the phone to Jill. "Interesting," he said as he went back to his cold breakfast.

"What do you think?" Jill asked.

Jamie didn't reply until he finished his meal. Wiping his mouth, he said, "I have learned something from you two."

"Really?" Jill asked. "What is that?"

"I need to speak to Liz before I announce a decision."

Jill laughed and stacked her bowl on top of my empty plate. "What are you going to tell her?"

Always stoic and stone-faced, Jamie stared at me. "I'm going to ask her how she'd feel about being married to a federal cop and possibly moving to Denver."

Jill reached out and squeezed Jamie's hand. "I hope I haven't backed you into a corner."

Jamie shook his head. "Not into a corner. You've opened a door that hadn't been there before." Jamie stood and smiled at me. "Why don't you pay for breakfast while I make a call?"

I pulled out a charge card as he left. "Do you think Liz might be happy with this opportunity? He'd be away from home quite a bit."

"I think she'll be thrilled that he's finally made a decision and he's consulting her on it. If I remember correctly, Liz's parents moved to Colorado Springs, so Denver might be an appealing relocation."

"I imagine it'd be helpful to have a family support network as the kids get older," I suggested.

"Kids? They only have one child."

I gestured toward the door. "I think we both know that they'd like to expand their family."

"There aren't any Park Service locations near Denver," Jill said as we threaded our way toward the door.

"Maybe Liz would like to stay at home and raise children for a couple of years. If not, I'm sure there are more job options in the Denver area than in Flagstaff."

Jamie was waiting for us outside the restaurant. In an uncharacteristic move, he hugged Jill. "That's from Liz." After releasing the hug he added, "And maybe from me, too."

I shook his hand. "Welcome to the National Park Service Investigative Services Branch."

"I still have to pass a federal background check."

Shaking her head, Jill said, "I don't think that will be a problem."

A smirk appeared as Jamie said, "I promise to not be an *Ivanbito*."

"Thanks for reminding me that I sometimes stampede through investigations like a buffalo."

Thinking he'd hurt my feelings, Jamie looked embarrassed. "Doug, you always do what needs to be done."

Jill shook her head. "Despite how much wake he creates or how many egos he bruises..."

Jamie raised his eyebrows. "Like an *Ivanbito*."

Laughing, Jill nodded. "Yes, like a charging buffalo."

The End

Other Dean L. Hovey mysteries from BWL Publishing Inc.

Whistling Pines cozies

Whistling up a Ghost
Whistling Pirates
Whistling Bake Off
Whistling Artist
Whistling Fireman
Whistling Wedding (late 2024)

Doug Fletcher mysteries

Stolen Past
Washed Away
Dead in the Water
Death in Shifting Sands
Devils Fall
Prairie Menace
Down River
Burnt Evidence
Gator Bait
Grave Survey
Dead End Trail
The Last Rodeo
Peril in Paradise
Western Justice
Strung out to Die

Pine County Mysteries

Killer Secrets
Deadly Mixture
Fatal Business
Taxed to Death
Conflict of Interest

Dean Hovey is the award-winning and best-selling author of three mystery series. He uses his scientific background, travel, extensive research, and consultants to add reality and depth to his stories. One reader said Dean's characters are like people he'd like to invite over for a beer and discussion.

Hovey's Doug Fletcher mysteries follow U.S. National Park Service investigators Doug and Jill Fletcher as their investigations take them to national parks from coast to coast. The Whistling Pines mysteries are humorous cozies set in a northern Minnesota senior residence, following Peter Rogers, the Whistling Pines recreation director, as he stumbles through the investigation of murders in his small town. The Pine County mystery series follows sheriff's deputies Pam Ryan, Floyd Swenson, and CJ Jensen as they investigate murders in rural Minnesota.

Dean and his wife split their year between northern Minnesota and Arizona.